*The Hundred-Year Diet: Guidelines and
Recipes for a Long and Vigorous Life*

*Doctor Tales: Sketches of the Transformation of
American Medicine in the Twentieth Century*

DOC LUCAS USN

A NOVEL OF THE VIETNAM WAR

BLAIR BEEBE

iUniverse, Inc.
New York   Bloomington

Doc Lucas USN
A Novel of the Vietnam War

Copyright © 2010 Blair Beebe

iUniverse books may be ordered through booksellers or by contacting:

iUniverse
1663 Liberty Drive
Bloomington, IN 47403
www.iuniverse.com
1-800-Authors (1-800-288-4677)

ISBN: 978-1-4502-3257-9 (pbk)
ISBN: 978-1-4502-3259-3 (cloth)
ISBN: 978-1-4502-3258-6 (ebook)

Printed in the United States of America

iUniverse rev. date: 6/11/10

For the members of VAP 61

We of the Kennedy and Johnson administrations acted according to what we thought were the principles and traditions of our country. But we were wrong. We were terribly wrong.

—Robert McNamara, 1994

Contents

Preface.. xv

Acknowledgments xix

I

FROM PHILADELPHIA TO GUAM

Chapter 1:   INTENSIVE CARE 3

Chapter 2:   HOME OF THE BLUE ANGELS 15

Chapter 3:   WELCOME ABOARD...25

II

THE GULF OF TONKIN

Chapter 4:   NIGHT PHOTORECONNAISSANCE 41

Chapter 5:   HEMORRHAGING AT SEA...................................50

Chapter 6:   FIRST MED 59

Chapter 7:   IT'S NOT MUCH OF A WAR 66

Chapter 8:   TWENTY SECONDS OVER HAIPHONG 71

Chapter 9:   FORBIDDEN TARGETS..79

III

DA NANG

Chapter 10: THE MILKMAN DELIVERS 89

Chapter 11: THE SEA IS EMPTY.....................................99

Chapter 12: THREE DEVILS FROM HELL 109

Chapter 13: A VISIT TO NAM HOA 118

Chapter 14: NAM HOA REVISITED..126

IV

BIEN HOA

Chapter 15: DOCTOR TRAN'S CLINIC...............................137

Chapter 16: TRAUMATIC STRESS.....................................148

Chapter 17: BONSOIR, DOCTEUR...156

Chapter 18: ANOTHER KIND OF MASH HOSPITAL............164

V

THE SOUTH CHINA SEA AND BEYOND

Chapter 19: TWENTY SECONDS OVER HANOI..................175

Chapter 20: THE SUMMIT.....................................186

Chapter 21: DOWN IN THE SOUTH CHINA SEA.................196

Chapter 22: THE BLACKBIRD 208

VI

FROM BANGKOK TO GUAM

Chapter 23: BANGKOK...219

Chapter 24: CONFLAGRATION 230

Chapter 25: GOING HOME 238

Afterword..245

Glossary 247

The Author..255

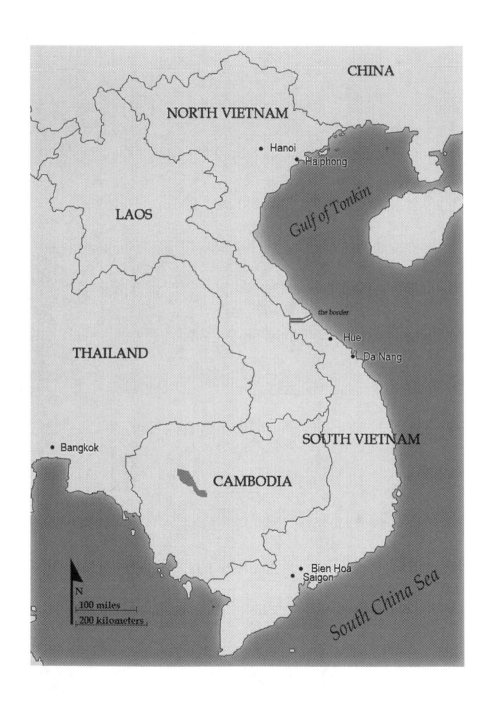

The RA-3B Skywarrior near Vietnam in 1966. The A-3 was the biggest aircraft ever to land on a carrier during the Vietnam War. Fully loaded, it weighted thirty-five tons, eight tons more than a World War II B-17 Flying Fortress, and it could fly at a speed of 610 knots, three hundred miles an hour faster than a B-17. Vice Admiral (ret.) James E. Service wrote: "The RA-3B was exceptionally versatile—one of many spin-offs from the initial bomber design. Air bosses were never enthusiastic about the A-3 platform due to the deck space it occupied, but the fighter and attack guys loved the tanker version, and the intelligence guys loved the photo product—couldn't get enough of it."

The USS *Enterprise* in the Gulf of Tonkin in 1966. Note several A-3s on board, including the "Blackbird" parked on the port side.

Preface

Many years had passed before I felt comfortable about resurrecting memories of the war in Vietnam. Even then, there were occasions when it was necessary to put this manuscript aside for a while. Certainly, I enjoyed the camaraderie in the navy carrier squadron, but the war itself cast an inescapable darkness over life. We didn't know why we were fighting, except for the abstract notion of stopping the spread of communism. But we also knew that the elected government of South Vietnam had not set a good example promoting human rights. Most Vietnamese people were poor farmers trying to survive in a country torn by centuries of conflict, where shelter and the next meal consumed all of their attention. They were not part of a cohesive nation and understood little about political ideology.

Religion gave them an identity, but it also separated them into two mutually suspicious groups, the Buddhists and the Catholics. The Buddhists hated the Catholic governments of Premier Ngo Dinh Diem, and later Premier Nguyen Cao Ky, and accused them of corruption and persecution of Buddhists. The Saigon government cared little about anyone outside of the capital, and consequently, much of the rural population felt alienated from their national leaders. Most Vietnamese people assumed we Americans were protecting the government that they hated, and that we were just the most recent in a long string of foreign invaders interested in exploiting them. We did very little to convince them otherwise.

Doc Lucas USN follows the experiences of a navy physician who is empathetic toward American servicemen and women trying to do the right thing, and it also looks at his friendship with a Vietnamese doctor caught in the crossfire of conflicting interests. The naval aviators on whom much of the story is based were professionals, but many privately questioned why we were there. Their carrier task force represented enormous destructive potential that had doubtful relevance in a war against an enemy dispersed among farmers living in bamboo huts. Airplanes could flatten any target, but in Vietnam, President Lyndon Johnson and Secretary of Defense Robert McNamara absolutely forbade attacking the most significant ones, for fear of further escalation of the war.

American involvement began as financial aid and military advice to help the South Vietnamese government combat the Communist insurgency. But on August 2, 1964, a minor encounter involving three North Vietnamese motor-torpedo boats and two American destroyers triggered a massive American military retaliation based on misinformation.

The USS *Maddox* was cruising alone in international waters in the Gulf of Tonkin off the coast of North Vietnam on a surveillance mission, when, to the dismay of the skipper, Captain Herrick, the North Vietnamese boats began to shadow the destroyer, closing almost to within torpedo range. The *Maddox* attempted to evade the small boats, but Captain Herrick believed his destroyer was in danger and fired warning shots. What followed remains unclear, but a sonar operator on the *Maddox* reported hearing torpedo propellers, and Herrick ordered the destroyer to open fire on the North Vietnamese boats. Aircraft launched from the USS *Ticonderoga* joined the attack.

Two days later, another destroyer, the USS *C. Turner Joy*, joined the *Maddox*. During rough weather at night, both ships picked up radar, sonar, and radio signals that they interpreted as another attack by North Vietnamese motor-torpedo boats. The two American ships began firing on radar targets and zigzagging to avoid torpedoes. However, no one on either ship could confirm a visual sighting of any North Vietnamese boat, nor did anyone actually see a torpedo. Captain Herrick began to doubt whether there were actually any motor-torpedo boats in the area and requested daytime aerial reconnaissance.

He sent a coded message to Washington and the *Ticonderoga*: "Freak weather effects on radar and overeager sonarmen may have accounted for some reports of North Vietnamese motor boats. No actual visual sightings by *Maddox* during the night. The first boat to close the *Maddox* two days ago probably fired a torpedo that was heard but not seen. All subsequent torpedo reports are doubtful in that I suspect that our sonarman was hearing ship's own propeller beat. Herrick."

Whether a North Vietnamese motor boat had ever fired a torpedo remained in doubt, but word had already leaked to the press from the previous messages sent by the *Maddox* two days earlier. Secretary of Defense McNamara told Congress there was "unequivocal proof" of "unprovoked attacks" on U.S. ships. The American public was enraged that North Vietnamese naval vessels had attacked American ships, and Congress quickly passed the Southeast Asia Resolution, also known as the Gulf of Tonkin Resolution, which granted the president the authority to "aid any Southeast Asian country threatened by Communist aggression, including the commitment of American forces without a declaration of war."

President Johnson had been a hawk, already having sent an increasing number of military advisors to Vietnam, but he also doubted the gravity of the Gulf of Tonkin episode or whether any North Vietnamese boats had ever fired a shot. He thought Congress was overreacting and had taken a completely unwarranted step.

"Those sailors out there may have been shooting at flying fish," Johnson said.

Nevertheless, he signed the bill and gave his approval for American troops in Vietnam to engage directly in combat against North Vietnam and to begin air operations, including strikes against targets in North Vietnam. Johnson's approval rating with the American people rose from 42 percent to 72 percent, and he won the presidential election against Senator Barry Goldwater by a wide margin three months later. Secret documents released in 1994 revealed that the CIA had been conducting raids on coastal North Vietnam before the Gulf of Tonkin incident.

Doc Lucas USN begins in 1965, at a time when lack of commitment and heavy losses had led to high rates of desertion among South Vietnamese troops. President Johnson sent in the U.S. Marine Corps to stabilize the precarious situation, but soon the marines themselves needed reinforcements. By the end of 1965, two hundred thousand American troops would be fighting throughout Vietnam, almost completely displacing the South Vietnamese Army. The number of American personnel in Vietnam would ultimately reach more than half a million, in a country with a population of only thirteen million.

I based much of the action in the novel on real people and events, but I made substantial changes to protect the privacy of my confreres and to advance the story. Sometimes I reversed the chronology. For example, Lyndon Johnson's meeting with Premier Ky on Guam actually occurred after the *Oriskany* fire, not before. Most of the scenes come from the historical record, interviews of Americans and Vietnamese involved with the war, and my own experiences. The result is a collage of incidents, compressed and attributed to a handful of fictional characters whose stories propel the plot and show the war through the perspective of the physician narrator.

Blair Beebe
Portola Valley, CA
2010

Acknowledgments

Vice Admiral (ret.) James E. Service was a former commander of the U.S. Naval Air Force, Pacific Fleet, and later Executive Assistant to the Vice Chief of Naval Operations. He was the executive officer of VAP 61 during the early days of the Vietnam War. He provided encouragement and crucial technical advice.

Jim Newcomb was a lieutenant commander during the war and naval aviator with VAP 61. He contributed the story about his A-3 snapping an arresting wire on the USS *Ticonderoga*.

David Farrar, former lieutenant commander and photo navigator in VAP 61, supplied details about photoreconnaissance and the missions flown during the war. He was awarded the Distinguished Flying Cross for a hazardous mission over Haiphong Harbor.

Ted Kubista, MD, surgeon, was a lieutenant commander during the war and served in the U.S. Navy Support Activities Hospital at Da Nang beginning in 1969. He elaborated on the conditions at Da Nang and added technical surgical information.

Richard Geist, MD, surgeon, was a colonel in the U.S. Army Medical Corps who served at Walter Reed Hospital during the war and later as chief of surgery in a mobile frontline army hospital, MUST 403d CSH, during Operation Desert Storm. He supplied technical information regarding the details of surgery in a frontline hospital.

I

FROM PHILADELPHIA TO GUAM

Chapter 1

INTENSIVE CARE

My friends call me Luke, but my real name is William Osler Lucas. My father was a doctor, and he had always wanted a son to become one too, so he named me for the celebrated Johns Hopkins physician, William Osler. From my earliest memories, I had tried to live up to my father's expectations, and in kindergarten, I called myself the "doctor child." I would rush immediately to attend any screaming classmate that had suffered sand in the eyes or a scraped knee and say, "Stop that crying and let me take a look at this." They would stop, too. Back then I was William, but much later, when I entered medical school, I feared my pretentious name would be ridiculed. So I became Luke.

Whenever I was sick as a boy, my mother always worried that I might die. She never actually said it, but I knew. She had good reason to be concerned, because her father and older brother had both died young of tuberculosis. I was certain I had to become a doctor in order to save her and my sister. All of that existed hidden in my subconscious, but I never seriously considered any other career option. By the time I entered high school, the only important decision remaining was selecting the kind of doctor I might become.

My father was a general practitioner, respected in the community, but he worried about a future for me in the same role.

"Times are changing," he said. "You will need to specialize."

"Why can't I be a family doctor like you?" I replied.

"Heart disease and cancer are increasing with the aging population. You should choose either cardiology or surgery."

"Won't we need general practitioners anymore?"

"Maybe not. My patients only want to see a specialist these days."

Having decided to become a specialist, I turned to worrying about the small things, like cosines and tangents, Boyle's law, the subjunctive of the verb *paraître*, and the travails of David Copperfield. Every spring, my grades took a tumble. I bathed in the warm sun radiating through the window next to my desk, only vaguely aware of the strange mathematical equations and lengthy conjugations on the blackboard. Each June brought a reckoning with my irate father.

"Penn State will never accept you with these grades, let alone Princeton."

Princeton had been my father's first choice, and Penn State was only a backup. That was the plan.

My backup plan turned out to be necessary, but Penn State did admit me after all. In my yearbook, my high school classmates wrote "To a future doc" and "Good luck when you get to med school." I began to fear what would happen to me if I were not accepted to medical school; I didn't know what other people did for a living, except maybe for lawyers or teachers, and I didn't want to become either of those. I decided I'd better study harder, at least until I had a better idea of the alternatives to becoming a doctor. No other option ever came to mind.

My four years at Penn State all seemed a long detour before the real preparation could begin. My grades were good, so my admission in 1959 to Jefferson Medical College in Philadelphia was assured. My father had attended Jefferson, and he was ecstatic.

"Congratulations. Jefferson is a great school. I know you'll do well there."

Students weren't supposed to enjoy medical school, but to my surprise, I loved it, even the basic science courses. The clinical years were the best. I especially liked working in the operating room and became the most enthusiastic of retractor holders. The time passed quickly, and in June 1963, I received a diploma that said "MD" and a promotion to intern. I was taking care of "my patients," although I no longer possessed the same self-confidence that I once had in rushing to rescue a sandbox victim. Nurses and patients called me "Dr. Lucas," although they often looked as if they were about to ask, "Just how old are you, anyway?" After four years of being called "hey you" in medical school, I still wasn't used to being addressed as "Doctor," and I sometimes caught myself looking around to see who the nurse or patient was talking to.

I had just started a rotation in the hospital's brand new experimental ICU, and I carefully read the instruction manual for each new apparatus. Few doctors had any experience with the new high-tech equipment and techniques; interns, residents, and senior staff physicians all had to learn from scratch. I had attended conferences, read journal articles, and examined the equipment and new intravenous catheters used in the ICU, but none of us, not even the faculty members, had yet provided hands-on care for very many intensive-care patients.

"The Unit" contained only four beds; Philadelphia General was the one of the first hospitals in the city to even have an ICU. Most of the regular staff physicians maintained a safe distance with only faint curiosity about the noisy equipment That reminded them of Dr. Frankenstein's laboratory. Like vines in an overgrown garden, twisted tubing sprouted from machines surrounding the beds and invaded every orifice of the cadaverous patients.

The residents and staff physicians liked to make rounds on the patients during the day, but we interns were the only ones present in the evenings and at night—and nighttime was when everything happened. At 11:00 PM on my first night on call for the ICU, the page operator called me on the loudspeaker system, "Dr. Lucas to the ICU stat!"

My pulse raced, and my hands were sweaty from the anxiety of being responsible for the care of an unstable patient. I had seen a few critically ill patients, but I had never before made decisions regarding their treatment.

The patient, Mr. Craig, had come to the emergency department during the evening with crushing chest pain and had suffered a cardiac arrest while an emergency physician was examining him. Up until 1963, not many patients had survived a cardiac arrest, but we had all recently been trained to use CPR, and we had also received one of the new cardiac defibrillators. Mr. Craig had been in the right place at the right time. He was ashen, but alert, when he arrived in the ICU. I sat down next to his bed.

"Am I going to die, Doctor?" he asked.

I tried to sound reassuring. "I know you had a scare, but you're better now. You still have a little problem with your heart rhythm, but we're controlling it with some medicine in your IV tubing."

"That's good." He spoke without looking at me, continuing to stare at the ceiling.

"Your nurse is watching your heartbeat on this EKG monitor," I said.

"I'm frightened."

So am I, I thought. I cleared my throat and took a breath. "Are you having any more chest pain?"

"Just a little," he said.

"But it's still there?"

"It's not nearly as bad as it was in the beginning."

I turned to his nurse, Sally Barton. "What was his last blood pressure?"

She didn't look away from the monitor. "Still about eighty systolic. I can't hear the diastolic," she whispered.

"Let's give him two milligrams of morphine intravenously every two minutes until the pain goes away."

She frowned and looked at me. "Won't that lower his blood pressure more?"

Sally had been working in the new ICU for three full weeks, making her a relative veteran. She seemed to sense my insecurity. My sweaty palms and persistent rapid pulse told me she was right. Nevertheless, I worried that if the patient remained tense, his body's oxygen demands would increase, robbing from his injured heart muscle.

"It's a risk," I said, "but he'll get worse if we don't relieve the chest pain. I'm going to put in an internal jugular catheter so we can monitor the effect of his drugs and calibrate the dosage more accurately."

Sally turned fully toward me, still frowning. "I've only seen the insertion of a catheter like that once before, and it was a vascular surgeon who did it," she said.

"Is everything okay?" Mr. Craig asked.

"You're doing fine," I said, "but we want to eliminate your pain with some medicine, because you'll be more comfortable, and it will help you recover faster."

I motioned for Sally to move away from the patient's bed a little so we could talk in private. I whispered, "I feel like we're flying blind without some way to measure the effect of the morphine and the other cardiac drugs that we're using, and I don't think I can entice a vascular surgeon to come in late at night to insert a venous catheter into a patient with such a poor prognosis."

She hesitated but then went to get a tray for the procedure and arrange the instruments. When everything was ready, she put on sterile gloves and gave me a weak smile. She prepped Mr. Craig's neck while I put on my gloves and tried to recall how to insert the catheter, trying to envision the diagram that I had studied a few days before. The critical moment arrived: she handed me the introducer for the venous catheter.

My voice cracked slightly. "Mr. Craig, I'm going to put a needle into your neck so that we can adjust the dose of your medication more precisely. It will only hurt a little."

He didn't respond. He kept staring at the ceiling while I felt around for the landmarks in his neck. I began to question whether this was a good idea, but I was committed. What would Sally think if I said I couldn't do it now?

Mr. Craig's neck was slender, and I could feel the pulse of his carotid artery next to the jugular vein. I just did it: I inserted the introducer. To my astonishment, I located the internal jugular vein, and the catheter slipped in, just as in the diagram. We attached IV tubing and a monitoring device and found everything working. I felt a huge exhilaration and flashed a thumbs-up sign to Sally. She rolled her eyes, but then she gave me a real smile.

"Let's start the morphine now," I said.

We both watched the gauge attached to the catheter and noted no worsening of Mr. Craig's severe congestive heart failure. Within ten minutes, he was asleep. His vital signs weren't good, but at least they weren't deteriorating. We had to give him more medicine to interrupt a dangerous cardiac arrhythmia during the night, but he slept through it.

Finally, a faint glow of dawn appeared through the lone window. Sally and I had been up all night watching Mr. Craig.

"I'm going to the cafeteria to grab something to eat before morning rounds start," I said. "Can I get anything for you?"

"No, thank you," she responded. "We're short of ICU nurses, so I brought a thermos and a sandwich in case I had to work extra hours." Then she said, "Luke—nice work. Most patients as sick as Mr. Craig don't make it through the night."

I dashed to the cafeteria, glowing, and ran into my friend Roger Casey. He and I were on duty together every other night, and we shared the same on-call room at the hospital, although neither of us spent much time there. While I was on my rotation in the experimental ICU, he was assigned to the surgery service. We sometimes saw each other in the cafeteria for a quick breakfast before sprinting to morning rounds with our respective residents and staff physicians. I found him there among the other interns and nurses, all wearing hospital uniforms: crumpled white coats adorned with stethoscopes for the interns and equally wrinkled light blue uniforms and caps for the nurses.

"How was your night?" I asked.

Roger was grinning broadly. "I had two patients with appendicitis—two—the same night."

"I hope they came in early."

"One of them did," he said.

Interns occasionally got to do appendectomies, if the right resident were on duty, but many interns never got to be the primary surgeon for an operation during their entire year's internship.

"Did you get to do the case?" I asked.

"The chief surgical resident was still here. He talked me through it."

I smiled about his good fortune and hoped I would get my own case some night. "Congratulations," I said. "You can put a notch on your holster."

"Two notches," he said with a little laugh.

"You did the other case, too?"

"The second patient came in at 2:00 AM, and I called the surgical resident." Roger stopped and took a big swig of coffee. "He sounded sleepy."

Roger paused again, and I said, "So?"

"He knew I had done the first appendectomy earlier, and he said, 'You do it,' and hung up."

"He never came down to the OR?"

"Nope."

No law prohibited interns from doing an operation, but we all knew the unwritten rule that a surgeon or surgical resident was supposed to scrub in to supervise.

"You did the case solo without a surgical resident?"

Roger gave an exaggerated nod. "Yep."

"You rascal!" We both laughed.

He opened his eyes wide, wrinkled his brow, and spread his arms. "I was just following orders."

I gaped at Roger and shook my head.

"I couldn't make the resident come down," he said.

I had to admire Roger's boldness. "Two appendectomies the same night. You'll be able to teach the rest of us pretty soon."

Ordinarily, the surgical residents would fight to get cases, and I suspected the resident who had slept through the night would be a little embarrassed—if he even remembered that he had ordered an intern to do an appendectomy. Meanwhile, Roger was gaining experience and confidence, although not in the way that the designers of the teaching program had intended.

Roger asked, "What's up in the ICU?"

"I've been a little busy. I have a patient who came in with chest pain and arrested right in the ER."

"Wow! Is he still with us?"

"Barely," I said. "He's alert enough to answer questions, but he's sleeping most of the time."

"What's his blood pressure?"

"If you listen very carefully, he has a systolic of around seventy or eighty."

"Whew!" He shook his head. "You can't get much sicker than that."

I turned to get up. "I can't stay. I just want to grab a banana and some coffee and get back to the ICU before morning rounds."

When I returned, Mr. Craig was still asleep, and Sally said that nothing had changed during the few minutes that I was in the cafeteria. I joined the entourage that was forming, led by a gray-haired staff physician, Dr. DePalma, the only one wearing a suit instead of a white coat.

The chief medical resident, Tony Ramirez, asked, "Who's presenting Mr. Craig?"

"I am," I said. "I was on duty during the night."

"What's his story?"

"He's a sixty-one-year-old man with an acute myocardial infarction who had a cardiac arrest witnessed by the ER staff."

Dr. DePalma interrupted Ramirez. "Why the bandage on his neck?"

"That's for an internal jugular catheter," I said. "I'm monitoring his central venous pressure to adjust his IV meds."

Dr. DePalma raised his eyebrows. "Who inserted the catheter?"

"I did," I said.

"Did anybody help you?"

"I didn't know anyone to call who had ever done one." I didn't want to imply that it might have been impossible to entice someone to come in the middle of the night, even if I had been able to find a physician experienced in inserting internal jugular catheters.

"Who taught you how to do it?"

I hesitated before answering. "I watched one a few weeks ago."

In fact, I had only watched a film. Roger and I had examined one of the catheters in our room and figured out how to insert one by reading the package insert and looking at the drawings. I didn't mention that part.

Dr. DePalma glared at me and shook his head. "An experimental ICU isn't the same thing as a dog lab."

I spread my hands and said, "The patient was in cardiogenic shock—and still is—with a blood pressure of only about eighty systolic. I didn't want to just guess at the doses of the drugs I was using."

"What's happening with the patient now?"

"He has severe congestive heart failure, and he's still having occasional short runs of ventricular tachycardia."

While Dr. DePalma was quizzing me, Tony Ramirez had been examining the patient with his stethoscope and said, "He's got a gallop and crackles halfway up his chest. With his story, it's no surprise that he has congestive heart failure." The gallop rhythm indicated that Mr. Craig's heart was struggling. The crackles came from fluid accumulating in his lungs as a result of the heart's weakened pumping action.

Dr. DePalma looked sideways at me. "What do you think about his prognosis?"

"Well, he's still alive," I said. "I've never seen a cardiac arrest victim survive to leave the hospital, and I know Mr. Craig has end-stage heart disease, but he could surprise us and recover. Isn't that what we're trying to find out with this new ICU?"

Dr. DePalma murmured something about new medical technology being a toy that wasn't going to help much with quality of life before leading us on to see other patients.

At lunchtime, I found Roger sitting in the cafeteria with two of the nurses, Jill Sandler and Sally. Their sandwiches looked soggy, so I reached for a banana again and some cottage cheese. Roger took a bite from his sandwich and then pushed it away. He leaned over and picked up a copy of the *Philadelphia Inquirer* that someone had left on an adjacent table and noted the headline: "More Marines to Vietnam."

That was bad news for us. Congress had just passed a law authorizing a doctor draft a few months before. Both Roger and I had already been accepted to begin surgery residencies at the end of our internships, but the news from Vietnam cast a pall over our plans. I didn't understand why our government would demand that Roger and I sacrifice the completion of our training for some conflict in a small Asian country. The United States hadn't been attacked. American involvement in Vietnam sounded more like an adventure than a defense of our country.

Roger began reading aloud: "President Johnson affirmed that Communist forces from North Vietnam led by Ho Chi Minh were reinforcing the Vietcong, threatening the overthrow of the democratically elected government of South Vietnam. According to Johnson, unless Western nations came to the defense of small, fledgling democratic nations, one state after another would fall like a row of dominoes.

Additional marines and equipment are needed to ..." He stopped reading and looked up.

Sally said, "It's strange. Until recently, places like Vietnam, Cuba, North Korea, and Red China meant no more to me than if we were talking about the Peloponnesian Wars. I'm still not absolutely certain where Vietnam is."

"We shouldn't be involved in this," Jill said.

I agreed with Jill. "I never imagined that we would risk another war with China after our experience in Korea."

"I think as we commit more advisors and equipment," Roger said, "the North Vietnamese and Chinese will do the same, and the conflict will spiral out of control."

"Let's hope this all blows over," I said.

He stared back. "Have you checked your mailbox?"

"What's going to be in my mailbox?"

"I don't know," he said. "But in mine, there was a little greeting from the Selective Service Administration."

I stopped. "Damn!"

I had been ignoring newspapers and had convinced myself that President Johnson would never allow further escalation in Vietnam. Roger's residency plans had just gone up in smoke, and mine would probably follow.

He said, "I have to report in July."

I looked down at the floor. "Which service?"

"Navy."

I headed straight for my mailbox. There was the letter. I was to become an officer and a gentleman in the United States Navy in July, and I would soon receive further information about duty assignments.

Another letter arrived a few days later from the navy's Bureau of Medicine, better known as BuMed, inviting me to apply for admission to the Naval Air Training Command in Pensacola to become a flight surgeon, which would obligate me for an additional year's service. Or I could be assigned to the general doctor pool, which usually meant the Fleet Marine Force. I didn't want to spend an extra year in the navy, but I also didn't want to go to Vietnam with the marines, either.

I had no intention of wavering from my planned medical career, but learning to fly in the navy did have some appeal. My two uncles had been naval officers during World War II, one of them a naval aviator, and I respected their service to the country. My curiosity about the navy had increased with the election of President Kennedy in 1960. He had been a naval officer in World War II, and later supported Project Mercury, the launching of an astronaut into space. I could become both a naval officer and a doctor. Flight surgeons received six months of training that included not only learning to fly, but also a basic education in the fledgling specialty of aerospace medicine.

I told Roger about Pensacola.

He frowned. "I can't picture you as a fighter pilot."

"Doctors receive only basic flight instruction. Most of the time in Pensacola is spent on training in aviation medicine."

"Are you serious about this?"

"Wouldn't you like to learn to fly and study aerospace physiology?"

"First of all, no!" he replied. "I'll keep my feet firmly on the ground, thank you. Secondly, last night, I asked Jill to marry me, and she said yes. She would probably change her mind if I said I was going to fly off aircraft carriers."

Jill was the best-looking nurse in the hospital, hands down, and came from a wealthy family from the fashionable Philadelphia Main Line suburbs. Her parents had wanted her to attend Bryn Mawr College, but Jill had decided that nursing was for her. She increased her offense by accepting a poorly paid position at Philadelphia General. Worse, she was now going to marry Roger, an orphan who had attended Girard College, a prep school in Philadelphia endowed by the Girard Trust for academically promising orphans. He was tall, blond, handsome, and poor. We had been best friends since our first year at Jefferson Medical College, where he had received a full scholarship.

"Well, I'm not surprised," I said. "When's the big date?"

"Because of this war thing, she agreed that we shouldn't wait. The wedding's next month."

"You're sending me an invitation, aren't you?"

"Invitation? More than that, Luke—you're going to be the best man."

"I'm honored." I shook his hand and laughed. "Just let me know how I can help."

As long as I was going to be in the navy, I thought I might try to make the best of things. Naval aviation might prove a great adventure, so I applied to the School of Aviation Medicine and took a physical exam. A month later, they sent a letter accepting me. Roger received orders to report to the U.S. Naval Hospital on Guam. He was allowed to take Jill with him.

"We're eligible to live in navy housing," he said.

I was happy for them. "Congratulations. What a great assignment."

"Jill is sad about leaving Philadelphia, but at least I'm not going to Vietnam." He seemed embarrassed and hesitated for a minute. "I hope the school in Pensacola works out for you."

I smiled. "I'm looking forward to it."

Chapter 2

HOME OF THE BLUE ANGELS

"Howdy. If you're going to the naval air station, we could share a taxi."

A tall blond man in cowboy boots tipped his ten-gallon Stetson. We had both just arrived on different flights at the Pensacola civilian airport, and we were both headed to the air base. We climbed into the backseat of an ancient taxi. The elderly man behind the wheel looked as if he might have been a retired chief petty officer.

"Administration building?"

The driver didn't bother to turn around or to ask if we were going to the naval air station. He could tell just by looking at us that we were green recruits. We headed off.

The cowboy turned to me. "My name's Colt. Colt Benson. Dallas, Texas. I'm going to the School of Aviation Medicine. I'm a doctor."

With a real Colt on his hip, he could have passed for a movie actor ready to enter a saloon for a gunfight. Even leaning forward, his head touched the top of the taxi, so he moved a little sideways and then sprawled back in the seat.

"I'm Luke Lucas," I said. "I'm from Philadelphia, and I'm in the student flight surgeon program too. Did you go to medical school in Texas?"

"Yep. University of Texas Southwestern in Dallas."

"Why did you apply to the School of Aviation Medicine?"

"I don't think I want to practice medicine. I've figured out that being up all night taking care of sick old people isn't my thing."

I laughed. "In aviation medicine, we won't have sick old patients."

"True, but I'm going to try to get into the regular flight training program and become a naval aviator, not just a flight surgeon." He turned to look me in the eye. "I want to fly supersonic jets and forget about being a doctor."

We stopped at the gate. I noted the huge sign while the marine guard checked our orders.

UNITED STATES NAVY
NAVAL AIR TRAINING COMMAND
PENSACOLA, FLORIDA
HOME OF THE BLUE ANGELS

The big Texan silently took in the sign. "I don't know about aviation medicine, but flying with the Blue Angels would be hot."

"You'd like to barnstorm around the country doing air shows?"

"I'd do anything if I could fly with the Blue Angels."

The driver passed brick buildings like those on a college campus, and moved on to the administration building where he dropped us. Inside, a petty officer at a desk gave us a map and directions to the BOQ, bachelor officers' quarters, where we would live for the next six months. He instructed us to be present for a roll call in front of the building at 7:00 AM the next day. I felt like a college freshman moving into the dorm.

The next morning, we found ourselves in a group of about fifty doctors from around the country, all of whom had just finished internships.

At exactly 7:00 AM, a marine sergeant with gleaming black shoes and a perfectly pressed uniform marched up to us.

"Line up!" he yelled.

He was the nutcracker, straight from Tchaikovsky's ballet, with his dazzling brass buttons, red coat, and blue trousers. He glowered at us from under a stiff, wide-brimmed hat that reached down to his eyebrows, held captive by a leather chinstrap that partially concealed his deadpan face. His every movement was squared like a robot or a dancer playing the part of a marionette.

In contrast, we were in alien territory, diffident and shivering in the cold morning. None of us had known which uniform to wear, so we variously chose white, navy blue, or khaki, pulled straight from overpacked suitcases and wrinkled just like the white coats we had worn in our hospitals. After fumbling around for several minutes, we arranged ourselves in a single straight row of fifty doctors facing the sergeant.

"I can't see you when you're spread out from here to Alabama; form five rows," he bellowed.

There was no course on how to line up in medical school, and it seemed to be an unsolvable problem for us. The sergeant shook his head and addressed us.

"Ladies, you are the worst-looking group of recruits I have ever seen. Thank God you aren't going to be marines. It would be too embarrassing."

He taught us how to do "dress right" and pushed us into five rows, more or less, and began to march down each row examining each of us from head to toe.

"Name."

"Lucas, sir."

"I'm not a 'sir,' I'm a sergeant, Mr. Lucas."

He put a checkmark on a clipboard that he carried like a baton and continued strutting through the five rows, stopping in front of each victim. When he had completed his rounds, he yelled, "Where's Mr. Watson?"

At that moment, the last of our colleagues emerged from the BOQ with one shirttail out under the blouse that he continued to button as he rushed to our formation. The unfamiliar lines confused him as he desperately searched for a spot to hide.

A roar came from the front of the group. "Did you have a good sleep, Mr. Watson?"

"No, sir—I mean, yes—sir."

"Do you show up late for the operating room too, Mr. Watson?"

"Uh—no, sir."

The sergeant put another mark on his clipboard and glared at the group. He shouted, "Left face!"

I found myself standing face-to-face with the doctor next to me.

He yelled, "Do any of you doctors know which direction is left? God help us if you ever have to do an amputation."

Several of us made 180-degree adjustments. Then we made a few more feeble attempts at left face, right face, about-face, and moved on to the salute. The sergeant shook his head and pronounced us hopeless.

A marine corporal who had been standing behind the sergeant started passing out folders containing maps, instructions on naval dress code, naval regulations, class schedules, and information on how to avoid venereal disease. Apparently, the navy assumed that doctors who couldn't tell left from right would probably be unfamiliar with how VD was transmitted, too. After an exhausting year of being on duty every other night, they may have been right about that.

The navy had assigned us all the rank of lieutenant, the lowest rank for any doctor, but we outranked the marine sergeant, so he had to act more like a scoutmaster than a boot camp drill sergeant. It must have been painful for him. He discharged us to begin our aviation medicine classes, which were to start immediately. In the afternoon, we would begin ground school for the aviation part of our training.

Late in the day, we trudged back to the BOQ, each toting a stack of instruction manuals and books and more homework than we had seen since our first year as medical students. I passed the open door of Colt's room and found him sitting staring at a bottle of Budweiser next to the stack on his desk. The pile of books was taller than the bottle of beer, a bad sign. Still, the long hours studying aviation medicine and learning how to fly an airplane would seem almost like a vacation after an internship taking care of critically ill patients. I thought the next few months might even be fun. I liked the idea of going back to being a college student, at least for a while, and I didn't mind at all the idea of sleeping every single night.

Almost every day during the first two weeks, the navy entertained us with some sort of swimming pool game, including one that remains a lasting memory: the parachute drag. It simulated being tugged through the water by a parachute canopy filled with wind. A big drum with a motor sat on the far end of the pool with four parachute cords attached.

They floated on the water, extending to our end of the pool where a chief petty officer held them.

He said, "Each of you will take a turn. First, you climb into one of the parachute harnesses on the hooks next to the pool."

The harnesses looked just like ones in Hollywood movies, with straps around the upper thighs and shoulders to form a kind of sling that would hang below a parachute.

"The clips that attach to the parachute couple and uncouple by squeezing. Try it a few times."

"This seems simple enough," I said to Colt.

"Piece of cake," he responded, but the way he said it did not sound convincing. I looked at him and wondered if I had underestimated this little exercise.

The chief petty officer continued, "If you bail out or eject into the sea, you must immediately detach the parachute from your harness. You have four clips. You must release the bottom two first and the top two last."

I repeated out loud to myself several times, "Bottom two first, top two last."

The chief asked, "All right, who wants to go first?" No volunteers. Colt was standing nearest, and the chief pointed. "You're first."

Colt slowly moved to the edge of the pool and climbed in. The chief handed the parachute cords to a swimmer, who attached the four cords and moved away.

The chief called out, "Ready?"

Colt signaled with his hand. The motor started, and the sudden tug of the winch on the cords yanked him forward toward the far end of the pool. He panicked and grabbed at the top clips first. The bottom cords, still attached, flipped and dragged him feet-first, rewarding him with a nose full of water. A rescue swimmer jumped in and pulled him sputtering and coughing out of the pool. The rest of us stood wide-eyed and silent. Colt was mortified. I felt sympathetic and wanted to console him, but there was nothing to say.

Several of us edged a little farther away from the chief, and I repeated my rosary to myself, "Bottom clips first, top clips last."

My turn came. I climbed down into the pool, the swimmer clipped on the cords, and I signaled, awaiting the execution. The tug came suddenly, but I remembered to grab first at the bottom clips. They fell off, and I found the top two. I was free and let out a whoop.

Everyone else made it, except for Colt. He had been sitting on a bench with his head in his hands, unable to look at us or the pool.

Then it was time for the notorious Dilbert Dunker, a contraption that looked like an airplane cockpit resting at the top of two rails forming a steep slide into the pool.

The chief announced, "Each of you will take a turn. You will climb up into the cockpit and attach your parachute harness to the straps."

A worried look passed around the group.

He continued, "When you're ready, I'll release this lever, and the cockpit will drop down into the water."

He demonstrated with the cockpit empty. The contraption plunged down into the pool with a giant splash, flipped over headfirst in a forward somersault, and began to sink. Some of my classmates grabbed the top of their heads and looked upward for divine guidance, while others turned around, taking a step away from the pool and closing their eyes.

It occurred to me that we were doing this in a nice, quiet swimming pool. What if we went down in the ocean? What was I thinking when I volunteered to fly in navy airplanes?

The chief petty officer said, "Underwater, you will be upside down. Release the four clips on your harness and swim toward the bottom of the pool to get clear of the cockpit."

We didn't look at each other. I assumed everyone shared my slight state of shock.

The chief continued, "Don't panic if you become disoriented. A scuba diver at the bottom of the pool will be watching and will pull you to the surface."

"I don't feel very reassured," I said to no one in particular.

I started repeating a new rosary, "Release the clips and swim to the bottom."

"Lucas, you're first," the chief said.

I hesitated before shuffling like a zombie toward the ladder leading up to the scaffold. I climbed in, and a sailor in a bathing suit checked out the clips that strapped me into my coffin. The release of the cockpit came suddenly, and I was underwater upside down. My rosary was directing me, "release the clips," and I was free, swimming toward the bottom. I cleared the cockpit and bobbed to the surface.

Somehow we all got through it, except for Colt, who refused to try or to talk to anyone and left the pool. I tried to find him later, but he wasn't in class or at the BOQ, and the next day, I checked his room and found it empty. A yeoman in the administration office told me he had left the air training command and been reassigned to the Fleet Marine Force.

After a couple of months, the real flying began. Student flight surgeons would spend each afternoon for the next four months at Saufley Field, ominously named for Lieutenant Richard C. Saufley, who was killed in a crash in 1916. Unlike gray operational aircraft, the trainers were painted white with bright orange areas on the nose, wings, and tail, flashing a warning to any other airplane that strayed into the area. When I first arrived at Saufley, dozens of those brightly colored planes were circling the field overhead, and both takeoffs and landings were happening at close intervals.

We were grouped with all of the other students, including some from the Naval Academy. The flight instructors did not give us any dispensation or special accommodation just because we were doctors and full lieutenants. Appropriately, we spent the first hour of instruction learning how to bail out. Once again I had a marine instructor, this time an aviator with the rank of major.

"The most important thing to remember about bailing out is that you must open the canopy first. Failure to do this will result in a significant delay in exiting the aircraft. Better yet, in order not to tax your memory, you will perform all takeoffs and landings with the canopy already open."

A smirk spread around my group of novice aviators.

"In case of an emergency, your flight instructor will order you to bail out. He will give you that order only once. There will be no question and answer period, as your instructor will no longer be in the aircraft."

The jocularity we had once shared was gone. We were a somber group. I had never before seriously considered the possibility of having to jump out of an airplane, and I didn't like the idea. Then I thought of the Fleet Marine Force. Maybe I could jump if I had to after all.

Climbing up into the cockpit of "my" airplane, number 136, I remember thinking how big it was, even though it was small compared with operational carrier aircraft. I strapped in, connected my microphone to the intercom, and went through the cockpit checklist.

The instructor in the backseat said, "Start the engine and go through the warm-up procedure."

I cycled the engine as prescribed in the manual while listening to the air traffic control transmissions. Each flight identified itself as originating from Saufley Field and by the airplane's number, in my case "SF 136," but instead of saying "Sierra Foxtrot One Three Six," they required us to say "Snowflake One Three Six." The navy was giving us a subtle reminder of the ephemeral life of a student naval aviator.

I heard one of my classmates radioing the tower.

"Uh—this is Snowflake—uh—One-Two-Two—uh—Over. Request permission to—uh—taxi."

Silence.

"Uh—this is Snowflake One-Two-Two—over. Requesting permission to taxi."

Silence again.

"This is Snowflake One-Two-Two. Request permission to taxi. Over."

"That's better, One-Two-Two. Permission to taxi."

Somehow I made it through the contact with the tower without humiliation and taxied, very slowly, toward the runway to get in line for take off. The instructor came on the intercom.

"Go to full throttle, kick in hard right rudder, rotate at fifty-five knots, and get us airborne."

I released the foot brakes, eased the throttle forward, and we started our roll. At exactly sixty knots, I pulled back on the stick to rotate.

From the backseat came a scream: "Fifty-five knots, not sixty!"

It was far from perfect, but we were airborne, and nobody had died yet.

About two minutes later, the voice from the backseat sounded again: "Do you think you might want to raise the landing gear?"

I had wondered why flying felt like driving a car with the emergency brake on. I raised the landing gear, and the rest of the flight went surprisingly well. I managed some turns, climbed and descended with the correct speed, and maintained the altimeter exactly on the altitude that my instructor dictated—at least some of the time.

My instructor corrected my little faults over the intercom.

"Fly into the break at 120 knots, not 116, goddamit. Gear down at ninety knots, not ninety-four. Aren't you ever going to lower the flaps? Were you planning to stall on final and get us both killed? Why are all of you doctors so bent on suicide?"

Rarely, he would extend a compliment. One time, when we were doing aerobatics, he yelled, "I want you to do a loop now. For a perfect loop, the pilot should feel his own prop wash at the bottom, but I've never seen a student do it. Doc, you haven't got a prayer, but try it anyway. I'll give you an A-plus for the course if you hit it, but you won't."

Performing a loop in an airplane is like doing a full gainer off a diving board with the bottom of the aircraft facing outward and the cockpit inward. The spot where the loop should finish is exactly the same as where it began. The airplane had to come down somewhere. In my case, it just happened by chance to come down in the prop wash. It was one of my better days.

"My god, Doc, you did it! I hope you're that good with a scalpel."

The day of my first solo flight dawned. The instructor and I flew our plane to an outlying practice landing strip several miles away from the traffic of Saufley Field. The Naval Air Training Command quarantined student pilots making their first solo takeoffs and landings so that the inevitable crashes would affect just one sole victim. The instructor and I landed the plane at the deserted airstrip, and then he stepped out.

"It's all yours."

Weak-kneed, I taxied into position for takeoff, stopped to check for any other aircraft in the landing pattern, released pressure on the foot brakes, and pushed the throttle forward. The plane started to roll and pick up speed. I eased back on the stick, the nosewheel came up, and the noise and vibration from the landing gear stopped—I was airborne. My fear evaporated and overconfidence arrived.

"Bring on the Red Baron!"

I completed my three prescribed practice landings, coming down each time squarely on the simulated aircraft carrier arresting wires painted on the runway. I wanted to go around again and do some more. Realizing that my instructor would not be amused, I stopped to pick him up for the flight home.

"I'm certifying you safe to solo," he said. "Next time, you can check out an aircraft on your own to practice."

I took it as an enormous compliment to be told by a marine major that I was safe enough to pilot a naval aircraft. I framed my flight certification and planned to hang it on my office wall—if I survived to have an office.

After six months in Pensacola, I received orders to the fleet. I was going to a carrier squadron that specialized in photoreconnaissance, VAP 61, based on Guam, with detachments on several carriers cruising in the South China Sea and the Gulf of Tonkin. Roger Casey and I would cross paths again, but unlike the hospital where Roger was stationed, my squadron would move around, mostly off the coast of Vietnam.

Chapter 3

WELCOME ABOARD

After a long air-conditioned flight, Guam greeted me with blinding sunlight and a blast of suffocating hot and humid air that sapped all of my remaining strength. Upon descending the portable stairs from the airliner, I entered an inhospitable landscape. Navy Seabees had constructed the runway, aircraft parking areas, roads, and buildings out of concrete composed of fine sand and crushed coral that reflected the burning heat from the sun, creating visible waves dancing from the surface. A fine grit penetrated my hair, clothing, and teeth. Sweat began dripping from my face, and my surroundings began to slowly revolve.

A navy hospital corpsman appeared. "Welcome to Guam. Here, I'll help you put your luggage into my jeep."

I wobbled toward the parking lot.

"You feeling all right?" he asked. "You look pale."

I felt like I was going to hurl. "It was a long flight. I'm just a bit woozy."

He frowned. "Would you like to sit down?"

I waved him off. "Is it always this hot?" I asked.

He laughed. "This is the best part of the day. You might want to stay out of the sun in the afternoons. That's when it really gets hot."

Hotter than this? It already felt like I was roasting on a barbecue spit.

"I'll be sure to stay out of the sun," I said.

"Don't worry, everyone who comes in from the States takes a couple of weeks to acclimate. We all get used to it."

He put the jeep in gear. The tires squealed, and we tore off.

"Where are we going?" I asked.

"The dispensary. That's where you can see patients when you're on the island. It's right across the street from the VAP 61 administration offices."

"Shouldn't I check in with VAP 61 first?"

"Two other flight surgeons work in the dispensary, but Dr. Hackett is the only one there today. He'd like to meet you. Then you can spend the whole rest of the day with your squadron."

"What's the dispensary like?"

"Small. But we can handle most of the problems of the patients that come in."

I looked at the palm trees and bleached concrete buildings that we passed. "Why are all of the buildings made of concrete?"

"Typhoons," he answered. "About one a year."

I had been on Guam for only a few minutes, and already I wanted to get back on that airplane. Guam did not resemble at all the Hollywood depiction of a tropical island. I saw jungle from the air before landing, but the naval air station was a burning desert.

"Everything looks deserted," I said. "I haven't seen any people walking around."

"They say only mad dogs and Englishmen go out in the sun in the tropics. The square building up ahead is the dispensary." He grinned. "It's air-conditioned. You'll like it."

The dispensary, a plain, concrete-block building, was attractively landscaped with hibiscus, palm trees, and a lawn. I noticed that no one ventured outside into the heat to greet us. We went in.

"Hi, I'm Glenn Hackett. Welcome to Guam."

Dr. Hackett wore a khaki uniform with an open-collar shirt, short pants, and knee socks like British soldiers in Southeast Asia during World War II. He was about my age, friendly, and a lieutenant like me. He held a cup of hot tea.

We shook hands. "Luke Lucas."

"How was your trip?"

"Long. I feel like I've fallen off the edge of the earth."

"You have—Guam is beyond the edge," he said. "The jet lag and heat will leave you fatigued for a few days, but you'll recover. Stay hydrated."

"I already feel as if I could drink a gallon of water."

"Would you like some tea?" he asked.

"Water would be fine, thank you," I said. "How's your medical practice here?"

"Pretty boring. Active-duty naval personnel are a healthy bunch, so we have very little to do."

The smell of disinfectant emanated from all corners. This was a well-scrubbed building. In the small surgical treatment room, the instruments looked as if they were arranged for inspection. Dr. Hackett said that neither doctor performed surgical procedures very often. I saw two doctors' offices that shared three exam rooms, all empty, but noted that three doctors working at the same time might trip over each other if the volume of patients were high. Three hospital corpsmen in pressed white navy uniforms were talking in a small coffee alcove. Two sailors sat in the waiting room. No one seemed in any hurry.

We looked at a small ward with six beds. "Usually we have no patients in the infirmary," he said, "never more than two or three. They mostly have just the flu, back strain, or some other minor problem. We only keep them here because they're not allowed to lie around the barracks when they're sick."

Practicing medicine as a navy doctor at the naval air station on Guam was the exact opposite of my internship at Philadelphia General. I decided that boredom might be worse than being overworked.

"It sounds as if you don't need another doctor," I said.

He smiled. "That's true, but you'll probably be away on detachment with your squadron most of the time. Their planes are scattered around the Western Pacific and often aboard a carrier."

"I could cover you in return when I'm on the island."

"Don't worry, we're not exactly overworked. We each see only a handful of patients a day."

In just a few minutes, we had seen the whole building. "You should go over to your squadron's administrative offices now to report in," he said. "They're right across the street by the large hangars. The commanding officer is Stan White, a Naval Academy graduate and a real gentleman. He looks like a young John Wayne."

"Thanks for the tour," I said. "I'll look forward to working with you."

I reemerged from the wintry dispensary into the steamy heat and crossed to the hangars where the VAP 61 offices were located. Inside, the heat was only slightly less oppressive than out in the sun. Mechanics swarmed over a large aircraft, an RA-3B Skywarrior, and electric tools screamed intermittently, forcing the mechanics to shout in order to communicate. The workers moved quickly, intent on their tasks, unlike the relaxed atmosphere in the dispensary across the street.

Since the mission of VAP 61 was photoreconnaissance, the group flew only the RA-3B model of the Skywarrior. Originally, the navy had designed the A-3 as a bomber, but many had been modified for specialized missions. A-3s in other squadrons had been adapted as tankers for in-flight refueling or for electronic surveillance.

On the second floor, I found the administrative offices, which were filled with government-issue gray metal desks and worn chairs. A large, noisy fan struggled without success to create a breeze. Yeomen banged away at typewriters and telephones rang. A large chalkboard on a wall listed the squadron's planes with their locations and flight data. I showed one of the yeomen my orders. He took a copy and pointed to two officers standing nearby.

Like the rest of the naval aviators in the squadron, Commander White wore a khaki uniform, but with long trousers, perfectly pressed despite the heat. His shirt was adorned only with the wings of a naval aviator and the silver oak leaves of his rank. He was talking to another lieutenant as I approached. When he saw me, he looked down at my flight surgeon's wings and extended his hand.

"Welcome aboard," he said. "I'm Stan White. You must be our new flight surgeon."

"Luke Lucas. I just arrived on the Pan Am flight."

I was surprised that the commanding officer of the squadron would introduce himself using his first name, and that saluting was apparently unnecessary in VAP 61. Superficially, there seemed to be a relaxed atmosphere here, but at the same time, the hangar and administrative offices were beehives of activity.

"Are you finding your way around?" he asked.

"I've only seen the civilian terminal and the dispensary."

He laughed. "You've seen most of Guam then."

"I noticed only three or four A-3s parked outside," I said.

"Most of our aircraft are on detachment. Right now, three are flying out of the Royal Australian Air Force base in Townsville, and five are either at Cubi Point on Subic Bay in the Philippines or aboard the *Coral Sea* in the Gulf of Tonkin."

"Townsville must be a nice place."

"We do a kind of specialized photoreconnaissance and have been experimenting with nighttime photography using flares. The deserted coastline near Townsville provides us with a good place to practice, and the RAAF has been generous in allowing us to use their air base."

My imagination began to invent reasons for taking night aerial photos, but discretion called for restraining my curiosity at first. It almost certainly had to do with the war in Vietnam.

"Where do you think I can be of most help to the squadron?" I asked.

"You may want to spend the next few days getting acquainted here; this is our home port, but we're away most of the time. Next week, you can check in with our training detachment at Townsville. After that, you should fly to Cubi Point to learn about our carrier operations and missions in Vietnam."

"How do I get around?"

"We have aircraft flying back and forth all the time, and they often have the third seat empty. We carry a photo technician on reconnaissance missions, but they have no need to fly with us if we're not taking pictures."

Commander White introduced me to the lieutenant standing next to him, his regular navigator, Dave Andrews.

"Dave knows everything there is to know about photoreconnaissance. He's also our legal officer."

Dave gave a big smile and held out his hand. "Welcome to the squadron."

He looked the part of a professional naval officer, trim, short hair, but not tall like Commander White. Underneath his smile, he had a thoughtful and studious air.

"You're a lawyer and a navigator?" I asked.

"No. When I first joined the squadron, I mentioned wanting to go to law school someday, so Stan decided that I was the perfect candidate to be the squadron legal officer."

"If I ever get thrown in the brig, I'll know who to call."

He laughed. "I only get to do boring legal stuff like wills. Do you have one?"

"No, I've never thought about it."

"Everybody should."

"Do I really need one?" I said. Up until going to Pensacola, I had barely enough money to pay for my laundry. I didn't have much more now.

"None of us is rich, but if you're going to engage in dangerous practices like flying in naval aircraft, you ought to have a will. We do some crazy things in this squadron; we land big airplanes on little ships that are moving. It's not like landing on simulated arresting wires painted on a nice, long stationary runway in Pensacola."

I enjoyed Dave's gallows humor, but all the same, it was rather ominous to be asked about a will in my first few minutes as a member of the squadron. My misgivings about opting for naval aviation kept bubbling up in my mind. Roger's decision to "keep both feet on the ground" appeared increasingly more prudent. I reflected that my assignment was not only much more dangerous, but that I had agreed to an extra year of service just for the privilege.

"How do I sign up for a will?" I asked.

"Here, fill out this form and sign it. We'll get it typed up for you."

Dave introduced me around, and I finished filling out forms, including the questionnaire for a will. It was the first time in my life that I had ever seriously considered my own mortality. I was a long way from home and feeling a bit lost.

I decided to find Roger at the large naval hospital, which stood on a hill overlooking the Philippine Sea. I tried telephoning and was connected to the page operator. Within a few minutes, Roger answered.

"Hi, Luke," he said. "It's terrific to hear from you. I have a car. Why don't I come down at lunchtime and pick you up? You can make rounds with me this afternoon."

Seeing Roger was just the medicine I needed. He seemed happy and relaxed. I got into the rusty old car that he had bought used on the island. After the barren naval air station, the road through the town of Agaña up to the hospital looked more like my imagined tropical island. Around the hospital were spacious lawns, flowers, and tall coconut trees that diminished the oppressive heat.

Roger said, "I'm taking care of marines evacuated from Vietnam, mostly with malaria."

"Are they very sick?"

"No, they mostly have the milder form of malaria, but they still spike intermittent fevers."

I knew that patients with malaria could have recurrent fevers for months, and sometimes even for years, but they didn't usually need hospitalization.

"So, why do the patients continue stay in the hospital?" I asked.

"They have to," Roger explained, "because to the Marine Corps, a marine is either fit for full duty, or he isn't—in which case, he must stay hospitalized until he becomes fit."

I struggled to see the logic. Convalescing malaria patients could just as easily be at home or lounging around the barracks.

"And as a result, you end up babysitting for a bunch of healthy marines just waiting for their fever to disappear?"

"Yes, but if they are still spiking fevers after one month, we evacuate them back to the States. Even so, I have a lot of patients."

"How many?" I asked.

"I'm taking care of patients on four wards, each with sixty patients," he said.

"Whew! That's a lot to see every day."

"My nurse and I have become very efficient. We concentrate mostly on patients with problems out of the ordinary. The corpsmen are well-trained to handle routine care. The treatment programs recommended in textbooks don't work, so I'm trying some different combinations to see if I can find a more effective regimen."

Roger had converted what might have been a boring practice into something quite interesting: finding an effective treatment for an old nemesis.

"Do you ever receive any patients with the more severe forms of malaria?"

"Once in a while. Serious complications like convulsions or kidney failure develop rarely, because these marines are in such robust physical condition. Our one death occurred in an older consulting engineer from Douglas Aircraft."

After we made rounds, Roger suggested a stop in the lab. One of the microbiologists wanted Roger to look at a blood smear from a marine who had just arrived from Vietnam. "It might be interesting to check on what she's got."

The new microbiologist turned out to be a slender brunette with an engaging smile and wearing a neatly pressed uniform sporting shiny gold ensign bars.

She introduced herself. "My name is Lynn; I just arrived on Guam a week ago."

"I'm Luke. I just came in this morning. I'm attached to a squadron at the naval air station."

"I haven't had much experience looking at malaria slides, but this one looks different from any of the others I've seen so far." She had the slide in question mounted in a microscope.

Roger peered at the slide for several minutes. "This one might be *P. falciparum* and not the usual *P. vivax*," he said. "*P. falciparum* parasites usually disappear from the blood quickly, which is why we don't often see them after the patients arrive on Guam, but *P. falciparum* can also be more dangerous."

Lynn asked, "If you're going back to the wards, would you show me which patient he is?"

"Sure. Let's go talk to him," Roger said.

The patient was easy to spot. He was shivering with a chill and had a blanket pulled up over his shoulders, not the usual picture of a patient on a ward lacking air conditioning on Guam. Roger asked him where he had been in Vietnam.

"Near to Da Nang."

"When did the chills start?"

"About an hour ago when they came in to get my blood test."

"No, I meant, when was the first time you had a chill?"

"Oh. Three days ago."

Roger turned to us. "He must have been evacuated right after the onset of the malaria. That explains why we're seeing someone with *P. falciparum* on a blood smear."

While Roger was writing orders to begin treatment, I talked a few minutes with Lynn and learned that she had grown up in San Francisco. She had attended the University of California at Berkeley, commuting from home, and later earned a master's degree in medical microbiology at UCSF, the University of California, San Francisco. She had never been far from home, except for one trip with friends to Hawaii, and felt confined peering through a microscope all day. She loved her work, but her college friends had scattered, leaving her feeling isolated. A tropical island similar to Hawaii had been alluring to her, although she was suffering misgivings about Guam, just as I was.

Roger finished writing. "Since you're both new on the island, why don't you come to my house for dinner? My wife, Jill, would love to hear about what's happening back in the States. You can meet the newest member of my family. We have a new baby daughter."

That was the best idea I had heard since arrival. Lynn said she would be delighted to come. We both accepted.

Roger and Jill's duplex in the officers' housing area near to the hospital was downright luxurious compared with the BOQ. I was glad to see Jill again and asked her how she liked Guam.

She looked around. "We're very comfortable living here."

"You have a tropical garden for a yard."

"Yes, the hibiscus grows almost like weeds."

"It sounds as if you'd like to stay."

She waved her hand. "Oh, no. Roger was lucky to receive orders to come here, and it has been like a long honeymoon for us, but I miss home. Paradise can be boring after a while."

"What's in Philadelphia?"

"My parents, brothers, and sisters all live there, and I miss the cultural activities that were part of our lives. I'm looking forward to going home at the end of Roger's service obligation."

I had a chance to talk more with Lynn and called her several times over the next few days. We went beachcombing and watched movies at the outdoor cinema that the navy had set up. Then we went surfing.

In San Francisco, Lynn had lived near Ocean Beach and had become an expert surfer. She had quickly discovered that Talofofo Bay on Guam was the perfect spot and talked me into renting a surfboard from the navy's special services. We borrowed Roger's rusted-out old car, and off we went. Lynn put on a dazzling display "hanging ten," and I survived without drowning.

Several times, we had dinner at the officers' club, called the Top O' the Mar for Marianas. The club had a spectacular view of the Philippine Sea and the dazzling tropical sunset. Being with Lynn was the most fun I'd had in years. Guam started to look just fine.

Commander White was flying to Australia with Dave Andrews the next week and requested that I go with them. He wanted to get an update on the training of new flight crews.

I told Lynn, "The squadron CO wants me to spend some time in Townsville and then aboard ship, so I may be gone for a few weeks."

She was quiet for a few minutes. "You'll write and call once in a while?"

"Every chance I get," I said. "Don't worry. I'll be back. Meeting you is the best thing that's ever happened to me."

"I'll miss you," she said. "I wish you didn't have to go."

I promised I would write and call often. Through medical school, internship, and flight training, I had practically lived as a recluse in a monastery. My first days on Guam were my happiest in years. I found it wrenching to leave Lynn, but off I went.

Townsville was a place out of time. It had something of the atmosphere of the American West of a hundred years before, with a saloon as a gathering place and communication center restricted mostly to male company. A man could order any kind of beer he wanted, as long as it was one of the two Australian draughts on tap. The bar served no other beverages, and none was wanted. If a man were hungry, he again had two choices: hard-boiled eggs or steak-and-kidney pie. The hard-boiled eggs were the smarter choice.

Dust swirled around the main street, coating the facades of the wooden buildings that opened onto raised wooden sidewalks, just like in towns called Tombstone or Durango in Hollywood movies. The street led down to the beach, where two cooks in a shack sold fish-and-chips that customers could enjoy at picnic tables while watching the ocean waves roll in. No one was swimming. A kind of picket-fence enclosure extended through the breakers from the beach into the ocean. When I asked one of the cooks about it, she said, "It's a shark pen—swimmers inside; sharks outside."

The Australians were gregarious and would not think of allowing an American visitor to eat alone, even at a fish-and-chips establishment, so a group of them signaled to me.

"G'day, mate, come and join us."

"Thanks, I'd like to," I said.

They were all tanned and wearing shorts with long, white socks, typical of all young men in Townsville at that time. Each wore a hat with a broad brim, a survival necessity for anyone of British descent in the intense sunlight.

"Will you be in Australia very long?"

"I don't think so, but I'm enjoying my visit."

One of my new Australian friends asked, "What are you American blokes up to out at the air base? Is it a big secret?"

"No, we're taking long rolls of aerial photographs to use for mapping uncharted areas of the outback as a goodwill project for the Australian government. It's almost like a vacation for the flight crews."

"Yeah, there're places in the outback where nobody's ever been."

The Australian government had indeed asked us to do the mapping, but I didn't mention that the real reason for our being at Townsville was to practice the new low-level, nighttime photoreconnaissance.

"Where'ya from?" one of them asked.

"I'm from Philadelphia."

"Philadelphia?" He wrinkled his brow. "That's where the Liberty Bell is, isn't it?"

"Yes," I said.

He thought for a few minutes. "You had to fight earn your independence. We've had to fight to protect ours, too. World War II was a frightening time here."

"I'm sure it was," I said. "I have two uncles who fought in the Solomons during that war. They told me about the Battle of the Coral Sea."

"We remember. You Americans stopped the Japanese from invading Australia."

One of the other Australians offered a suggestion. "We're going to have our annual Anzac celebration in two days. You might enjoy it."

"What are you celebrating?"

"ANZAC stands for Australian-New Zealand Army Corps. World War I was a kind of coming of age for our two countries. After we fought at Gallipoli in 1915, we had more of a national identity. Anzac Day is something like your Independence Day."

I thought for a minute. "Wasn't the battle at Gallipoli a great tragedy for Australia and New Zealand?"

"Yeah, it was. But it also showed our courage, our pride, and our independence."

"I'll look forward to celebrating with you," I said.

The big celebration of Anzac Day arrived. The flight crews took the day off, and I watched the festivities with Dave Andrews. Marching bands and long lines of Australian Army Reserve troops in khaki marched in their digger hats with a strap around the chin and one side of the brim turned up. They moved their arms in an exaggerated fashion—very British—while their boots made a swishing sound in the dust. It seemed festive and patriotic, but I felt a little uneasy about their romanticizing the carnage at Gallipoli.

The Australians had requested that a unit of American sailors from our squadron march in their parade. I suspected that the war clouds gathering in Vietnam worried the Australians, who were happy to have a group of visiting American naval aviators to reassure them that allies were around, in case the dominoes began falling farther south. The memory of a threatened invasion during World War II was still very much on their minds. The Americans appeared in dress whites, marching in perfect formation and looking more sober and professional than the Boy Scout-like Australian reserves. The sailors did not seem to be celebrating. I felt a chill about what might lie ahead for us.

Booths on the street sold food throughout the day while people watched sack races, dog shows, and young girls in kilts performing

Scottish dances. Toward evening, Dave and I went out to the place where, in 1942, the Australians had built a solitary gun emplacement facing the ocean to defend against an expected Japanese invasion.

While we sat watching the surf, I asked Dave how the training was going.

He kept staring at the surf with his elbows on his knees and didn't answer for several long seconds. Then he said, "It's scary—really scary."

I had no idea. I had thought that photoreconnaissance would be relatively safe. "Can you tell me about it so I can understand what the flight crews are facing?"

He looked at me. "As Stan told you, we're photographing the ground at night using flash bombs."

"Yes," I said. "I remember."

He stared out to sea again. "The flash bombs ignite one after another for up to a minute. It's like having a series of giant flashbulbs go off in your face. We're blinded, so I have to navigate with my face in a hood over the radar scope."

"Is that dangerous?"

"Very," he said. "We have to fly at low altitude to get the pictures. It's not too bad here in Australia, but we may be doing this in Vietnam. They have some pretty big mountains there."

"Oh. I understand."

"That's only part of the problem." He hesitated again, still looking out at the horizon as if he were trying to visualize a plane coming in from the sea. "The flash bombs not only light up the ground, they light us up, too."

I looked at Dave. "So that makes you an easy target."

"Scary thought, isn't it?" he said.

I couldn't imagine the courage that it would require to take off from a carrier at night and then fly low over hostile territory bathed in the light of their own flash bombs. It seemed almost suicidal to me. I had been living in a cocoon, concerned with my own minor discomforts. The VAP 61 flight crews were probably going to be in mortal danger. I wasn't sure what I could do as a doctor for them, because what they needed was a priest. If that was supposed to be my role, I felt completely unprepared.

While we were walking back, Commander White found us. He said we would have to leave Townsville the next day and fly to Cubi Point in the Philippines.

"The Vietcong are threatening to overrun the marines defending the U.S. Air Force base at Da Nang," Commander White said. "We will be closing down the training detachment in Townsville and increasing the number of reconnaissance flights over Vietnam."

Stan and Dave did not plan to stay long at Cubi Point. They would pick up a photo technician as a third crewman and continue on to a carrier, ironically the USS *Coral Sea*, off Vietnam. I would follow a day later on the COD, a shuttle aircraft that provided carrier onboard delivery.

Meanwhile, I got a letter off to Lynn. I wrote about what a nice place Australia was and let her know I would be flying to the Philippines, but I didn't mention anything about a carrier or VAP 61.

II

THE GULF OF TONKIN

Chapter 4

NIGHT PHOTORECONNAISSANCE

The COD from Cubi Point reached the *Coral Sea* while Stan and Dave were flying a high-altitude, daytime photoreconnaissance mission. Since they were due to land a few minutes later, I found a spot where I could watch them trap aboard. The large number of aircraft crammed closely together shrank the huge deck, making the ship into a giant Gulliver covered with swarming Lilliputians, each with a pair of sound-suppressors over his ears to protect him from the deafening noise of the jet engines. Each member of the deck crew wore a jersey in a bright color designating his job, and they all carried out the little communication necessary through a kind of sign language. They were in perpetual motion, moving from one task to another and back again, creating purposeful but bewildering chaos.

Suddenly the movement stopped, and every crewman turned to face the stern. In the distance, I could see the familiar outline of an A-3 on final. The huge jet aimed straight for the deck, slammed down with a reverberating thump, and roared as if in triumph. Stan pushed the throttles forward upon feeling the impact to assure enough airspeed in case he had missed all four arresting wires. The tail hook caught the number two arresting wire, yanking the monster aircraft to a stop.

Stan cut back on the power, and the engines calmed to a high-pitched whine.

Standing next to me was a chief petty officer who had stopped to gawk at the giant with the rest of the deck crew. "We call that airplane 'the Whale,'" he yelled at me over the din.

"I can see why," I replied.

"There's no such thing as a routine carrier landing for an A-3," he said. "It's a 'controlled crash' every time."

The landing gave me a thrill. I looked over at the chief, who obviously enjoyed watching, too. He stared at Stan's airplane and continued talking. "Two years ago, one of them broke the number two arresting wire on the *Ticonderoga*."

I turned toward him. "That must have been terrifying."

"Damn right. The frayed end went supersonic in a whipping motion that sprayed the airplane—made hundreds of little holes—like they were pierced with an old beer can opener."

"Was anybody killed?"

"No one was killed, but the cable broke both legs of a sailor who was in the wrong place."

I grimaced and wondered if I had been standing in a dangerous spot.

"What happened to the airplane?" I asked.

"It bolted off the angled deck and dropped down almost into the water—seemed to just hang there—then it picked up enough speed to stay airborne. It was a miracle."

"I wonder why the navy needs to land such a big airplane on a carrier," I said. "Can't an A-3 fly its missions from land bases?"

The chief looked at me and then down at the medical corps oak leaf on my collar; in a lowered voice he said, "You don't know about the A-3?"

I leaned toward him to hear.

"It was designed to carry a nuclear bomb."

"Jesus!"

I was stunned. I knew that the United States had nuclear weapons, but I assumed they were mothballed in silos somewhere in North Dakota or Kansas, or carried on missile-launching submarines. The possibility that naval aircraft might carry nuclear bombs had never occurred to me, certainly not my squadron's planes. I didn't like that. Photoreconnaissance and making maps were more my speed.

Stan folded the wings and followed the directions of a deck crewman to taxi toward a parking slot. He shut down his engines, and different crewmen began unloading the large film cassettes, handing them down through the bottom hatch. As soon as Stan and Dave climbed out, the deck crew attached a small electric cart to the nose gear to push the plane backward toward the edge of the deck with the tail hanging out over the water. Even so, the huge A-3 consumed as much space of any two other aircraft.

When Stan spotted me, he and Dave came over. "Welcome to the Gulf of Tonkin. Come on with us; we'll help you get squared away."

"That landing entertained the whole flight deck crew," I said.

"My flight suit is soaked with sweat during every carrier landing," Dave said. "I'm always amazed to find myself still alive after trapping aboard in an A-3."

If a professional like Dave were scared, there was no hope for me. Trapping aboard in the COD had been easy, because the landing speed was slow, with plenty of time for the pilot to make corrections, but an A-3 had a fast landing speed like an express train roaring through a small town. It seemed a miracle that the violent jerk on the tail hook hadn't ripped the airplane in two.

"We're having a meeting in the war room with all the VAP 61 officers on board in one hour," Stan said. "Captain Leigh will be there. He's the air wing commanding officer. We call him the CAG, which stands for Commander, Air Group. You should attend so you can learn more about our missions, Doc."

I was assigned a bunk in Dave's compartment, paid a mandatory fee for meals in the officers' mess, and then followed Dave to the war room.

Two of the squadron's RA-3B Skywarriors were aboard the *Coral Sea*, mapping areas bordering on North Vietnam and Laos, sanctuaries and supply routes for the North Vietnamese Army regulars (NVA, in our clipped military language), who were flooding south to join the Vietcong, often just called the VC, who were South Vietnamese Communist insurgents.

In the war room, I met Jason Lockhart, the soft-spoken pilot of the other RA-3B and his navigator, Stuart Blake. Dave told me Jason had several years of experience in many types of naval aircraft and a reputation as a good pilot. Jason had a wife and two children living in officers' housing back on Guam. Stuart wasn't married and had been with the squadron for only a few months.

Six of us sat around a metal table with pull-down maps at the head behind Captain Leigh. The captain welcomed us and described the current situation.

"Operation Rolling Thunder hasn't stopped the Vietcong or the NVA. They seem to be getting stronger in spite of the air force attacks. Now they're threatening to overrun the marines defending the air base at Da Nang."

He got up, lowered a large, detailed map of the area around Da Nang and continued, "The marines haven't been able to find the NVA supply bases or their routes coming down from the North. Helicopter crewmen can see nothing through the jungle canopy during the day, and the VC and NVA avoid open areas until night. They're like dancing bantamweight boxers, always on the move."

He looked at Commander White. "Stan, tell me about your experiments with nighttime photoreconnaissance."

"Our flight crews are all adequately trained now to go operational with the high-intensity flash bombs to photograph the ground in long strips at night."

"How's the detail?" Captain Leigh asked.

"The pictures are beautiful," Stan responded.

"Good enough to find a line of NVA soldiers?"

Stan nodded. "We could tell you their hat sizes."

Captain Leigh sat down again. His eyes met Stan's for a few seconds. "Can you find those supply lines?"

"Yes, sir, if they're out in the open."

I thought of Dave staring out to sea, expressing his fears about using the flash bombs.

Captain Leigh looked up at the ceiling, apparently thinking. "There are some problems, aren't there?"

"Sure," Stan said. "We have to fly low to get our pictures, and we've never tried it in mountains like the ones around Da Nang."

"But you can navigate using radar, can't you?"

I saw Dave cross his legs and look away from Captain Leigh.

"Yes," Stan said, "but because of all the twisting and turning between the mountains, we'd have to fly slowly to shoot our strips of film."

Captain Leigh frowned and rubbed his forehead. "And the flash bombs would make you an easy target for triple-A."

"That's exactly right. An antiaircraft artillery gunner's dream. Triple-A may be old technology, but the NVA couldn't ask for an easier target."

"So far, we've seen triple-A only north of the border," Captain Leigh said.

"Yes," Stan said. "So we shouldn't have any problem with triple-A as long as we stay south of the border. The mountains are the bigger problem around Da Nang."

I noticed Dave and Stuart Blake exchanging worried glances.

Captain Leigh began playing with his pen. "How soon would we know what you get on film?"

"After we returned to the ship," Stan said, "we would process the film and have our analysts give you their assessment of possible targets. Anything obvious they would spot immediately, but a detailed analysis of a long strip would take some time."

"So that means a half-hour return flight from the target," Captain Leigh said, "and say, another half hour to process and analyze the film."

"That's right, more or less, but my guess is that our analysts would spot any big target within minutes after coming out of the developing machine."

Captain Leigh was silent and continued playing with his pen. Then he said, "The information would be more than an hour old from the time you take the pictures until we could send target coordinates to our attack planes."

"Yes," Stan said, "it could take more than an hour."

Captain Leigh leaned back in his chair. "An hour is a lot of time for the enemy to leave the area. On the other hand, we might get lucky and find massed numbers to attack from the air—or at least we could point the marines in the right direction."

Stan nodded. "It's worth a try."

There was another brief period of silence, and then Captain Leigh asked, "How soon could you launch?"

"My plane and crew could be ready anytime after dark. We just need to know the areas that the marines want photographed."

Captain Leigh hesitated one last time. "I'll radio the marine commander at Da Nang to ask him what he thinks and let you know shortly."

He left, and we all looked at each other. Dave Andrews said, "Damn! Those are big mountains near Da Nang."

I asked a basic question. "Can you even do it?"

"Yes, we can," Stan said. "Unfortunately, during our training with the flash bombs in Australia, we didn't see mountains like these. There's a risk, but the marines on the ground are at greater risk than we are."

I had been on the *Coral Sea* for only an hour. Here I was in a completely foreign world wondering, again, why I ever wanted to become a flight surgeon. My knowledge about the war so far had been acquired at a safe distance. The reality of what the VAP 61 aircrews might face stunned me.

We all met again in the war room about an hour later.

Captain Leigh said, "The marine commanding officer at Da Nang says he'll take any help he can get. He's plenty worried over his mounting casualties."

"Did he suggest any specific targets?" Stan asked.

"His intelligence staff had been listening to debriefings of marine patrols and poring over maps for several months, so they suspect certain areas as highly probable locations for Vietcong supply routes and bases."

Captain Leigh turned to the map of the area around Da Nang. "The NVA are mobile and could be anywhere in a big arc around the air base." He indicated a large semicircle with his hand. "It's a big area, and they could disperse their supplies and constantly change their routes."

"We can't photograph all of that," Stan said.

"Yes, I know." Captain Leigh pointed to the map. "There is a river called the Vu Gia that cuts through a gorge southwest of Da Nang. It runs from the Laotian border to within about eight miles of the air base."

Dave blurted out, "My god, look at those mountains! Sorry, sir, I was thinking out loud."

Stan tried to repair the damage. "It wouldn't be easy, but I think we could get some good pictures."

Captain Leigh looked at Dave for a few seconds and then continued, "The marines suspect that some supplies are coming in along that river, and they think that the VC may have a supply base at the point closest to Da Nang."

"Have marine patrols on the ground probed the area?" Stan asked.

"No, and helicopters flying over the area during the day haven't spotted anything. But the intelligence people are certain that the NVA are in there somewhere—possibly in large numbers."

"Why haven't the marines attacked?" Stan asked.

"Too many casualties. The rugged terrain would be easy for the NVA and VC to defend."

Dave asked about the reaction of the marine commander when he found out about the time needed to return and process the film.

"They understand," Captain Leigh said. "They're hoping we get lucky and identify a supply dump, or maybe we might surprise the VC with the delayed attack an hour after a flash-bomb run."

Stan turned from the map and looked at Captain Leigh. "We'll be ready anytime you say."

Captain Leigh met his eyes. "Plan for midnight. We'll launch a flight of A-4 Skyhawks about twenty minutes later. They'll be over the target ready to attack by 0100. The flight deck will be clear to recover your aircraft right after they launch. Thank you, gentlemen." Everyone stood, and Captain Leigh left.

Dave continued to stare at the map. "I can handle the night navigation between the mountains with our radar if we come in slowly. But I'll need some time to study the chart to anticipate the turns."

"You have about eight hours," Stan said.

"I want to spend some time with the chart now, and then I'll brief the photo technician. Do you want me to talk to the maintenance crew chief, too?"

"No, I'll take care of him. You go to work on the route over the target."

At 2330, it was pitch black. I watched the three-man crew walk out onto the flight deck to begin the preflight check on their aircraft. I thought how peaceful it was and found it hard to imagine that a battle was raging around Da Nang over the horizon. The air was still warm and humid, but a fresh, salty breeze swept over the deck, augmented by the speed of the ship, which was turning into the wind to capture extra lift for the aircraft about to take off. The combination of the catapult and the ship's movement directly into the wind would vault the thirty-five-ton airplane forward in only 1.2 seconds and produce an immediate airspeed of well over one hundred knots.

At 2350, the deck crew brought over two starter motors, and the jet engines roared to life, obliterating the tranquility on the flight deck. Crewmen pulled the chocks, and one of the yellow shirts, an aircraft director, guided the plane to a catapult. Stan unfolded the wings, and the catapult crew attached the RA-3B to the catapult and scurried out of the way.

At exactly 2400, I saw the catapult officer, or shooter, give the signal to rev up the jet engines. When they reached full power, Stan clicked the switch on the throttles that flashed all of the navigation lights to order the launch. The shooter signaled to open the catapult launch valves, and seconds later, the huge aircraft lunged forward. They were airborne. Da Nang was only about one hundred miles away. Barring something going wrong, they would trap back aboard in about forty-five minutes.

As soon as they were gone, I heard other jet engines come to life. A squadron of twelve A-4 Skyhawks that were assembled on the flight deck prepared to launch. Their engines resolved into a scream that reached the threshold of pain. Each of the planes carried bombs, yet these aircraft were not even half the size of an A-3. They were the worker bees with powerful stingers following their scout to a target. The deck crew manipulated them to the three steam catapults, firing each in sequence. One launched every minute with a loud hiss, followed by a deafening bang that caused the whole ship to shudder. A cable then slowly dragged back the catapult, clanging against the deck and reverberating in all of the compartments in the ship. Within twelve minutes, the whole squadron was airborne.

After the attack planes were gone, the ship seemed eerily quiet. In only a few minutes, Stan, Dave, and their photo technician would return. I stared at the darkness behind the stern of the ship and strained to hear the sound of the A-3 returning. I knew the crew would have endured a frightening minute twisting and turning over the river. Now they would face a night carrier landing.

The plane suddenly reappeared out of the black and immediately slammed onto the deck as before. Stan caught an arresting wire and brought the engines back to idle. Before the deck crew moved the plane, they opened the bottom hatch, and the photo technician began passing down bulky film cases. Other crewmen ran to the small lab where machines would develop the long strips of film, and analysts would search the banks of the river.

I walked with Stan and Dave to the war room to await the report. Within minutes, the voice of a photo analyst blurted out from the speaker phone, "NVA supply column near the start of the run. They're fording the river in the direction of Da Nang."

"How many?" Stan asked.

"About twenty, but I can only see the ones in the river. The banks are covered with foliage, so I can't see much beyond the river itself, but you might consider hitting the area on both sides."

Captain Leigh said, "Most likely the NVA will have scattered, but maybe with the hour delay, they'll think it's safe again. Let's attack the ford and the banks on either side."

The *Coral Sea* radioed the coordinates to the airborne flight of A-4 Skyhawks to begin their attack.

After dawn, the marines sent a message that their helicopters had flown over the area and saw devastated foliage but no evidence of destroyed supplies or dead Vietcong. The enemy had been there during the recon run, but where they were during the attack was anybody's guess. The mission had been a great technological feat. But the marines were no safer as a result, and the North Vietnamese troops and supplies almost certainly continued to pour in.

Chapter 5

HEMORRHAGING AT SEA

Although the first night mission near Da Nang had not paid off, the technique seemed promising, so more missions followed. The CAG began ordering missions north of the border, and the flight crews started experiencing close calls with triple-A fire and surface-to-air missiles, called SAMs. Our intelligence officers told us that both the Soviets and the Chinese were supplying the North Vietnamese with technological support and equipment, including more advanced radar-controlled triple-A, and the *Coral Sea* had already lost one A-4 to triple-A. The RA-3Bs from VAP 61 were especially vulnerable to triple-A fire, but they had the element of surprise during their flash-bomb runs.

I was sitting in the sick bay of the *Coral Sea* when the phone rang. "Doc, it's for you—the CAG wants you."

Captain Leigh had never before called for a flight surgeon during combat operations, so this meant something bad had happened.

"Get up to the flight deck on the double," he shouted into the phone. "We have a damaged aircraft with an injured crewman who is bleeding badly. They can't make it back to the ship and are going to bail out. I want a flight surgeon on the helicopter for the rescue attempt."

I grabbed an emergency bag and the flight helmet that we kept in the sick bay and ran for the deck. During flight operations, a helicopter always hovered next to the carrier in case a damaged aircraft was unable to land and the flight crew had to eject. The helicopter crewmen had plenty of practice rescuing downed airmen from the sea, and a flight surgeon ordinarily only got in the way. But with a hemorrhage, every second counted.

The helicopter was already settling down on the flight deck as I completed my dash and jumped on board. We immediately lifted back off in the pitch darkness. Through the big, open hatch, I saw the disappearing carrier below, completely blacked out, ghostlike, and nearly invisible. Because the deafening noise of the engine and rotor blades made conversation impossible, one of the two crewmen used sign language to direct me to a seat.

I plugged in my helmet's microphone and yelled, "What's up?"

The helicopter pilot shouted back through the intercom, "Doc, it's Jason Lockhart's plane. They took some triple-A and are losing altitude."

"Where are they?"

"Over North Vietnam—about forty miles north of the border."

"Are we going to try to land in North Vietnam to pick them up?" I screamed into the microphone.

"No, Jason is trying to reach the coast to bail out into the gulf. I'm talking to him now. Listen in."

I heard a string of static and then Jason's voice. "Angel One ..." The radio squawked. "Shrapnel ... cockpit ..." The radio squawked again. " ... bleeding ..."

"Where is the wound?" I yelled.

More static and then Jason's voice again: " ... tourniquet ... can't stop ..."

Anxiety gripped me in the same way as the first time I was called to the ICU as an intern, but now I only had an emergency bag, no ICU. I strained to hear the voice again, but the only sounds came from crackling static and the racket and vibration of the helicopter.

The helicopter pilot came back on. "If they made it to the coast, we'll be over them in less than three minutes."

Because an A-3 had no ejection seats, the crew's only option was to bail out through the hatch in the bottom of the fuselage, just as bomber crews had done during World War II. The aircraft's designers had omitted ejection seats to reduce weight, in order to make carrier landings possible. The navigator would have to push the wounded crewman out first. Even if he survived the bailout, one of the helicopter rescue crewmen might have to jump into the water to detach the wounded man's parachute and rig the sling on the hoist, using illumination from the helicopter's spotlight. All that assuming that we could find them in the dark.

"Doc, a second helicopter is on the way, so we'll fish out the injured crewman first and return directly to the carrier," the helicopter pilot said.

The crewman might need multiple blood transfusions in a hurry, and we had no blood bank on the carrier. "How much time would it take to Da Nang?"

"Da Nang?" The pilot asked. "Why?"

"They have a blood bank and experienced surgical teams to handle major battlefield trauma."

"About thirty minutes from where they will try to bail out—half that much time to the carrier, but in the opposite direction," the pilot said.

Fifteen minutes. It was risky when every second counted. On the other hand, what good would the fifteen minutes do if the carrier didn't have the right facilities and equipment to save his life?

"Go to Da Nang," I said.

"Roger, Da Nang. I'll let them know we'll be paying a visit."

A short time later, the helicopter pilot came back on. "We should be over Lockhart and his crew in less than a minute."

The sea was fairly calm, so the helicopter was able to hover just a few feet above the water. One of the rescue crewmen was getting ready to jump in case the bleeding victim needed help. The other rigged a sling that would loop behind the victim and under his arms, attaching in front to the hoist. We had all practiced rescues like this in a swimming pool, but a victim with a major injury, struggling with a parachute and trying to strap into the sling, would probably be exhausted. The two crewmen weren't counting on the victim having any capacity to help himself.

We peered into the blackness. Finding three tiny specks at night on a vast ocean didn't seem possible. I imagined the pain and terror of the injured crewman, wondering if he would be able to inflate his life jacket and turn on his strobe light.

"We'll lay the victim on his back," I yelled into my microphone to the crewman on the hoist, "and then I want you to focus the hand spotlight on the wound."

Jason had used the word "tourniquet," so the bleeding had to be from the victim's arm or leg. He had implied that the tourniquet wasn't working, so the wound probably was high up in his groin, or maybe near his shoulder.

Once in the operating room at Da Nang, a surgeon could stop the bleeding and do a proper repair, and maybe save the leg or arm, too. Plenty of extra hands would be available for starting an IV, hanging the blood transfusions, and checking blood pressure. But for now, I would be working with only a rescue crewman to assist on the floor of a vibrating helicopter—and I had never taken care of a patient hemorrhaging from a major injury. What if I failed and the patient died because of my inexperience? I felt like an imposter.

We were over the area that Jason and his crew had targeted for bailout, but I could see nothing except the main spotlight's small circle of light skimming on the water. We had no way to know whether they had made it to the coast or whether they had been able to bail out safely. If we were going to save that air crewman, we would have to find him quickly.

All of us saw it at the same time, and we shouted together over the noise of the engine and rotor blades. "There's a flare!"

The helicopter veered toward the flare. The spotlight found the downed pilot, navigator, and photo technician, all lined up about a hundred yards apart, with the one farthest away still attached to his parachute and being dragged through the water.

"Get ready to jump," the helicopter pilot yelled.

We descended and hovered only a few feet over the injured man, so that the rescue crewman could jump without waiting for the hoist. No orders were necessary; everyone knew his job.

In a blink, lifeguard and victim came together. After another second, the light breeze separated the now-free parachute from the victim. The second rescue crewman had already lowered the sling into the water using the hoist, and the pilot began maneuvering to drag it toward the victim. In another few seconds, the rescuer in the water had secured the victim into the sling and waved his hand in the air. The hoist pulled the injured man up to the helicopter, and the second crewman and I dragged him in. The helicopter roared, and we lurched forward. We were on our way to Da Nang.

The victim was alive and conscious, barely—shivering, moaning, hemorrhaging, and staring blankly. Without a word from me, the helicopter crewman shined the portable spotlight on the victim's right thigh, which was already covered with blood just after he'd been pulled from the sea. The patient was obviously in shock. I froze for just a moment, aghast at the amount of bleeding.

I shook myself and mopped away the blood with gauze pads. There in plain view was the femoral artery, lacerated and exposed in the gaping wound high up in his thigh. The artery was partially divided, with blood pouring out as from a spigot. I pressed hard with my thumb directly on the artery just above the bleeding site, and the flow ceased. Blood was still oozing from the wound, but at least the major hemorrhaging had stopped.

"Shine the light on my medical bag," I yelled at the rescue crewman.

I picked out a scalpel, a hemostat, and an arterial clamp.

"Okay, now back on the wound."

With my left thumb still pressing on the artery, I tried to enlarge the wound slightly with the scalpel in my right hand. I needed to expose the artery enough to place the clamp above the laceration. The helicopter jumped suddenly from some turbulence, and I almost cried from frustration. How was I going to stabilize the bleeding? With a clearer view of the artery, and less turbulence, I might be able to attach the arterial clamp.

"Hold the spotlight a little closer to the wound," I said to the crewman.

I tried to enlarge the wound again with a quick motion in case we hit more turbulence—still not enough visibility to clamp the artery. Twice more I enlarged the incision. Finally I could see more clearly above the laceration. I used the hemostat to dissect around the artery and took a deep breath—time to clamp.

"Damn!" The clamp wouldn't go on. I had to dissect more to free up the artery. The spotlight kept jiggling, and I couldn't see well enough. It was taking me a long time, and my left thumb pressing on the artery was starting to ache. I tried the clamp again. This time it worked! I gave a whoop.

I slowly released the pressure with my thumb, and the clamp held. No more arterial bleeding. I packed the wound with gauze pads and said to the crewman, "Here, keep some mild pressure on the wound to reduce the oozing."

I needed to get an IV started. I knew that might be difficult, because the patient's blood volume was so depleted that his veins would be collapsed. The best choice would be to insert an internal jugular catheter in the way that I had done as an intern in the ICU. I grabbed an introducer from my emergency bag and felt for the carotid artery pulse right next to the internal jugular vein. I took a deep breath and prayed that we wouldn't hit any turbulence.

I hit a bull's-eye with the introducer and threaded in the large-bore catheter that would allow running a bag of normal saline wide open. As soon as the surgical team at Da Nang poured five or six units of blood into him, they could put him to sleep with a general anesthetic while the surgeon repaired the artery. Meanwhile, the patient would have to make do with the saline rushing into his veins to expand his blood volume and buy time. But he was going to need many units of blood.

His heart was racing at 180 beats per minute, and I wanted to see if he had any measurable blood pressure, but the din of the helicopter prevented my hearing anything through my stethoscope. His weak pulse didn't even bounce the needle on the dial of the cuff. I put a blanket on him and took over maintaining pressure on the wound.

"Take off the patient's boots and raise his feet to help maintain blood flow to the head," I yelled to the rescue crewman.

I clicked on my microphone to talk to the pilot. "I got lucky and was able to stop the bleeding, but the patient needs a lot of blood in a hurry. Connect me with the hospital at Da Nang."

"Sure, Doc," the pilot said. "I'll switch channels."

"Da Nang, this is Angel One. Over."

An air-traffic controller from Da Nang answered, "Roger, Angel One."

"Request patch to First Med. Over."

The air-traffic controller connected us to the hospital, and I clicked on my mike.

"We have a patient in shock with a lacerated femoral artery that's partially divided. I've stopped the bleeding and have an IV running wide open, but he's barely conscious. He needs blood in a hurry. Universal donor would be great, but if you don't have any, his dog tags say A-positive."

"Roger, Angel One. Wilco on the blood. We have an OR open, and we'll be ready for him."

A few minutes later, the helicopter pilot came back on the intercom.

"The VC and NVA are attacking the air base. There's a mortar barrage going on right now. When we approach Da Nang, I'll have to put out all lights back there. This might be a hairy landing."

Oh, god, no! What if the Vietcong shot down our helicopter? What if they overran the air base?

"How's the patient?" the pilot asked.

"He's lost a lot of blood," I said, "and he's barely conscious, but he has a chance."

"You're a good man, Doc."

I thought about Jason Lockhart, Stuart Blake, and the helicopter crewman still in the water. "Have you heard anything about the second helicopter?" I asked.

"Yes, we left a flare to mark the spot for them. They already have Lockhart and his navigator. They're picking up our crewman right now. They're all okay."

"That's a relief."

The injured air crewman was still clenching his teeth and moaning while staring at the overhead. In spite of the warm air temperature, he was still shivering, no doubt from the pain and depleted blood volume. I couldn't imagine how much discomfort he was in, but at least he was still with us. I knew that giving him morphine might suppress his feeble blood pressure even more, but we wouldn't reach Da Nang for another fourteen minutes, and he was becoming agitated. I gave him some morphine anyway.

Thirteen minutes to go.

I took over applying pressure to the wound and noted that the gauze pads had more blood again. I quickly removed them and found that the arterial clamp had slipped a little, probably because of all the jolting around in the turbulence and the pressure on the wound. The failure of the clamp made me want to scream. A queasy feeling hit me, as I realized that I would have to reposition the clamp, and do it fast with a minimum of blood loss. Too far from Da Nang to allow any more blood loss.

"Hold the spotlight close to the wound again," I said to the crewman. "The clamp moved a little, and he's bleeding again."

I took a deep breath and pressed hard again with my left thumb on the artery above the clamp. Then I released and repositioned the clamp in one motion. It held! I gradually released pressure on the artery with my thumb. No further bleeding. A huge sense of relief washed over me.

Ten minutes to the hospital.

I began talking—or rather shouting—to the patient, uncertain whether he could comprehend anything through his distress and the noise of the engine.

"You've lost some blood, but we're only a few minutes from the hospital at Da Nang."

Miraculously, the injured man nodded his head a little, just enough to notice. He never looked at me but still stared at that same overhead spot.

"I'll hold the light," I yelled to the rescue crewman. "You get more blankets and more saline."

The first bag of saline emptied, and I hung a second. His pulse still raced at about 180 beats per minute, and again there was no detectable blood pressure. Seven minutes to go.

"Do you remember bailing out?"

This time he didn't respond. Perhaps the pain was too severe. In any case, my asking him questions to divert his attention was futile.

"The morphine hasn't worked," the rescue crewman said.

"I know; he's still in a lot of pain. Let's give him another dose."

I checked his pulse again: no change, 180 beats a minute. I became conscious of my own pulse hammering, too—so much for my being the calm, cool flight surgeon. Paradoxically, the clock seemed to slow.

Eventually we reached four minutes to go, and the second bag of saline finished, to be replaced by a third.

I stole a glance toward the land, but everything was black; not a light shone anywhere.

The pilot came on the intercom. "We're approaching Da Nang. I'm turning the lights out in the back. We'll be on the ground in two or three minutes."

The helicopter became black as death, and it was turning and bouncing more. The lack of vision completely disoriented me so that I had trouble with balance. I could hear explosions that seemed to be getting closer, and I began to panic a bit. After this frantic rescue, were we going to die caught in the middle of a battle?

Suddenly, we plunged to the ground like a high-speed elevator. I couldn't breathe, paralyzed with fear. A hand immediately reached through the hatch offering a unit of blood. At first, I was confused and thought I was hallucinating, but I could feel it; it was real. As if in a dream, I attached it to the IV tubing, while more hands appeared and lifted the patient onto a gurney. A nurse wrapped a pressure cuff around the bag of blood to speed the infusion, and another checked his blood pressure—still nothing. Everyone knew his role, and no one spoke as they began rolling the patient on a wooden boardwalk directly toward a large tent only a few feet from the helicopter pad.

Chapter 6

FIRST MED

My heart was still racing as I got out of the helicopter in the dim light—I felt like I might faint. My legs didn't want to move. There were a few Quonset huts, a large cluster of tents, and a group of doctors and nurses in scrub suits. I staggered after them into the tent only a few feet from the helicopter pad. The surgical team moved the patient onto an operating table, inserted an endotrachial tube to control his breathing, and started the anesthesia immediately. The surgical light, instruments, and scrub suits looked just like those in the operating rooms at Philadelphia General. But away from the surgical field, the walls made of olive-drab canvas stretched over a wooden frame, the plywood floor, and the combat boots worn by the surgical team confirmed that this was a different world.

"Second unit up," a nurse announced. "A third starting in about a minute."

She had hung another unit of blood using my catheter and was starting a second IV. In just a few more minutes, the patient would have received three or four units of blood. The vascular surgeon had already examined the wound and started calling for instruments.

The circulating nurse, a kind of gofer for the scrubbed-in surgical team, gave me a mask and gown and pointed for me to stand back from the table.

She said, "Dr. Steiner, the flight surgeon who came with the patient is here."

A doctor, presumably Dr. Steiner, spoke to me from behind his mask. "Nice job, Doc. I couldn't have clamped that artery any better myself. I think I can suture it without resorting to a graft. In a few months, we'll give you back a two-legged crewman."

"I'm glad you're here," I stammered. "This is the first time I've seen an injury like this."

"You passed with flying colors. What's the patient's story?"

I told him what happened.

"Your air crewman is lucky to be alive," he said.

"The helicopter crew fished him out of the water not long after he bailed out. That's what saved him."

"That may be," Dr. Steiner said, "but this is a major arterial laceration. Without your stopping the bleeding, the patient would have died. The artery is incompletely divided, and he would have bled out very quickly. If the artery had been completely severed, it would have retracted, stopping the bleeding. This injury would have been fatal without the clamp. You did nice work."

I felt momentary exhilaration. The patient was going to live. The surgeon began the operation, working quickly as more units of blood arrived. The circulating nurse was now standing next to me, telling me about their recent experience. Dr. Steiner had operated all night for the past four nights in a row. She had lost count of the number of surgical procedures they had performed, mostly on marines, but also many on South Vietnamese soldiers and even on Vietcong and NVA prisoners.

She said the attacks against the air base always happened at night, so casualties began coming in just before midnight. After dawn, helicopters often brought in more wounded from the firefights during the night.

"Sometimes twenty-five or thirty casualties arrive on the same night," she said.

While Dr. Steiner was operating on my patient, hospital corpsmen and nurses rushed another wounded man onto a second operating table that I hadn't noticed before. The new arrival was a young marine who was still actively bleeding from a mortar wound. He was nearly dead.

A surgeon accompanying the patient yelled out to a nurse, "Give me an introducer; I'm going to do a subclavian stick."

"I've never heard of that," she responded.

"Just give me the same introducer that we use for internal jugular catheters."

He jabbed the introducer into the patient's chest just under the middle of the collarbone and began threading in the catheter.

"I want eight units immediately," he said. "Fast as you can. This patient is still bleeding, and we need to stabilize him to start the surgery."

Less than a minute later, the circulating nurse called out, "A unit of universal donor is running wide open, and a second unit is ready to follow. The rest will be here in a few minutes."

The surgeon had grabbed some instruments and was beginning to work. Without looking up, he spoke to the nurse. "In a patient whose blood volume is as depleted as this one, the subclavian is the biggest, fattest vein around. If we hadn't been able to pour some blood into him fast, he would already be dead."

I realized that the circulating nurse was probably also the chief operating-room nurse. Her surgical mask hid her emotions for the most part, but her raised eyebrows showed her anxiety. Nobody spoke for a few minutes, and then she started talking to me in a low voice, apparently trying to relieve the stress.

"They sometimes give twenty or thirty units of blood to a patient with extensive trauma," she said, "but that many always causes serious coagulation problems. Patients get a complication from coagulation particles that the surgeons call 'Da Nang lung.'"

Soon, a hospital corpsman came in and told me the helicopter pilot was pressing to leave.

My patient was stable, so I had no excuse to hang around. "All right. I'm coming." I was so grateful that we didn't lose the patient that I wanted to thank Dr. Steiner and the surgical team for their efforts. "Is there anything we can fly in for you from the Philippines or Guam?"

Dr. Steiner didn't bother to look up from the surgical field. "We haven't had any fresh milk in months."

The joke was a sign that the operation was going well. I recognized the laconic humor typical of someone who had recently been an overworked vascular surgery resident. Now he was an overworked surgeon in a frontline hospital. Fresh milk was an ordinary commodity back in the States, but an unobtainable luxury in Vietnam.

"Fresh milk." I frowned. "Okay, you've got it—airmail, special delivery."

It was going to be hard to find fresh milk in the Western Pacific, but I couldn't pass up the challenge. Fresh produce and dairy products were almost as hard to get on Guam and in the Philippines as they were in Vietnam. The Department of Defense sent all food supplies for the Far East by cargo ship from ports on the West Coast, a trip of several weeks. Suppliers had to sterilize milk at high temperature, not just pasteurize it. The milk cooked further in the tropical heat, first aboard ship, and then in commissary warehouses. The only places for us to obtain fresh dairy products were the States, Australia, or Japan. I didn't know if our planes would be going to any of those places any time soon.

I knew that when our flight crews landed in Japan or Australia, they would ask immediately for fresh milk, surprising the natives. The Japanese didn't drink milk; they produced it mostly for the American armed forces stationed there. The Australians considered beer the only appropriate beverage for a man.

"Milk? You mean to drink? You could ruin your health with that stuff."

Out on the landing pad, I became conscious again of the mortar explosions in the distance that had caused me to panic as we were landing. Gunfire was audible, too. A fuel truck was refueling the helicopter, and I found the pilot in his seat calmly conducting his preflight ritual. He turned around toward me.

"Doc, we have to go as soon as they finish refueling."

The carrier would have combat flight operations going on for the next several hours, and we had to get back. The ship had only two helicopters and might need us again.

I climbed into my seat. The crewman had already washed away the blood on the deck of the helicopter and returned everything to its place, as if the rescue had never happened. But I was still shaking as I thought about my airman's devastating injury—and the huge responsibility handed to me for his survival. Taking care of the young airman whose leg had been blown apart was far more disturbing to me than attending to the usual knife and gunshot victims in the emergency department in Philadelphia.

As we lifted off, I stared through the open hatch at the glowing hospital tents below, framed by the night. During the forty-minute flight back to the carrier, my earphones crackled with air traffic control jargon, but no one spoke on the intercom. We were each buried in our own reflections. As we neared the *Coral Sea*, the pilot clicked on the intercom.

"Doc, I just received a message that Captain Leigh wants to see us as soon as we land. He was impressed by the rescue."

"So was I," I said. "You all pulled that air crewman out of the water quickly."

"My crewman told me that you stopped the bleeding immediately."

"He probably could have done the same thing," I said.

The helicopter crewman clicked on. "I could never have done that."

"We were really glad to have you on board, Doc," the pilot said.

I had nearly panicked while trying to stop the bleeding in the helicopter. I didn't want anyone to single me out for praise for just barely doing my job. The whole event felt more like a nightmare than heroism. Being responsible for that airman's life still weighed heavily on me. I knew the rescue could have gone either way, and I had no confidence that I could ever pull off a repeat performance.

We settled down on the flight deck, and the helicopter pilot and I went up together to the war room. A group was waiting for us, including Stan, Jason Lockhart, and Stuart Blake. Another naval aviator from VAP 61 was there, Lieutenant Commander John Grayson, and his navigator, Lieutenant Ted Hanley. Everyone stood up when we walked in.

Captain Leigh greeted us. "That was a remarkable feat you two pulled off." He looked directly at me. "I hear that you saved that airman's life, Doctor."

"We were lucky this time. Another minute or two in the water and he would have bled to death. The quick action of the helicopter crew made all the difference."

The helicopter pilot shook his head and waved his hands. "My crewman tells me that no hospital corpsman could have stopped the bleeding. We were damn glad to have a doctor on board."

Jason came around the table to look me in the eye and shake my hand. When he extended his hand, I noticed a slight tremor. I wasn't the only one who had gone through a bad night. "Thanks, Doctor. That rescue meant a lot to me. I felt responsible for what happened to my crewman."

"What you all did tonight was heroic," Captain Leigh said. "Jason, those marines at Da Nang are getting clobbered, and missions like the one you flew tonight are the only means we have to interrupt the supply lines from the North."

Jason bowed his head. In a quiet voice he replied, "I know the marines are at great risk, sir."

Captain Leigh looked at the helicopter pilot and then at me. "The helicopter rescue was heroic, too, because you two saved the life of one of us. You can call it luck, but the way I see it, that air crewman wouldn't have survived without your quick actions."

He looked around the table. "The only way we can get through this war is by helping each other. The Pentagon works with strategy and numbers—abstractions—but our war is on a personal basis. For us, there is no greater heroism than trying to save the life of a comrade."

I looked at John Grayson, the other naval aviator, sitting quietly, frowning. He had flown a mission over the North at about the same time as Jason's flight. The two looked like twins and had been close friends for several years, flying A-3s. Like Jason, John had a wife and children living in officers' housing at the naval air station on Guam. Ted Hanley, the youngest officer in the squadron, was watching everything. He had married an Australian girl in Townsville just a few weeks before starting this detachment.

We went over the details of the event, and Captain Leigh told us to write up an incident report with a copy to BuMed.

When we broke up, Commander White spoke to me. "Is there anything I can do for you, Doc?"

Without having to think, I said, "Yes, there is. I asked the vascular surgeon the same question in the operating room at Da Nang. He said they would appreciate receiving some fresh milk."

"Milk?"

"It was a joke, of course, but maybe we could pick some up somewhere civilized and find an excuse to stop at Da Nang. That would be the best joke of all."

Commander White laughed. "So they'd like some fresh milk? I think we can take care of that. I may be flying to Japan in a few days to install some new equipment on my aircraft. It wouldn't be much trouble to load up a few cases of milk for the hospital. You can come with us."

Chapter 7

IT'S NOT MUCH OF A WAR

I spent the next few hours trying to write the flight surgeon's portion of the incident report. Writing it up proved difficult for me. The rescue had been an intense emotional experience rather than some technical procedure. I wrote, *I recommend avoiding reconnaissance missions in areas where the enemy is shooting at our airplanes*, but tore that up. Next I wrote, *I engaged in no thought process during the entire rescue and relied solely on reflexes, so I don't remember it very well. If I had thought about what I was doing, I probably would have made a mess of it.* That version ended in the waste can, too.

The flight surgeon's report was not supposed to be a scientific paper; it was just to complete a dossier that the navy would file for aviation medicine research. I tried again. *The airman suffered a shrapnel wound, hemorrhaged from his femoral artery, and bailed out into the sea. We picked him up with a helicopter, clamped the artery, and delivered him to a vascular surgeon in a tent.* Perfect! Now all I had to do was elaborate a little. I delivered the report to Commander White, who approved it without bothering to read it.

I asked him if he had heard anything from Da Nang.

"He's going to be all right," he said. "The operation went well. We got a radio message a little while ago. Why don't you catch some sleep? You haven't been to bed since yesterday."

Weariness had indeed set in, and flight operations would end at noon, in just a couple of hours. We were on a twelve-hour, midnight-to-noon schedule, while our sister ship, now the USS *Midway*, conducted flight operations from noon-to-midnight. The sick bay was nearly empty, and two other flight surgeons were on board, so I expected a little uninterrupted sleep.

While walking to my cabin, I felt the stares of a number of sailors in the passageways. A few spoke to me.

"Nice work, Doc."

"Thanks for saving our shipmate, Doctor."

Captain Leigh, and now one of the sailors, had called me "Doctor," not just "Doc." I felt uncomfortable being singled out as someone who warranted a more formal address. I was still very inexperienced as a physician and feeling insecure about the responsibility.

I shared a compartment for junior officers with four bunks, although two of the bunks weren't taken. Dave Andrews was poring over maps and making calculations. He looked up when I walked in.

"Doc, what you did during the night gave us all a big lift."

"It was a close call," I said. "Don't you count on our being lucky again. Navigate your airplane somewhere a little less unfriendly."

"I'll relay your recommendation to the CAG, and he can inform the president."

"Stupid war," I said.

I lay down on my bunk and examined the springs of the mattress above. Fatigue poured over me, and I closed my eyes. I knew what Dave was doing.

"You're planning another mission?" I asked

"That's the only reason for staring at these maps."

"Where this time?"

"It's a military secret. Navy regulations. Article 13, Section 5."

"I was thinking about joining the navy," I said. "You can tell me."

Dave scowled at me. "All right, we're going somewhere in Southeast Asia."

"That's what I was afraid of," I said.

I was quiet for a few minutes, and then I asked Dave a question. "How long does it take you to plan a mission?"

"For two minutes over the target, about four hours. For four minutes over the target, all day."

"That's daunting."

"With these low-altitude flights, I'm more worried about the mountains than the triple-A. If we hit a mountain, we're dead. If the triple-A gets us, you'll be there to patch us up."

"Go to hell."

"I need to get some work done, Doc. Get some sleep."

I passed out. When I awoke, it was early evening, and Dave was gone. No doubt he was meeting with Stan White and the photo technician to prepare for that night's mission. They would probably launch soon after midnight. As I was dressing, two unfamiliar officers entered the compartment carrying duffel bags. One was a lieutenant who wore the wings of a naval aviator, and the other was a navigator with a single silver bar, a lieutenant, junior grade. They were here to claim the two vacant bunks.

"Welcome to the presidential suite," I said. "I'm Luke Lucas. Those two bunks are empty."

The lieutenant extended his hand. "Rex Foster. I fly F-4 Phantoms. This is Mike Williams, my RIO, radar interceptor officer."

"Did you just come in from Cubi Point?"

"We flew from San Diego to Cubi yesterday and to the ship today. We're hoping for some action before the end of the tour. We hear it's not much of a war, but it's the only one we've got."

That stopped me for a moment. I said, "Yeah, just a few partisan peasants."

Rex didn't understand my satire. He said, "I'd love to get a shot at a MiG."

"I don't think the North Vietnamese have attempted any attacks from the air on the carrier task force."

"Not the North Vietnamese," he said. "The Russians are bound to show up sometime in their new MiGs." Rex became animated. "Have you ever flown in a Phantom?"

"No."

"The initial rate of climb is 35,000 feet a minute." He zoomed his hand up in the air. "Four hundred miles an hour straight up, heading for outer space."

"Hot airplane," I said.

"The Phantom is the hottest airplane in the world. We're going to kick their tails all the way back to Moscow."

"If anyone sees a MiG, I'm sure he'll let you know," I said. "The flight crews in my squadron are a little more worried about the ordinary triple-A that these peasants are using quite effectively. Is this your first operational tour?"

"Yeah, and the ship will be heading back to the States soon." He sounded disappointed.

Mike Williams had been unpacking his duffel bag while we were talking. He had placed a bottle of scotch and a bottle of gin on the table that Dave Andrews had been using to plan his flight earlier. The navy forbids alcohol on board any of its vessels, an unambiguous rule that no one misunderstood. Unopened bottles of alcoholic beverages were a breach of discipline, but not a medical problem.

I hadn't eaten anything for almost twenty-four hours. After a shower, I went down to what the flight crews called "the bowling alley," a long, narrow compartment where cooks served a short-order breakfast to airmen, twenty-four hours a day. Flight suits and "dirty shirts," the flight deck officers' color-coded shirts, were permitted in the bowling alley, while the mandatory uniform of the day in the regular officers' mess was service dress whites. No one was admitted to the officers' mess after the executive officer was seated. Some naval aviators ate nothing but breakfast for an entire cruise.

In the evening, flight crews with night missions congregated in the bowling alley, and the aroma of bacon and eggs filled the mess deck. John Grayson and Ted Hanley were sitting with a group of aviators from another squadron. They made space for me at their table and invited me to sit down.

"Are you holding sick call in the helicopter tonight, Doc?" John asked.

"I hope not," I said. "Do you have an especially dangerous mission?"

"No, we drew an easy one—just like Jason's last night."

I didn't know how to respond. My problems paled compared with the enormous risk these flight crews had to face. We would likely be suffering more casualties soon, and these airmen knew it.

No one mentioned politics or the growing dissent about the war back in the States, but the flight crews knew about it. They felt isolated and alienated from people at home. They were also becoming more distant from the regular ship's officers, who ate in the officers' mess and were not exposed to the risks of flying in combat areas. The flight crews had nowhere to turn for support except themselves. As a result, they were bonding into a close-knit community, almost a family, and they looked after each other. I wore the wings of a flight surgeon, but that wouldn't have gained me entry into their inner circle. My participation in the rescue of an air crewman was different, something they respected. As a result, I was one of them now, whether I liked it or not.

After leaving the bowling alley, I went to the ready room to pick up any information I could find about the night's missions. Stan and Dave were flying low in the mountains again and would launch at midnight. They would land back on the ship in just over one hour, so I decided to wait. They trapped back aboard at 1:15 AM without having encountered any triple-A, and we talked until 3:00 AM.

By then I was tired again. I walked with Dave back to our compartment to get some rest. The bottles of scotch and gin were still on the table, but now they were half empty. We learned that our two new shipmates had just launched to fly CAP, combat air patrol, a protective cover of fighter-interceptors to defend the carrier task force against any surprise attack from Chinese or Soviet airplanes. The alcohol had just become a medical problem. I would seek out the F-4 squadron's flight surgeon again the next day.

That afternoon, the commanding officer of the *Coral Sea* briefed the CAG and squadron commanders. A number of cargo ships had entered the North Vietnamese port of Haiphong.

Chapter 8

TWENTY SECONDS OVER HAIPHONG

Stan White called all of the VAP 61 air crewmen to the ready room. The rumor about the ships in Haiphong Harbor had spread to all of the carrier's compartments at the speed of sound. The ship was buzzing.

Stan said, "The Pentagon wants to know the nationality of those ships and what sort of cargo they're unloading."

Stuart Blake gave a small cheer. "At last. It'll be like shooting fish in a barrel."

Jason had a big smile. "Haiphong is less than two hundred miles away, a short hop for us."

Stan's serious expression hadn't changed. "President Johnson has ordered that no attack be made on any of the ships without his authorization. Sinking Soviet or Chinese ships could escalate our involvement in Vietnam into a world war. Nevertheless, the Pentagon still wants better intelligence about the ships."

Stan looked directly at me. "I hope you got some sleep this afternoon, Doc, because I may need you. We're short a photo technician."

Stan's photo technician had come down to sick bay a few hours before because of a fever and cough. X-rays had shown pneumonia. I had no choice but to ground him, leaving Stan without a third crewman for an important mission. The squadron had lost two photo technicians

71

in twenty-four hours, and there was no replacement on the ship. Flying one from Guam would have taken too much time.

Stan's eyes bored through me. "I need to patch a crew together tonight."

"You want me to fly a mission as an air crewman?" I asked.

"With your training, you are qualified to fly as a crewman on our aircraft."

I dreaded flying in an A-3 off a carrier enough, but this was worse—much worse. He wanted me to fly a mission over North Vietnam. The major port of Haiphong would certainly be one of the targets most heavily guarded with triple-A and SAMs. Fear gripped me.

"I don't know anything about running cameras or dropping flash bombs," I stuttered.

"Dave Andrews knows more about our cameras and flash bombs than any photo technician, and he says he could teach you all you need to know for this mission in fifteen minutes. Will you do it?"

My heart was racing. There was no time to reflect. I answered impulsively, "Sure, if I can help. What do you want me to do?"

"As soon as we finish here, put on your flight suit and come back to the ready room to meet with Dave and me. We'll explain the mission, and Dave can take you to the plane and walk you through the procedure with the cameras and flash bombs."

I passed on the bacon-and-eggs dinner that evening, as the aroma had suddenly become repulsive. I didn't think that I would ever be able to tolerate that smell again, because I now associated it with intense fear. At Pensacola, we had heard that a fighter pilot's breakfast was "a cigarette and a cup of black coffee followed by vomiting." I didn't smoke, but I was experiencing the nausea part.

I went directly to sick bay to alert the two other flight surgeons that I would be busy for a few hours. I found Dr. Steve Eliot.

"Commander White asked you to fly a combat mission?" he said. "Those A-3s make perfect target practice for the triple-A gunners."

"I had some firsthand experience with that two nights ago."

He frowned and spread his hands. "Then why are you doing this?"

The surgeon I had met at the hospital at Da Nang, David Steiner, had been up all night for four nights in a row trying to put wounded marines back together. The doctors and nurses there weren't even sure whether the marines would be able to hold the perimeter around the air base. The more I thought about it, I had no choice but to go.

"I told Commander White I would do it," I said.

Steve shook his head. "The sick bay is quiet. Go get your tail shot off."

I went back to my compartment to change into my flight suit and then headed back to the ready room. Stan explained that we were going to photograph the ships in the harbor at Haiphong to find out what flags they were flying and whether they were carrying any military cargo. We could take high-level, daytime pictures, but the North Vietnamese would probably try to unload under cover of darkness, so we were going to come in low and take some pictures using flash bombs. We would have the element of surprise, and the whole run over the harbor wasn't supposed to last more than about twenty seconds.

My anxiety and the accompanying nausea increased. A dense ring of antiaircraft artillery surrounded Haiphong, and our big whale was going to hang over the harbor for a stretch of time that seemed long enough for the triple-A gunners to zero in. I didn't need to ask Stan White about the risk.

Stan said, "Dave, you take the doc to the airplane to go over the cameras and flash bombs. Let's meet back here at 2100 hours. The launch is set for 2200, and we should be over the target about thirty minutes later."

Out on the flight deck, Dave and I glanced in the direction of North Vietnam. I took in the deep red glow of the tropical sunset that reflected off the windows of the parked aircraft. If this had been a pleasure cruise, I might have called the setting serene. But these were warplanes, and we weren't tourists. I felt more like an ancient Greek soldier worried that Zeus was sending a dreadful omen.

Our airplane was backed up to the edge of the deck with its tail extending over the water. On the tail were painted the large black letters SS, which the flight crews asserted stood for "Saturdays and Sundays." But in reality, the navy assigned the letters as a code to identify each squadron, in our case, VAP 61. On the wings and fuselage, the word NAVY was painted in block letters. We climbed through the hatch in the bottom, and Dave directed me to the photo technician's seat.

"Your job is fairly simple," he began. He explained that all of the cameras were fully loaded, and the bomb bay was filled with the flash bombs. Then he reviewed the buttons and switches I needed to know. The cameras would already be turned on and ready to run at the time we launched. It wouldn't take us long to reach the target.

"Is that it?" I asked.

"You have one other task."

He pointed to a set of controls labeled ECM, meaning the electronic countermeasures device installed in the tail of the aircraft. I was already familiar with ECM from my training and prior flights. Theoretically, it foiled radar-controlled triple-A and SAMs. The flight crews were a little worried that the Soviets might have found a way around our countermeasures, but nothing better was available at the moment.

"Don't turn it on until after we make our run over the harbor. It might reveal our presence, and surprise gives us the best chance."

"It shouldn't be too difficult to remember to turn on our only defense," I said.

"The success of the mission depends on getting the pictures. The cameras are the highest priority. Concentrate on them."

"What will you be doing?"

"I'll be concentrating on the radar," Dave said. "We won't have the option of making a second run."

We rehearsed a number of times, which seemed unnecessary to me, but Dave said that I needed to operate by reflex, and that everything had to be quick and perfect. We climbed back out of the aircraft, and he left to spend more time revising his flight plan. At least he didn't have to worry about crashing into a mountain this time. I went back to my bunk to lie down and read, but the words just blurred. The time remaining until we launched passed slowly, and my anxiety increased.

At 2100 hours, other flight crews were gathering in the ready room, talking quietly and pointing at charts. I looked at the map of Haiphong Harbor. If triple-A hit us over that bay, only the North Vietnamese would be there to rescue us. Then I realized that it didn't matter, because we would be flying so low that we wouldn't have time to bail out.

Stan and Dave entered the ready room and began to discuss the mission.

"The weather-guessers predict clear skies over Haiphong all night," Dave said.

We would be able to get good pictures. I got no reprieve from the weathermen.

"Give me your proposed route to the target," Stan said.

"I have us steering well away from the coast and then dropping down under their radar just above the waves before we make our turn for the run into the target."

"Good, that's fine. After the run, I'm going to turn back toward the gulf and increase our speed before we begin to climb out."

Stan wanted to stay low to avoid the SAMs, which we believed were ineffective at low altitude. We wouldn't have to worry about triple-A over open water, either.

Stan turned to me. "Did you understand Dave's explanations?"

"Yes, I have it." At least I thought I did.

It occurred to me that Stan was putting a lot of faith in my ability to learn quickly. Perhaps that was a compliment, but I felt a heavy responsibility to carry out my assigned tasks with precision. As I had learned from my flight instructor in Pensacola, even when instructions seemed simple, it was easy to make a mistake. I remembered the dunking that Colt Benson had suffered in the swimming pool when he panicked about which clips to release first.

We walked out to the plane together, and I climbed into my seat while Stan and Dave did their walk-around preflight check, giving me time to reflect on what we were about to do. I had only wanted to be a doctor somewhere safe. But now I found myself part of an extremely hazardous mission. I didn't care about the flags on some cargo ships in a port in a small Southeast Asian country. Did it really matter whether supplies were coming into North Vietnam by ship, rail, truck, airplane, or mule?

Stan and Dave climbed into their seats and finished their preflight check. At exactly 2150, two jet-engine starters lit off our engines, and the deck crew pulled the chocks and guided the plane to one of the catapults. There another crew prepared us for the cat shot. The drama of the preparation fascinated me, but at the same time I felt as if I were being led to my execution.

We were going to leap from a ship and fly to a target two hundred miles away at more than six hundred miles an hour. If we weren't killed during the cat shot, plenty of other hazards awaited us like the antiaircraft guns at Haiphong, or perhaps just human error or mechanical failure. Everything about the mission was unnatural and otherworldly, and I wanted to be somewhere else, anywhere but on that airplane.

At 2200, the catapult officer signaled full power, and the engines roared. Stan clicked the navigation-lights button to order the launch, and the catapult shot us into the black of the night. As we climbed up to high altitude, I checked my pulse—hammering again, just like during the rescue two nights before. No one spoke on the intercom. Stan and Dave had worked together for a long time and had gone over this mission carefully, so no further words were needed. They left me to my own misery and dread.

Soon we dropped down just above the waves and turned to port for the low-level dash toward Haiphong. After about ten minutes of my pulse pounding in my ears, Stan's voice came on the intercom.

"Doc, I'm about to climb slightly before we begin our run over the harbor. I'll open the bomb-bay doors in about one minute."

I focused on the panel in front of me. I was sweating as I carried out one last mental rehearsal and prayed that I could do everything right.

I heard the bomb-bay doors open, and soon after, I could hear the flash bombs release, followed by blinding bursts as the flares exploded one by one. A mechanical whirring sound reassured me that the cameras were working. Everything changed to slow motion as we hung interminably over the harbor, surrounded by the popping sound of triple-A.

How could the North Vietnamese gunners have missed us?

I almost screamed from the agony of remaining suspended in the glare of the light. When we were almost to the end of the run, a loud bang with a different kind of light jolted the airplane, lifting us up like the most violent turbulence. We seemed out of control for a few seconds, and then Stan leveled the aircraft before banking hard to starboard, the change in direction pressing me into my seat. We were accelerating and heading for open water. I had fully expected to be killed, but we were all still alive!

Stan came on the intercom. "Everything all right back there? I think we made a good run."

"I'm fine," I yelped.

"We're going to start the climb up to high altitude in just a few minutes. Would you mind switching on the ECM?"

They had assigned me only three important tasks at my panel, and in my fear, I had forgotten the last one. A trained monkey would have been a better photo technician than I was. I felt really stupid and flipped on the ECM.

Stan was consoling. "No harm. The ECM blocks the radar-controlled SAMs—or so they say. We're probably out of their range already, but it can't hurt to use what little defense we have."

I felt giddy with a huge sense of relief like a prisoner with an eleventh-hour reprieve. The trip back to the *Coral Sea* passed quickly, and I didn't notice our approach to the carrier because of the darkness of the night and the blacked-out ship. The first hint that we had arrived was the sensation of the aircraft descending for the landing. Dave had told me that night carrier landings were always frightening.

"If we miss the arresting wires long," he had said, "we just go around again. If we miss short, well … we would never know it."

We banged onto the deck. The tail hook caught, propelling us forward violently against our seat harnesses. Stan pulled back on the throttles and folded the wings. The deck crew released the tail hook, and we taxied briefly to make room for more aircraft recoveries. Stan shut down the engines. Silence returned, but my knees were still too weak to move. Dave got up and started unlocking film cases, handing them down to deck crewmen who rushed them to the photo lab.

I looked at my watch: 2310 hours. Only an hour and ten minutes had passed since we had catapulted off the deck. I was emotionally drained, soaked with sweat, and my pulse was still a hundred beats per minute.

Stan and Dave were climbing down out of the cockpit and called for me to follow.

"Let's go, Doc," Dave said. "Do you want to see your handiwork?"

They were going to debrief with the CAG and the admiral in the war room, where the first photos would be coming out in just a few minutes. My legs began to move, and I climbed down. I didn't much care about the nationality of those ships. Still, I wanted to see the photographs that were so valuable as to be worth risking the lives of three people.

All three of us entered the war room.

Captain Leigh got up. "Congratulations to all three of you on your mission."

He looked at Stan. "Were there many ships in the harbor?"

"I couldn't see anything because of the flash bombs," Stan said. "How many did you see on the radar, Dave?"

"More than a dozen," Dave said. "Some of them tied up at piers. I think we got some good photos."

In a few minutes, an intelligence officer brought the first photos and a magnifying apparatus. The name showed clearly on one of the ships—it was painted in Cyrillic letters. We could also see cranes lifting surface-to-air missiles onto the dock.

Chapter 9

FORBIDDEN TARGETS

Within minutes, almost everyone who wasn't airborne knew that a Soviet ship—and probably ships—were unloading surface-to-air missiles in the harbor at Haiphong. They also knew that the CAG had not ordered an attack. VAP 61 officers onboard had all congregated in the ready room.

Stan saw me and pulled me out of the ready room into a passageway.

"Doc, we're having our own Cuban missile crisis here. The admiral told Captain Leigh that he has direct orders from the chief of naval operations in Washington not to bomb those ships. The admiral warns that if we were to attack, the marines might face an avalanche of Chinese soldiers pouring over the border, and we might see Russian MiGs swarming over our carriers."

"It's tough to ask the flight crews to ignore the chance to take out those missiles," I said.

"Everyone up the chain of command knows it. Meanwhile, we're stuck doing the best we can to take the pressure off our ground forces, particularly the marines around Da Nang. Meanwhile, navy and air force aviators flying over North Vietnam must accept the additional risk of those SAMs."

"Do you think anyone in Washington has considered withdrawal?" I asked.

"No, the situation is not that unstable. I think the president will continue the ban against attacking Chinese and Soviet ships, but I also think he will not order a withdrawal."

"So we're in a dangerous stalemate," I said.

"That's the way it appears at the minute," Stan said.

"How do you think I can help?"

"Keep your eyes open. The people in the Pentagon are asking a lot of us, and we could develop a major morale problem. You've earned the trust of the flight crews, and they might want to lean on your shoulder a little. You might start seeing more medical problems, too. I need you to make yourself available if anyone feels a need to talk."

"I'll do everything I can."

I had never thought of myself as a morale officer before, especially because, as a medical student and then as an intern, I had been at the bottom of the pecking order of the medical staff. Triple-A and SAMs were much more serious than medical-staff squabbles, anyway. I had no idea how to help airmen deal with their fear. That I knew from personal experience.

Stan and I went back into the ready room where members of the flight crews were grumbling.

"We put our tail ends on the line every night to try to find targets," Stuart Blake said, "and yet when we find a big one, it's off limits?"

Jason was usually quiet in meetings, but he was vocal now. "Those missiles are intended for use against our flight crews, and our own government is declaring us to be expendable."

John Grayson said, "We have the capability of sinking every one of the ships in that harbor in a single attack, but instead, our crews will have to continue flying dangerous missions and exposing ourselves to a menace that could have been avoided."

"We're just target practice for the SAMs and triple-A gunners," Jason said.

Everybody was looking at Stan. "Captain Leigh is aware of all this," he said. "If the Soviets and Chinese entered into the conflict the way they did in Korea. We would be in a much worse state than we are now."

"Does that mean we just continue to fly our missions the same way?" John asked.

"We may have to modify our tactics, like staying low all the way in and out, but yes, we have to continue to do what we can to interrupt the North Vietnamese supply lines."

There was a long silence.

"That's really hard to swallow, Stan," Stuart said.

I found myself feeling a little angry, too, but not at Stan. Everyone in the squadron respected him, and they would give him their loyalty. But the Haiphong incident had changed their trust in the leadership in Washington. We thought that every American serviceman and woman had a right to the full support of the government and the American people. We were making a huge sacrifice, and we shouldn't be "expendable," as Jason had put it. I didn't see how we could contribute to the war effort by getting shot down, nor did I understand our strategy in the war.

"I'm not any happier than any of you about this situation," Stan said, "but I promise you I'll do everything I can to assure that each mission that we fly is necessary. Meanwhile, we're going to experiment with a new system of imaging that doesn't require flash bombs."

"You mean something like ultrafast film?" Stuart asked.

"That's not exactly it," Stan said, "but you have the right idea. I'll tell you about it in a few days when I know more."

Dave and Ted Hanley hadn't said a word. As the newest navigator in the squadron, Ted probably felt reluctant to speak up. Dave was a senior navigator and the member of the squadron closest to Stan. He probably didn't want to add to the pressure on his partner.

Stan went on, "Meanwhile, I have more bad news for the squadron."

"Worse than what you've already told us?" John said.

"I'm afraid so. We're receiving more and more requests for night photoreconnaissance. We may have to increase our efforts."

I was stunned.

"There's more," Stan said.

Everyone listened.

"Even if we put six RA-3Bs and crews in the air every night, we still won't be able to meet all of the requests."

Jason gasped and spread his hands. "Six at once?"

"We've been keeping only two or three aircraft onboard," Stan said, "but the air boss still complains about how much space we take up. So we're going to try flying some missions out of Da Nang."

John Grayson said, "That means we would assume the same risk as the marines."

"That's not the intent, but it is the reality," Stan said.

The compartment was quiet.

"We will still keep two aircraft on the *Coral Sea,* and then later on the *Enterprise* when it relieves the *Coral Sea*, but we'll be basing at least four at Da Nang, maybe more."

Da Nang was a major U.S. Air Force base. I wondered why Stan had never mentioned the role of the air force in all this, so I asked him.

Stan explained, "For several years, the air force had emphasized strategic bombing and fighter-interceptors, so they weren't as ready for a ground war as naval and marine aviation were. We've had to pick up more of the load."

"What is the role of the air force now?" I asked.

"They're adapting to carry out ground support missions in South Vietnam, and their fighters patrol the areas of North Vietnam northwest of Hanoi, near the Laotian and Chinese borders. They don't see much triple-A, but they occasionally run across a MiG."

"We cover the eastern and central areas because of the closeness of the carriers to the North Vietnamese coast?" I asked.

"That's right. Right now, we're less than one hundred miles from Haiphong."

"Will we have full ground crew support at Da Nang?" John asked.

"With our four or five aircraft," Stan said, "we'll need to bring a lot of support people from Guam and Cubi Point."

There were tense looks and shaking heads as the meeting broke up.

Stan asked me to wait. "I want you to come with us to Da Nang, Doc. If you end up with some time on your hands, I'm sure the hospital there could use you."

I was going to become a hybrid: a flight surgeon to a demoralized carrier squadron and part-time doctor to marines fighting in the jungle. The flight crews in VAP 61 were flying some of the most dangerous missions of the Vietnam War, and the marines around Da Nang were fighting some of the bloodiest battles. Who could have imagined that a flight surgeon attached to a reconnaissance squadron based on Guam would end up in such a dangerous position? I had even agreed to an extra year's service for the privilege …

"But for now we have some unfinished business," Stan said. "I have to fly to Japan for the installation of the new imaging equipment that I mentioned. We'll be on the ground overnight. Dave and I don't need a photo technician on this trip, so you can come with us."

The plan was to fly to the air force base at Yokosuka on Tokyo Bay for the maintenance work and then directly to Da Nang the next day. I immediately thought of my promise to the surgeon at Da Nang.

"As long as we're there, will it be possible to pick up some fresh milk?"

"I've already radioed your milk order through the air force exchange. You can make your special delivery."

The milk may have been a small gesture, but my morale received a huge boost.

Stan, Dave, and I catapulted off the *Coral Sea* and flew the three hours to Yokosuka. A cat shot in an A-3 was starting to feel almost routine. As we approached Japan, I thought of the San Francisco shops selling pastel-colored Japanese prints that had perfectly captured the view of mist-shrouded Mount Fuji backed by streaked clouds. We glided over Tokyo Bay to land at the air force base; I was a tourist in an exotic land.

In climbing down from the aircraft, I felt the relief of being in a peaceful place instead of on an aircraft carrier in a world gone mad. It was as if Japan and Vietnam were on two different planets. I wasn't sure which one was real.

My first goal was finding a telephone. It took several tries, but I finally got through to Lynn.

"What happened?" she asked. "You haven't written or called for a long time. Where were you?"

"I've been on the *Coral Sea*, and there was no way to telephone. It's like living in outer space."

"What are you doing in Japan?"

"I'll be here only for a few hours," I said. "The plane is undergoing some maintenance."

"Is the plane safe?"

"There's no problem with the aircraft. Factory technicians are installing some special imaging equipment. I won't be going back to the ship, because I'm joining a new detachment at Da Nang early in the morning."

"Oh, no! Da Nang. That's in Vietnam, isn't it?" she asked.

"Yes," I said, "but I'll be on the air base where it's safe, not out in the jungle with the marines."

"Can't you come back to Guam sometime?"

"I'd like to come more than anything, but the squadron is flying a lot of missions right now. I'll be busy for a while."

"I miss you," she said.

"I miss you, too. I wish I could be with you," I said.

We hung up. I didn't know how to explain the contrast between the normal world on Guam and the insane world in Vietnam. I hadn't imagined how stressful the war would be.

Stan and Dave had been to Tokyo many times and wanted to stay at Yokosuka to oversee the installation of the new equipment, but as long as I was there, I wanted to see Tokyo, if only for an hour or two. I caught a shuttle to Atsugi, where I could board a commuter train for a quick trip into Tokyo.

The air base looked like any other, but outside the gate, everything was foreign. Tiny houses, seemingly made of paper and wood, crowded the narrow roads, but everything was neat and in good repair. Buses and a few small automobiles competed with pedestrians for the limited space, forcing the shuttle to weave in and out. Finally, I emerged in front of the train station, located only a short distance from a small U.S. naval hospital.

My curiosity forced me to look inside, where a doctor noticed me and introduced himself.

"Good afternoon, sir, I'm Luke Lucas," I answered. "I'm a flight surgeon with a navy carrier squadron."

"What can I do for you?"

Captain Smith, the commanding officer of the hospital, was a rounded man in his midforties and wore the eagle of a navy captain on his collar. Unlike the professional naval officers in VAP 61, his uniform fit poorly, his insignia were not perfectly aligned, and his shoes had not been shined any time recently. In his hand was a copy of the Far Eastern edition of *Time* magazine.

"This is my first trip to Japan, and I was curious about your hospital."

"We have very few inpatients here, because we transport anyone seriously ill back to the States. I'd make rounds with you, but there isn't anything to see right now."

"I didn't mean to intrude."

"It's no imposition. I was just about to go next door to the navy exchange, which would be more interesting for you to see than this hospital."

I didn't know how to decline gracefully, so I agreed. "Thank you, Dr. Smith. I'd like to see it."

I followed him into a large warehouse where acres of Japanese-produced merchandise and art objects were displayed, as in many of the import shops in San Francisco, but multiplied a hundred times in quantity. There were paintings, wooden carvings, dishes, silk fabric, kimonos, transistor radios, television sets, and Honda motorcycles. It was not at all interesting to me, and my mind wandered.

"You can see all the excellent bargains," Dr. Smith said.

I nodded, but I couldn't imagine what he would do with any of the articles for sale. After remaining the minimum time required for politeness, I said, "Thanks for showing me the navy exchange, but I will be in Japan for only a few hours and would like to see Tokyo."

"The train station is just a short walk and has frequent commuter trains into the center of Tokyo," he said. "The air force shuttle from the station to Yokosuka makes frequent trips when you return."

After I left, it occurred to me that he had not asked a single question about the war in Vietnam, as if he never thought about it.

The trains in Japan ran on time and wasted little of it sitting in stations. As soon as the doors opened, riders would dash on and off, and the trains would immediately move on. Because of the large numbers of passengers, most people had to stand, which made me notice the differences in height. I looked down on a sea of black hair and felt very much alone; my uniform and blond hair set me apart, but the other passengers were polite and did not stare.

The commercial center of Tokyo, called the Ginza, buzzed with people. It was Asian, but at the same time Western, with functional modern architecture, rock music, and businessmen in suits hurrying between appointments. The glare of neon signs rivaled the Strip in Las Vegas, beckoning tourists to discotheques, bars, restaurants, and boutiques. The contrast between the grim reality of the war that I had left just a few hours before and the extravagant, materialistic, garish life in Tokyo depressed me. We had taught the Japanese some of the worst characteristics of American culture. I didn't want to see any more. After a short time, I took the train back to Atsugi to catch the shuttle.

When I arrived at Yokosuka, technicians were still working on the installation. Stan and Dave were talking with one technician, who was explaining to them the operation of the new equipment. Stan said that we would leave in the morning, and that a truck would come just before takeoff with the milk packed in crates filled with ice to place in the bomb bay. I kept smiling as I thought about delivering milk to a tent hospital in the wilds of Da Nang.

The flight back the next morning passed quickly, and as we approached Da Nang, in daylight this time, I could see that it spread for several square miles, a moderately-sized city. The air base outside of Da Nang resembled a pockmarked battleground from World War I, with trenches and barbed wire surrounding the entire base. I looked down on the parallel runways, which were under constant repair because of the regular nocturnal Vietcong attacks. We made our turn to land.

III

DA NANG

Chapter 10

THE MILKMAN DELIVERS

Even though the weather was tropical on Guam, nothing could have prepared me for the brutal days of fire at Da Nang. Building a major air base required stripping a wide swath of land of all shade and converting the jungle into an unnatural and uninhabitable desert burning in the sun. My previous trip had been in the middle of the night. When we opened the hatch after landing this time, the sweltering midday air invaded the cockpit and turned it into a furnace. The long and wide expanse of runways, taxiways, and parking spaces captured the sun's heat and practically melted the rubber on our flight boots.

Air force planes roared down the parallel runways in pairs, punctuating the constant high whine of dozens of planes in the taxiways. Dust stirred up from booming engines mixed with the acerbic smell of jet fuel and tar, overwhelming the natural aroma of agricultural Vietnam. I was coated with sweat and grime within minutes in the merciless sun and suffocating humidity.

A different kind of torture would erupt at night as a result of mortar bombardments that seemed random and without aim. The erratic nature of the blasts made for a deadly lottery, reminding the defenders that everyone was at risk, no shelter was safe, and no one was exempt. I had awakened that morning in a comfortable air force BOQ in Yokosuka. I would spend my nights for the next few weeks in a tent, enshrouded with mosquito netting and tormented by the sound of irregular explosions.

Before landing, Stan had radioed the hospital to let them know we had an important package for them. A large, boxy ambulance was waiting for us at our assigned parking place. They had come to retrieve the precious cargo.

Stan said, "Doc, you should ride in the ambulance with the milk. Offer our thanks and high regards to the staff there."

The ice around our cargo had not melted at all, thanks to the frigid temperatures at cruising altitude, and the arrival of cold, fresh milk appeared as a mirage to the doctors, nurses, and patients in the tent hospital. Their limited refrigeration capacity would not allow storing all of it, so an immediate party erupted in the largest tent, where picnic benches were set up as a mess hall. Corpsmen carried the milk crates in, and then nurses helped them carry pitchers to serve each of the marine patients who could swallow. Finally, the doctors, nurses, and hospital corpsmen all received their shares.

David Steiner, the chest and vascular surgeon, came over to me with a big smile. "This is a miracle. We don't get much cause to celebrate here."

"Compliments of VAP 61 on board the *Coral Sea*."

"I was joking about the fresh milk, you know. Where did you get it?"

"We had to fly to Japan for some maintenance," I said.

"Well, please thank the members of your squadron. We appreciate your thinking about us." He cocked his head toward the tents and laughed. "Our idea of luxury around here is a hot shower."

Dr. Steiner had been at Da Nang for just a few months, but he had probably done more surgery in those months than in all of his six years of residency and fellowship in chest and vascular surgery at the Massachusetts General Hospital. He had operated on more severe trauma victims than any surgeon in the state of Massachusetts might have seen in a lifetime. He told me that he was a "Berry-Planner," drafted into the navy for two years immediately following the completion of his specialty training. The Berry Plan allowed certain physicians in specialties that were in short supply to complete their training prior to reporting for duty, an advantage for both the physician and the navy.

After we finished talking, I spotted a familiar face out of the corner of my eye. "Colt Benson, what are you doing here?"

Colt had exchanged his Stetson and cowboy boots for marine fatigues covered by a white coat. He looked more serious than when we had shared a taxi in Pensacola. A stethoscope hung around his neck—and he wore glasses—another disqualifier for flight training at Pensacola. Something else was different: he wore a real Colt in a holster under his white coat.

"Hello, Philadelphia. How's the flying business?" he said.

"If it weren't for the occasional moment of terror, it would be fairly quiet. Are you working full time in Da Nang?"

"I'm assigned to the marine command here, so I see patients for sick call and take care of the inpatients with medical problems, mostly infectious diseases."

I think it was the first time that I had ever seen Colt smile, and he seemed genuinely pleased to see me. Meeting someone I associated with home made me happy, too, even though we had known each other for only a few days in Pensacola. My trip to Japan and uneasy phone call to Lynn had generated a longing for anything associated with home.

"You must have a big inpatient load," I said.

"Enough to stay out of trouble. We have a lot of marines around this air base, and it seems most of them get sick sooner or later. Are you here for just a quick turnaround?"

His question reminded me that I would be stuck at Da Nang for a while.

"No, I'm here full time for at least a few weeks. Maybe more. My squadron needs to increase the number of our aircraft flying over the North, so we'll base some here for a while."

A corpsman handed each of us a frosty glass of milk. We touched glasses, and I said, "To the U.S. Marine Corps."

He looked at his glass. "You're a real magician."

"I've got a great squadron CO."

We sat down at one of the picnic benches in the mess tent.

He wrinkled his brow and tilted his head. "Will you be flying many missions?"

I had suppressed that thought. I had flown two combat missions: one in a rescue helicopter and the other in an A-3 over Haiphong, and I had been terrified both times.

"None, I hope. The missions are extremely dangerous, and we will probably start suffering more casualties."

"Yeah." He looked away. "I heard about the air crewman you fished out of the water."

"That was one of the most frightening experiences of my life."

He looked down at his glass. "Have you had other planes shot down?"

"The air wing had already lost one before I arrived on the *Coral Sea*."

He shook his head. "I thought naval aviation was supposed to be safe."

"Maybe it used to be."

Colt had downed his milk and looked around for a corpsman with a pitcher. "This chilled milk is terrific. It's funny; I never drank milk at home. How will you spend your time here?" he asked.

"Only about half of my squadron will be here, so I'll have some time to help at the hospital if you need me. I'd be glad to give you a hand with the marines if I could be of any assistance."

"As a matter of fact, all of us are overwhelmed. Besides malaria, I'm seeing a lot of dengue, infectious diarrhea, and plenty of diseases I don't recognize. With the heat and humidity, all of the marines have rashes that become infected."

We were both smiling again and happy to be talking about tropical diseases; they were natural and impersonal. Patients usually recovered. People trying to kill each other in a war was different. We couldn't smile about that.

"Do you have time to work on malaria prevention?" I asked.

"Most of the marines don't bother to take their malaria pills, because they are convinced the pills don't work; and I think they're right. They call our insect repellent 'mosquito candy.'"

"Do you have an infectious disease expert here?"

He grinned. "That's me. For all doctors assigned to the Fleet Marine Force, the navy gives four weeks of special training on tropical diseases, but it was practically useless, because standard treatments generally don't work even if I'm able to make a diagnosis."

"What do you do?" I asked.

"Anything that doesn't clear within seventy-two hours we transfer out, mostly to Guam, and mostly for malaria."

"Don't you have any expert help?"

"I'm in radio contact with other doctors embedded with the marines who are in the same fix. The marine CO here helped me patch together a regular radio conference with an infectious disease consultant at the Communicable Disease Center in Atlanta. A microbiologist at the U.S. Naval Medical Research Unit on Taiwan joins us, but what we're seeing often baffles them, too. So, mostly we're flying blind."

On my first trip to Da Nang, the battlefield operating room had been a foreign world that was unfamiliar, and now Colt was describing what seemed like diseases from a new planet, diseases that not even experts could identify.

He continued, "Several of us are experimenting with some combination treatment ideas. Since we send many patients to Guam, we've included a doctor there on the conference calls."

"Roger Casey?" I asked.

Colt smiled again. "Yeah, do you know him?"

I was laughing now. "Yes, he was my best friend in medical school," I said. "We were interns together at the Philadelphia General Hospital. I spent some time with him not long ago. My squadron uses Guam as its home port."

"Roger's been very helpful in coordinating the transfers."

"I'm not surprised. He's conscientious and will be a good contact."

"Small world," Colt said.

Colt had completely changed. In Pensacola, he had seemed adrift in the wrong profession, but now he had a role and a purpose. I was going to enjoy working with him, and I was glad to be back in a hospital environment. We were two green physicians together, far from being experts in the medical problems we were facing, but it might be easier to learn together.

Not long after my arrival in Da Nang, the marine commander paid a visit to David Steiner, and I received a call to come to the tent where they were meeting.

When I arrived, Dr. Steiner looked up at me. "We've occasionally been losing trauma patients coming in by helicopter, because the corpsmen can only start IVs, give morphine, and apply pressure dressings. By having a doctor in the helicopter, we could begin surgical treatment earlier when possible and save more lives, just as you did with the air crewmen. You are certified as a flight surgeon and can fly as a helicopter crewman, and you obviously aren't afraid to clamp an artery on a hemorrhaging patient. Would you be willing to try it?"

"You want me to ride full time in helicopters?"

Dr. Steiner said, "We have a senior hospital corpsman who could screen requests for when they specifically need a doctor in the helicopter."

The marine commander leaned forward toward me. "I can't tell you that these rescue missions aren't dangerous," he said, "but I have to explore every option to reduce our casualties. We have an impossible mission defending this air base, and we're losing enough marines to make up a whole company every week."

I didn't think I could save a company of marines, possibly not even one marine, but the commander sounded desperate. Moreover, it was likely that he was politely giving me an order. Under the circumstances, I responded in the only possible way.

"I'll do anything I can to help."

"Thank you, Doctor," the marine commander said.

He didn't say "lieutenant" or "Doc." Once again, I heard the word "doctor" used as an expression of respect and thanks; and once again, I felt the queasiness returning. Whenever a combat officer addressed me as "Doctor," I knew there would be danger attached. I had volunteered for naval aviation, in part, to avoid the Fleet Marine Force. So far, I had encountered the high risks of both.

The air ambulance dispatcher kept direct radio contact with the hospital and wasted little time calling me for help.

"We're picking up some casualties that may be critical. A helicopter will come get you in about three minutes."

"Wilco," I replied. I grabbed my flight helmet and an emergency surgical bag before dashing to the landing pad. A marine helicopter with a big red cross was hovering, and one of the crewmen reached down and pulled me up before the helicopter touched down. We were off.

We passed over the pockmarked trenches at the perimeter of the air base and headed toward the hilly, jungle-covered terrain at low altitude. Within minutes, we approached the landing zone, or "LZ," which the pilot said was in a relatively flat clearing. He came on the intercom.

"I have radio contact with the platoon leader. Listen in."

After a few seconds of static, a marine lieutenant on the ground came on. "We may have a hot LZ."

"What's the situation right now?" the pilot asked.

"It's quiet, but the helicopters coming in will stir 'em up."

"How many casualties do you have?"

"Looks like seven—two are real bad," the lieutenant said. "They're still alive, but barely."

The lieutenant was telling us we were going to be a target for the Vietcong mortars. Why didn't we turn around? I felt panic rising and couldn't get enough air. In the distance, I could see the large clearing, which was filled with shattered palm trees and craters. We were going to try to land there.

The pilot came back on the intercom. "The marines are setting off smoke bombs. We'll be on the ground just long enough for them to load the two critically wounded casualties. There's a helicopter right behind us that will pick up the other five."

Even before the helicopters dropped to land, explosions erupted around the clearing. I couldn't see any way to avoid them. Was the pilot really going to try to land in the middle of this inferno? Then the plunge, the blasts, the noise, and the smell disoriented me. We had landed without being hit, and we were enveloped in smoke, so I couldn't see anything. A soot-covered marine appeared at the hatch, lifting a wounded comrade onto the floor of the helicopter.

"CPR," he yelled, pointing to the victim and looking at me with an anguished expression. "Mortar blast!" he added.

At the same time, the helicopter crewman was helping to load a screaming combat casualty through the opposite hatch. We became tangled, and I couldn't get in position to examine the patient in front of me, let alone try to continue CPR. The concussion from a mortar blast very close by rocked the helicopter and sent me flying on top of the screaming victim. I had barely moved when the helicopter leapt into the air, tumbling me again. We were accelerating rapidly, and I still could not regain my balance. After several long seconds, we leveled off. I was more steady, but paralyzed with fright.

On the deck of the helicopter in front of me, the wounded marine that I had helped load was struggling with shallow, ineffective breaths, and he had a wild expression in his eyes. I tried to concentrate on him. Since he was alert, there was no reason for CPR, but his skin had turned the dark blue color of cyanosis, evident even under the black dirt of the battlefield. That meant that his blood was not picking up oxygen. He had an agonal look that I had only ever seen before in patients with cardiogenic shock from a massive heart attack.

Then I saw that the patient's trachea had deviated to one side, the classic sign of a collapsed lung. I grabbed a large-bore needle out of the emergency surgical bag and jabbed it into his chest. Next, I attached IV tubing to the needle and submerged the other end into a bag of saline on the deck of the helicopter. Air bubbled out of the tubing into the saline, and very quickly the patient began to take deeper breaths. His color gradually improved, and his anguished look faded.

I glanced quickly at the other patient, who was still screaming. He had suffered a nasty-looking shrapnel wound in his abdomen and was pounding the deck of the helicopter with his hands and feet. Blood swelled, filling the wound in the middle of a ragged hole in his blackened uniform, and I could see intestine. The air crewman had administered morphine and was trying to start an IV. I stole a few seconds to administer a second dose of morphine.

I clicked on the intercom to the pilot.

"Connect me to the hospital."

Almost immediately, I heard the voice of Colt Benson. "What have you got?"

"Two patients," I shouted. "One with a shrapnel wound to the abdomen, and one with a pneumothorax from a mortar blast. The one with the abdominal wound needs an operating room and blood right away. He's O-positive. I've rigged a siphon for the pneumothorax case, but he needs a chest tube."

Dr. Steiner was listening in and heard me. "Nice work, Doc. We might make a real surgeon out of you yet."

We had been so busy that I hadn't noticed our approach to the hospital. The helicopter descended more gradually this time, and welcoming hands reached for the two patients, lifting them onto gurneys. They wheeled the abdominal wound victim directly into a tent operating room and the pneumothorax patient off to X-ray. Surging adrenaline still drove my heart rate and weakened my knees, so I waited a few minutes before climbing out of the helicopter.

I was still wearing my flight helmet, and the pilot came on the intercom. "Are they going to make it, Doctor?"

"I don't know. I think so."

"I'm glad—we don't always get here in time."

"Do you often land in the middle of a barrage like that?" I asked.

"No, that's the worst I've ever seen." He hesitated. "I didn't think it would be that bad."

I felt overwhelming nausea but managed to avoid vomiting.

"I'm so weak I can hardly move," I said.

"You'll have to climb out, because the other helicopter will need to land in just a minute."

I had forgotten about the other helicopter. It was a miracle that both survived. The OR nurse had told me that sometimes twenty or thirty combat victims arrived at the same time. Back then, those were just numbers to me.

I wobbled after the pneumothorax patient into X-ray, where Dr. Steiner joined me.

He said, "The dispatch corpsman told me that your patient was undergoing CPR before you picked him up."

"That's right."

"The mortar blast knocked the patient unconscious and probably caused the pneumothorax, too, but the attempt at CPR may have made it worse. We'll have the chest X-rays in just a few minutes. Let's see if your patient can talk."

Dr. Steiner addressed the patient. "You're in a hospital. Do you remember what happened?"

"No, how did I get here?"

"This doctor brought you in his helicopter. You were knocked down from the blast of a mortar shell. You had a concussion, and you also have a collapsed lung. We're going to take a look at your X-rays."

The film showed a partially collapsed left lung and fluid in the pleural cavity.

"The fluid down low is probably blood," Dr. Steiner said. "You expanded his lung enough with your needle to save his life, but we'll insert a bigger tube into the upper part of his chest to evacuate the rest of the air from the pleural space and then place another down low to evacuate the blood. You can do it. I'll show you how and talk you through the procedure."

The room started to spin on me, and Dr. Steiner noticed my pallor. "Are you feeling all right?"

"I'm still shaking. We came down in the middle of a mortar bombardment."

"You look a little pale."

"Somehow, I managed to take care of the patient on the way back, but now I need to sit down for a few minutes. I wouldn't make a very good marine."

"Your patient and I can spare a few minutes; we'll get him cleaned up and set up the equipment. If you're going to keep clamping arteries and inserting needles into chests, I'm going to have to show you how to do the rest."

David Steiner wasn't going to let me off the hook and allow this learning moment to pass. It was an act of friendship and trust.

Chapter 11

THE SEA IS EMPTY

Over the next few weeks, I made more helicopter runs, but none into a hot LZ, and none requiring invasive treatment in a bouncing helicopter. I worried about the heavy responsibility that Stan carried, having to order night missions over North Vietnam, but morale did not fall apart as I had feared. The flight crews only had to look around the perimeter of the air base to see that we were all vulnerable in the event of a Chinese invasion. Since the incident with the missiles on the Soviet ships in the harbor at Haiphong, we had not suffered any casualties, or even any aircraft damage.

I suspected that Stan was using all of his influence to avoid accepting missions for the squadron that he considered to be too risky. He would always reserve the ones of highest risk for himself, so I felt especially sorry for Dave Andrews, although he was probably the most qualified of all of the navigators in the squadron and the one most capable of handling the difficult missions. I wanted to take the pulse of the squadron members to see how they were holding up, so I decided to start with Dave. As usual, he was studying his charts. He looked up and spoke first when I entered his tent.

"Hi, Doc. Nice to see you. What's happening over at the hospital?"

Dave seemed pretty calm—at least outwardly. But I knew that wasn't always the case, especially from hearing his story about his flight suit soaked with sweat after night carrier landings. I thought I'd try to chat a little before getting down to the morale issue.

"I assist in the operating room and help another doctor take care of the flood of marines coming in with malaria."

Dave smiled. "All of that in addition to riding in helicopters and pestering navigators."

I grabbed a chair. "I've already had to evacuate one of the aircraft mechanics back to Guam because of malaria, so keep your mosquito netting zipped up."

"Why can't you just treat malaria with pills?" he asked.

"None of the textbook treatments work. We're seeing resistance to every drug we have."

"Oh," he said. "That sounds bad. What would you do if I got malaria?"

"I'd send you back to the hospital on Guam and hope that your own resistance would ultimately eliminate the disease."

Dave thought for a moment. "Let me see if I understand this. If I forgot to use my insect repellant and got malaria, you would ground me from flying any more combat missions and send me back to Guam, where I would have to sit back in my easy chair and watch the sunsets through a veil of cabernet sauvignon. Is that right?"

"That's it, more or less."

"Doc, let me give you some lawyerly advice. Don't let that information leak out to the rest of the squadron."

I had to laugh. Dave seemed to be coping well, but I wanted to probe a little more.

"By now, you must have memorized every square foot of North Vietnam."

He looked down at his chart. "Just about. We go in and come out low—the whole way."

"Are you still flying in the mountains?"

"Always." He pointed to the chart. "The terrain is flat close to the coast, but it becomes hilly pretty quickly inland. It keeps me alert."

Only a few months before, Dave had obsessed about night navigation for a one-minute run over a target in the mountains close to Da Nang.

Now he was acting as if the longer and more dangerous missions over the North were everyday events. Of course, for him, they were, but I was surprised about his outward calmness.

"How's the new imaging equipment working?" I asked.

"We're learning," he said, "but there are still a few bugs. Stan says we'll be installing it in our other aircraft soon."

"How are you and the other navigators handling the stress?" I asked.

He looked up at the top of the tent and leaned back in his chair. "I'm tired. We're all flying more missions than we were a month ago."

"Have you had any rest days?"

"Rest days—ha!" he said. "A rest day is when we fly a mission over South Vietnam, but I don't get many of those."

"I should ask Stan about that," I said.

Dave turned completely around to face me. "Don't mention anything about me. Stan has plenty to worry about. I don't want to add anything to his sack of problems."

"I'll be discreet," I said.

"While you're talking to Stan about our missions, Doc, tell him about yours. I hear you've been riding marine helicopters right into the middle of VC mortar barrages."

Dave could tell that I was trying to play the role of the squadron psychologist. I was part of the squadron's inner circle of aircrews at high risk. The norm was mutual support. Shrinks and priests weren't allowed in. I gave up the questioning and became an airman again.

"My helicopter flights aren't as dangerous as your missions. What I'm doing is safe most of the time."

"Safe, hell!" he barked with a grin. "Do all doctors tell lies like you?"

"Sometimes," I said, "but only when we talk to lawyers."

"I'm only a pretend lawyer."

Both of us were more relaxed now. "Speaking of lawyers and helicopters, did you ever get my will typed?"

"Yes, and I stapled it to the handwritten form you filled out that has your signature, so it's all nice and legal. I made sure that if you died, I got all of the money."

I looked at Dave. "It's the 99 percent of lawyers like you who give the other 1 percent a bad reputation."

We both roared. I didn't know if my visit would improve Dave's morale, but I felt better. Dave was coping with the stress much better than I was.

We both left together to attend Stan's regular briefing for the flight crews. He introduced a new replacement naval aviator, who had experience flying the tanker model A-3 used for in-flight refueling of the carrier planes. The squadron was short of pilots, so the other naval aviators were glad to welcome him.

I noticed that the new pilot's pants were a couple of sizes too big and that he gradually emptied a large glass of water during the briefing. He looked wasted like someone suffering from a chronic illness. At the end of the meeting, I approached him.

"Welcome to sunny Da Nang. I'm Luke, the squadron flight surgeon."

"Hi, Doc. I'm Bill Spencer; nice to meet you."

"I'd be happy to see you any time for your flight physical."

"How about now? Commander White wants me to start flying right away. I just need to use the head, and I'll be right with you."

We went over to the hospital together and into an examining tent. I asked him a few general questions.

He wrinkled his brow. "Doc, I've been losing a lot of weight recently. I think it's all this heat and humidity. Do you have anything that could build me up?"

"Let me finish the examination, and then we'll talk about it. I'm going to need a urine sample."

"No problem. I have to go all the time lately."

I put a dip stick in his urine and noted the dark color—strongly positive for glucose—and then I looked at him, a career naval officer ready to do the job for which he had spent many years training.

"I don't know how to tell you this easily," I said, "but I suspect that you know you're sick."

He looked away toward the canvas wall of the tent. "What is it, Doctor?"

"You have diabetes."

"That's nothing," he said. "People just take pills for diabetes these days, don't they?"

"Some do, but not the ones who are losing weight rapidly and peeing all the time. I'll bet your vision hasn't been so good lately."

He didn't want to respond. I knew that a prolonged high blood sugar swells the lens and impairs vision. He stood up, took a couple of steps, and turned around.

"Are you going to ground me?"

"I have no choice."

He shook his head. "Damn! You're certain? Don't you need some other tests?"

"We'll be getting other tests at the hospital, but your symptoms are typical of type 1 diabetes. It usually begins during childhood or adolescence, but sometimes it starts later."

"What's wrong with just taking the pills?" he asked.

"All that weight loss tells us that you have an absolute lack of insulin. Pills don't generally work in such cases."

"Can't we try?"

"It doesn't matter whether you need insulin or pills," I said. "Any form of diabetes is an absolute reason for permanent grounding in the navy."

He glared at me. I felt badly for him, but Stan was going to feel worse. "Let's go talk to Stan," I said.

As we entered, Stan looked up. He seemed to sense that something was wrong. "What is it?"

"Bill has diabetes; I have to ground him."

"For how long? I need him."

"Stan, he has diabetes. As soon as he finishes talking with you and packing his bag, I'm going to admit him to the hospital, start him on insulin, and evacuate him back to the States."

"What? He's been flying every day."

"I doubt if he can even see the instrument panel clearly right now. With his high blood sugar, he could easily get himself killed along with his crew."

"It's not as serious as all that, is it?"

"I'm not talking about a minor technicality; he has diabetes. I can relieve his symptoms with insulin, but he can't fly again; and he will have to leave the navy with a medical discharge. I don't like delivering bad news, but I can't ignore a major problem of health and safety."

Stan bit his lower lip, glared at me, and then looked at Bill. "Okay, Doc, whatever you say. Give us a few minutes, and then you can have him."

"I'll be at the hospital waiting for him."

Stan came over to the hospital to see me the next day. "Thank you for handling the problem with Bill Spencer. I suspected that something was wrong with all that weight loss, but we're so short of flight crews that I had closed my eyes."

I worried that the disappointment of losing a replacement pilot before he even started would put a further damper on morale. When I first arrived on Guam, the flight crews carried on an easy bantering, full of jibes and jokes as they arrived for meetings. Now, the mood was more somber. Although one plane had been shot down, many weeks had passed since that incident, and in addition, morale was recovering somewhat since we discovered the Soviet ships at Haiphong Harbor. The flight crews were looking forward to when the new imaging equipment would be installed in the rest of the aircraft. My conversation with Dave Andrews had suggested to me that spirits might even be improving.

Then a few nights later, the worst possible news came in.

Stan White called me at the hospital. "Doc, John Grayson and his crew were on a night mission over North Vietnam and took a hit from triple-A soon after making a run with their flash bombs. I've sent a helicopter to pick you up."

Stan sounded dejected, as if he could hardly speak. I thought of John Grayson, troubled and silent, sitting in the war room the night that Jason Lockhart had been shot down. Now the situation was reversed. We had suffered no further incidents in the weeks since then, and I had even allowed myself to become complacent about the risk that the flight crews were taking. We may all have become too optimistic. Now I was jolted into facing the grim reality of the dangerous missions once more.

The helicopter appeared immediately, and we lifted off and started heading north along the coast. I clicked on the intercom to talk to the pilot.

"What have you heard?"

"John Grayson was trying to make it to the coast. They were all three wounded: John, Ted Hanley, and the photo technician. We lost radio contact."

"How long ago?" I asked.

"About fifteen minutes. The *Enterprise* has already dispatched a rescue helicopter. They're much closer than we are."

"Why are we going?"

"Commander White wanted a second helicopter at the scene—and you on it."

We had been very lucky with the first air-sea rescue, but I had a bad feeling about this one, especially the "all three wounded" part. The helicopter pilot said John was trying to reach the coast. I wondered how far inland they were.

"Were they near the coast when we lost contact?" I asked.

"I don't know," the pilot said. "I think it was a short transmission. The *Enterprise* picked it up."

"That doesn't sound good."

When Jason Lockhart's plane was shot down, there was a lot of static, but he stayed on the radio until just before they bailed out. If John Grayson reached the gulf, I hoped he had flares, because we had no other way to find them at night.

"Hadn't John been shot down before?" the helicopter pilot asked.

"No, that was Jason Lockhart. They're close friends—practically inseparable—and they look alike."

The pilot dialed in on the frequency for the *Enterprise* helicopter, and after a few minutes we heard them call back to the ship.

"This is Angel One. We're over the area—no flare so far."

"Did John give coordinates for an area where he would bail out?" I asked.

"I'll call Angel One to find out," the pilot said.

A minute later, the pilot came back on my intercom. "They guessed about the bailout area based on the coordinates for Grayson's photo run over the target. They're searching a section of the gulf nearest to his target."

"Wow! Talk about dead reckoning," I said. "They could be anywhere."

The pilot didn't answer. Even if they had reached the gulf, they were all wounded, and bailing out through the hatch in the bottom of an A-3 took strength and dexterity. The bleeding air crewman that we rescued several weeks before hadn't even been able to release his parachute, let alone light a flare or mount his one-man life raft. If John Grayson and his crew were in the water, we'd better find them quickly.

After about twenty minutes in the air, we joined the *Enterprise* helicopter. Both of us had search lights, but they were nearly useless in the large expanse of ocean. All we could see was the two small circles of light sweeping the waves. We had to fly a tight pattern because of the limited visibility, so we were covering only a tiny speck of the gulf below us. We could easily pass close by survivors in life rafts and never see them. Jason Lockhart had been able to light a flare on the previous air-sea rescue, and we found him and his crew almost immediately. This barren search frustrated and depressed me.

We remained mostly silent, straining to see the dancing circles of light in the blackness as the minutes slowly passed. In time, the constant vibration and racket of the helicopter became fatiguing, and I found my concentration slipping. Everyone at Da Nang suffered from chronic sleep deprivation, and I began to feel guilty that I wanted desperately to sleep while there may have been survivors below in critical condition.

The *Enterprise* helicopter radioed us. "This is Angel One. We're low on fuel. Our other helicopter will join you over the area soon. Good luck." I checked my watch: more than three hours since John Grayson's call had come in, a long time for injured airmen to be in the water.

The sky was beginning to lighten, and visibility was improving rapidly. We saw a destroyer at a distance arriving on the scene, but we could see no sign of John or his crew. After a while, the other *Enterprise* helicopter arrived, and as we were now low on fuel, the pilot turned us toward Da Nang. The sun was rising as we approached the air base. Before landing, the pilot called back to the second *Enterprise* helicopter.

"Angel Two, have you seen anything yet?"

"This is Angel Two. Visibility is good, but the sea is empty. We'll continue to search along with the destroyer."

As soon as we were down, I climbed out and found Stan White standing with his hands on his hips at the edge of the helicopter pad staring at the ground.

"Doc, the *Enterprise* will keep searching with their helicopter for the next few hours, but I want to launch ours again, too, just as soon at it refuels. The destroyer can remain in the area all day, but we have better visibility from the air. Can you handle another trip?"

I was dead tired, and my head hurt, but I said, "Sure, I'm ready to go."

I climbed back into the helicopter, lay down, and fell dead asleep during the refueling and flight back to the search area. Interns excelled at grabbing sleep in half-hour stretches. When the air crewman woke me, I couldn't recall where I was. I sat up, confused for several minutes, then everything became clear: the vibration, beating rotors, engine roar, whipping wind, and this time, the dazzling sea below.

I saw the *Enterprise* helicopter and destroyer way off in the distance making regular turns in an organized pattern. We were covering far more area than we could during the night, and we could search carefully in all directions, but by late morning we had seen nothing. The destroyer would still search for another twenty-four hours, but the chance of finding any survivors had faded. The *Enterprise* helicopter departed, and then later, with fuel critically low, we returned to Da Nang a second time, weary and disheartened.

Stan was again waiting on the helicopter pad while we landed. His lips were tight, and he wore a scowl. This time a circle of VAP 61 airmen surrounded him, watching me as I stepped out of the helicopter. I looked back at them and shook my head slowly. They turned away, gazing at the ground, at the sky, at nothing. Jason Lockhart was sobbing. I could have cried just looking at him, but I was too exhausted. The aircrews began to walk away.

Stan had tears in his eyes. "Doc, John Grayson's wife and three children are living in officers' housing on Guam. I don't want her to hear about this from anyone but me, and I'd like to have you along. We'll fly to Guam just as soon as you can get your bag packed with service dress whites."

Stan was going to tell Mary Grayson in person.

"Right after, I'll call Australia and the photo technician's parents in the States," he added.

Ted Hanley was the quiet young navigator who had been married in Australia only a few weeks before starting the detachment. His new bride had remained in Townsville awaiting a vacancy in officers' housing on Guam while Ted was at Da Nang. Stan hadn't known the name of the photo technician. He had just joined the detachment as a replacement, and it had been his first combat flight.

We were airborne in Stan's A-3 on the way to Guam thirty minutes later. I should have been glad about the chance to see Lynn, but it I wasn't fit company for anybody. She wouldn't have understood if I had returned to Guam, even for just a few hours, without telling her. I made a decision to let her know. I asked Stan to radio VAP 61 on Guam to request that they telephone Lynn at the hospital.

Chapter 12

THREE DEVILS FROM HELL

No one ever slept in a navy carrier plane, not even on a big one. Crew members shared their cramped seats with a parachute and a one-man life raft, and the Plexiglas canopy lacked shades and buttons for turning out the lights. For years afterward, I marveled at the spaciousness of economy class on commercial airliners with the luxury of reclining seats, pull-down trays, and flight attendants serving cold drinks. In the navy, instead of in-flight movies, we played with radar and electronic countermeasures devices, and rather than listening to music via the earphones in our flight helmets, we received occasional cryptic, low-fidelity entertainment from air traffic controllers.

The fatigue from having been up most of the night on two consecutive four-hour helicopter rescue flights was taking its toll. The tension from the events, the noise in the helicopter, the cramped space in the A-3, and even my flight helmet had become annoyances. Stan, Dave, and I had not used the intercom at all during the trip. We had just lost an entire crew, and no one wanted to talk.

We arrived red-eyed at dusk, backed by a fiery sunset in the direction of Vietnam, three devils emerging from hell to torment two navy wives and the parents of a young air crewman. After a quick shower and change from flight suits into service dress whites, Stan called Mary

Grayson to ask if we could pay her a visit. He told me he could almost feel the panic on the other end of the phone line.

Houses in the married officers' area on Guam were two-story duplexes, terraced so that each looked down from a bluff onto the beautiful Philippine Sea. The scene gave a feeling of calmness, peace, and security. Cool ocean breezes tempered the tropical heat. Papaya, banana, and breadfruit trees, along with hibiscus and birds of paradise, completed the serene picture of a Pacific dreamland.

Mary Grayson looked like a movie star, thirty years old, trim, brunette, and wearing shorts and a T-shirt. She was standing barefoot in front of her house waiting for us by the curb.

Before we had even stopped, she came toward us, raised her arms, and shouted, "What happened to him? Is he all right? Tell me!"

Stan stopped the car in the middle of the street and got out right next to her. I followed. He frowned and tightened his lips in a grimace that told her the whole story.

"Some antiaircraft fire hit his plane, and he went down," he said.

She pleaded, almost in a scream, for more information. "Did he bail out?"

"He radioed that he was trying to make it to the coast to bail out, but we lost radio contact with him."

"Oh, god! No!" she howled.

I had talked to the families of patients, including parents of children who had died, or were dying, but this was far worse. I had never seen agony as intense as this woman was suffering. Families understood a natural death, but there was nothing natural about dying in an airplane over Vietnam.

Stan said, "The doctor here spent the night and most of this morning in a helicopter searching the sea in the area where John may have gone down, and a destroyer is still continuing the search right now. Helicopters from the *Enterprise* have been involved, too."

She turned to me, pleading and using her arms again. "Did you see anything?"

"No," I said. "We looked all night and all this morning. We didn't find them."

She was sobbing out of control. "Well, he could have bailed out over land, couldn't he?"

"Yes," Stan said. "That's still possible."

She stopped crying and looked back and forth at each of us. "Where did it happen?"

"About a hundred and fifty miles north of Da Nang," Stan said.

"My god, that's in North Vietnam!" she screamed.

"I'm afraid so," Stan said.

She collapsed to the ground, sobbing loudly again. "Why did we become involved in this stupid war?"

We weren't doing a very good job of consoling. Mary's neighbor, Jason Lockhart's wife Sarah, arrived. She looked at Mary weeping on the ground and at us in our white uniforms; then she sat down next to Mary, and the two women embraced, both crying. Stan and I stood there dumbly like two mindless statues. I had to look away. It was then that I noticed three children who had just emerged from Mary's house and were standing in front of the door. All were young, and they were dressed in pajamas. They weren't moving, just staring at their mother on the ground with Sarah Lockhart.

Another neighbor that I didn't recognize came running. She went straight to the children, hugging all three at once.

The tallest child, a little girl, asked, "Is Mommy hurt?"

The neighbor started to cry and couldn't answer at first. Then she said, "Yes, she's hurt a little, but she will be all right soon. You'll be able to help her."

I leaned over Sarah Lockhart and offered her a small bottle of tranquillizers. "Please take these for her. She may want them later. Maybe you will, too."

She glanced at me quickly, removed one arm from Mary, and slipped the bottle into her pocket. She didn't look at me again.

It was getting darker, and I could just see a remnant of the red sunset in the clouds over the sea. My eyes were filled with tears, and I could no longer look at the two women on the ground or the three children with the neighbor. I focused on the clouds, trying to remain stoic. Stan and I couldn't share their grief. We could only be intruders.

Stan said to Mary, "I'll be at the squadron administrative offices most of this evening, and I'll call you tomorrow morning with an update."

We left and didn't speak right away. Eventually I asked, "What will happen to Mary?"

Stan didn't answer right away. "Navy policy requires that we assist the family members in returning to the States within twenty-four hours," he mumbled.

That surprised me. It didn't sound right. It was obvious that navy wives were a close-knit bunch who all lived with the terror of an official visit like the one we had just made. Only other navy wives could understand. They were the real extended family of a recently-widowed navy wife, just as the real extended family of the airmen was the other members of the squadron. I wondered who had made that policy. It couldn't have been someone who had served in Vietnam. There was a navy padre at the hospital. I would ask him later.

Stan came back to life slowly. "The navy will arrange for seats on the Pan American flight that comes through Guam every day, and Mary Grayson will be on it with her three children headed for San Francisco, probably tomorrow. Professional movers will pack all of their belongings and ship them back to the States."

We reached the BOQ, where Stan dropped me off and drove on to the VAP 61 hangar area to make a series of phone calls, beginning with one to Ted Hanley's bride in Australia. Stan would also be worried about whatever was happening in Da Nang, so he would be busy for a while. It was now dark, and I was depressed, exhausted, and alone in the BOQ.

I called Lynn, who sounded delighted and cheerful. No one had told her why I was on Guam.

"I'll come pick you up right now," she said.

After a few minutes, she arrived at the BOQ in Roger's rusted-out old car. She gave me a big hug and said, "You look awful. When was the last time that you slept?"

"I don't know," I said. "Not for a couple of days."

"Why are you dressed up in that white uniform?"

I couldn't form the words. "We lost a whole flight crew," I finally stuttered.

She gasped and looked at me wide-eyed. "How dreadful!"

Lynn had been on my mind ever since leaving Guam for Australia, and I had longed to see her. But that night I couldn't think about her. I kept seeing Mary Grayson and Sarah Lockhart clinched on the ground and the three children huddling with the neighbor in the background.

We got into the car and started off. "Stan White and I just finished telling the wife of the pilot," I said.

"How did it go?"

I broke down and cried right there in the car. I didn't know whether Lynn was embarrassed, and I didn't care. We remained silent while she drove slowly through Agaña. I stopped crying after a while.

"I'm so sorry. Did you know her?" she asked.

"No, but I knew him."

Lynn looked at me, not knowing what to say.

"They have three small children," I said.

We went quiet again, and then I said, "I spent all last night and all morning in a helicopter conducting a search over the Gulf of Tonkin."

"Was it an accident?" she asked.

"No."

"Oh." We were quiet again for a few minutes. I couldn't concentrate on our conversation. Finally, she asked, "Do you want to talk about it?"

"Not right now," I said. "I need a little time to sort out my own feelings."

"I'll be available when you're ready," she said.

I tried to smile.

"Have you had dinner?" she asked.

I realized that I hadn't eaten anything for twenty-four hours.

"Restaurants close early here," she said, "but I have some food in my apartment. Would you like to take a chance on my cooking?"

It dawned on me that I hadn't been in somebody's home in months. My meals had been at odd hours in the bowling alley on the *Coral Sea* and in a tent at Da Nang. Dinner had been bacon and eggs on board the ship and something unidentifiable with mashed potatoes at Da Nang.

"That's the best offer I've ever had," I said.

She drove to her apartment in the officers' housing area next to the hospital. "When do you have to go back?" she asked.

"Probably tomorrow morning," I answered.

"So soon?"

"Everybody is stretched thin."

She paused. "What you're doing is dangerous, isn't it?"

"The flight crews and marines have it much worse."

"But it's still dangerous for you, too?"

"Not really," I lied.

Her apartment contained a small kitchen area, table and chairs, and a bed, but her space was huge compared with a four-bunk sleeping compartment on a carrier or a tent at Da Nang. She had curtains, a poster of the Beatles, a small television set and stereo, and a bookcase that was filled with a mix of medical books and novels by Steinbeck, Heller, Vonnegut, and Faulkner.

"It won't take me long to put some dinner together. Why don't you lie down for a few minutes?"

That's the last that I remembered until morning when a ray of sun caught my eye, and I heard the shower running in the bathroom. She had taken off my shoes and covered me with a blanket. I had not been the romantic date of her dreams.

My watch read 7:00 AM. I called the VAP 61 administration offices and found Stan already there—or maybe still there. He said that he needed the third seat for a replacement photo technician, because they were short in Da Nang again. Jason Lockhart was bringing his plane to Guam for installation of the same new equipment that had been installed on Stan's in Japan. Jason's third seat was empty, so I would return with him in a day or two. Stan and Dave were going to take off immediately.

I felt a little guilty about staying, but was happy, because it gave me an opportunity to make amends with Lynn for the night before. She came out of the bathroom dressed for work, looking beautiful.

"I'm sorry about falling asleep on you," I said.

She waved it off. "You didn't have much choice. You were exhausted."

"Where did you sleep?"

"Right next to you."

I smiled and shook my head. "I can't believe I missed that."

She wrinkled her brow. "I heard you talking on the phone. Do you have to leave right away?"

"No. It looks like I'll have another twenty-four hours on Guam."

"Oh, wonderful! We'll make the most of it. I have to work today, but we can have lunch together, and I have the evening free."

Lynn seemed delighted. I was forgiven for my moody behavior and my failure to call during the past weeks.

"I'm sure that Roger won't mind my tagging along on rounds while you're working."

I drove the car back to the BOQ to shower and change to a khaki uniform, and then I returned to the hospital. Before contacting Roger, I looked for the padre, who was busy talking with a patient on the marine ward. He saw me, and when he had finished he approached.

"Can I help you?"

I told him my story and asked him what he knew about the policy of sending wives home to the States within twenty-four hours of becoming widowed. I wondered if the real reason was to cut short the exposure to the reality of the war for the other families living in navy housing.

He replied, "Don't you think sending them home to their families immediately would be the most humane decision?"

"I'm not sure," I said. "But I think their real families are the other navy wives who understand and share the same fears." I told him about the scene with Mary Grayson.

"I hadn't thought about that," he said. "I imagine there's some flexibility depending upon the circumstance."

"I had assumed that it was a strict rule," I replied. "Maybe you're right. I'll call the squadron administration offices. Thank you, Padre."

I immediately called the VAP 61 administrative area to ask what was happening with Mary and her children. A yeoman answered, "They're booked on the Pan Am flight at 2:00 PM."

I had no way to know what Mary really wanted, and I didn't want to do more harm than good. I let the matter drop but continued to wonder about it.

I found Roger nearby. He had compiled a large amount of data on the patients evacuated from Vietnam, some of whom I had seen there. His research was not progressing rapidly, however, at least not on the malaria patients. He couldn't yet demonstrate if any of the combination treatment protocols had shown any increased effectiveness. The best defense against malaria was still prevention: mosquito netting and staying out of malaria-infested jungles.

We all had lunch together, and I listened to Roger and Lynn talk about the research project. I mostly stared at the sea through a window in the cafeteria with only one ear on the conversation. After work, Lynn and I went for a swim, and in the evening, we sat on the veranda at the Top O' the Mar for a long time and watched the bloodred fire of the sunset reflected on the Philippine Sea. She talked about the hospital and the Beatles, and then about her visits to several small Guamanian villages, places with names like Inarajan and Tamuning. She had gone surfing on many of her free days. Her voice was musical and soothing, and even though I didn't hear most of the words, the sound had begun my cure. Later that night, she slipped into bed with me to begin another phase of my therapy.

The next morning, my mood had lifted somewhat, and I could concentrate better on conversation. I called in to the VAP 61 administrative offices and found that Jason Lockhart's plane had arrived while I was at the hospital. Factory technicians had worked on it all night. I talked to Stuart Blake, Jason's navigator, who told me that we would leave for Da Nang about 10:00 AM. A sense of sadness had been growing in me, knowing I would have to leave paradise for the Vietnam cauldron. I told Lynn about my trepidations.

"I can't know all you've been through," she said, "but I understand."

"You've been wonderful," I said. "I felt that I was on the edge of a black hole."

"You're looking into my eyes more, and I caught you smiling once. You're going to be all right."

"I wish I could stay," I said.

"I wish you could, too," she responded.

Lynn drove me over to the naval air station, and this time, when we passed through Agaña, I noticed more details. It looked very much like older, peaceful towns on some of the outer islands of Hawaii, with abundant tropical flowers and a farmers' market. Hibiscus was growing in front of an old Japanese pillbox in a park facing the beach where U.S. Marines had made an amphibious landing during World War II.

After we arrived, Lynn stared at the A-3 parked in front of the VAP 61 hangars. "I don't want to lose you," she said.

"I'll be back," I promised.

I watched Jason and his navigator perform their walk-around preflight check, and then they climbed up into the cockpit. I kissed Lynn and we parted, but she stood there a long time. She was still there by the hangar while we were beginning our takeoff roll. I was reentering hell.

Chapter 13

A VISIT TO NAM HOA

Jason hadn't responded when I said good morning. He ran through his cockpit checklist with a blank expression. I asked him about his wife Sarah, but he remained silent. Then, after we had been airborne for a while, he clicked on the intercom. "She helped Mary Grayson get ready for her flight to California yesterday afternoon."

I was surprised at such a late response to my question, but I knew that John Grayson's death would have affected Jason even more than the rest of us. I started to wonder about Jason's ability to concentrate on flying the airplane. There was no co-pilot in an RA-3B, because the navigator had the right-hand seat in order to guide the aircraft during photo runs. I decided to try a little more conversation to probe Jason's state of mind.

I looked at the new imaging equipment installed on the panel in front of my seat, which I recognized as the same as had been installed in Stan's plane in Japan. I thought that it might be a good way to engage Jason in some dialogue to get an idea of his mental status.

"What's the new toy, and may I play with it?" I asked.

After a delay, Jason said, "No, you have to be checked out first."

I tried to make light of his comment. "It looks to me like the kind of scope that we use in hospitals for radioisotope scans to detect tumors. We call it a rectilinear scanner."

Silence.

I waited several minutes and then said, "With this, I'll bet you can fly over North Vietnam and detect brain tumors on the ground."

Jason still said nothing. I began to worry if the psychological trauma of John Grayson's death had immobilized Jason to the point of making him unsafe as a pilot, and I had a very high stake in his competence at that moment. Navigators had no pilot training, and for landing the big whale, I had just enough training to cause major anxiety all around. In a screaming-purple emergency, an A-3 pilot could talk me through a landing on a nice, long runway, but no one would be more terrorized about it than me. I wanted to believe that Jason's mental status was clear enough to land the plane.

"I noticed the word 'infrared' on the instrument panel," I said. "That must mean it picks up warm truck engines and cooking fires, too."

Silence.

"It also means that maybe you won't have to use flash bombs anymore."

Silence.

"May I play with it now?"

"No," Jason said.

At least I had confirmation that he was alive, but I had gotten nowhere in trying to assess his ability to function. Jason was normally quiet, so I couldn't tell if his reluctance to communicate was just his normal way of dealing with grief, or whether he was depressed enough to be a danger. I decided to wait and see, since I had no other attractive alternative.

No one talked on the intercom for a long time, and I became increasingly worried. Then an air traffic controller contacted us, and after an awkward pause, Jason answered appropriately. As we approached Da Nang, Jason responded slowly, but correctly, to each air traffic communication and turned to land. I was more anxious than I had been on the night carrier landing returning from Haiphong, but he seemed to be handling the aircraft normally for the landing. I held my breath, and then we touched down. My flight suit was soaked. I closed my eyes and felt the relief pour over me.

After shutting down the engines, Jason remained sitting at the controls with his head bowed. He didn't move for several minutes, and then like an automaton, he climbed slowly out the airplane. I understood Jason's grief, but would I want a surgeon in his state of mind to operate on me? I planned to talk to Stan.

After I climbed down out of the aircraft, one of the ground crew handed me three messages: one from Stan, one from the marine commander, and one from the hospital. I went to see Stan.

He spoke first. "I've had phone calls from the marines and from the hospital. They wanted to know when you'd be back. Apparently, you had been doing the work of about three doctors."

"Everybody at the hospital does the work of three people," I said. "You do the work of about six."

"I told them when you would arrive, but I also had to tell them something else. We're moving the detachment closer to Saigon. The air force has expanded a big air base at a place called Bien Hoa."

"That's pretty far south," I said. "Aren't most of the missions over North Vietnam?"

"Bien Hoa isn't convenient, but we don't have much choice. The *Enterprise* will let us keep two RA-3Bs on board, and we can use Cubi Point, but that's much farther from targets in North Vietnam than Bien Hoa."

"Why do we have to leave?"

"Da Nang is a small air base, and we take up a lot of space, but we can still use it for quick turnarounds. Our A-3s can carry a big load of fuel and have a greater range than other carrier aircraft."

I didn't like having to leave my friends at First Med, especially David Steiner and Colt Benson, but Bien Hoa wasn't under siege, and there were no wounded marines to snatch from hot LZs, and no front-line naval hospital where operations on maimed combat victims lasted all night.

"No doubt the flight crews won't miss Da Nang," I said. "Bien Hoa might be a little safer."

"Maybe, but the VC have started firing mortar shells into the air base at Bien Hoa from time to time."

Stan folded his arms and looked down. I sensed that the loss of John Grayson and his crew weighed heavily on him and that he felt frustrated about having to move the detachment to an air base that would add more flying time on many of the missions. I wanted to bring up the subject of Jason Lockhart.

I said, "I suppose the squadron is taking the loss of John Grayson and his crew pretty hard."

Stan still stared at the ground. "No one is saying much, but we're all feeling the grief." He looked up. "How's Jason doing?"

Apparently, Stan had the same concerns that bothered me. "Not good. I'm worried about him," I said. "He's even quieter than usual, and very slow in responding to air traffic controllers."

Stan faced me directly. "These are high-stress times, Doc. The flight crews trust you; they're more likely to level with you than anyone else. Keep an eye on Jason."

"I will," I said, not knowing how I was going to assess Jason's mental competence as a naval aviator. I looked at the bags under Stan's eyes and turned-down mouth. "How are *you* doing?"

"I haven't had time to think about it."

We were both silent for a minute.

"We have one positive development at least," Stan said finally. "You've noticed the new infrared imaging gear, haven't you?"

"Yes."

"That should give us an edge."

"I hope so," I said.

"It'll reduce the risk," he said. "We should be able to install it in all of our aircraft in the next few weeks."

Using flash bombs had likely contributed to the loss of John Grayson and his crew, and also Jason's incident with triple-A. But substituting infrared imaging for the flash bombs wouldn't eliminate all of the risk. Still, the new equipment had arrived at the best moment to offset the despair, or at least to mitigate it a little.

"When do we move to Bien Hoa?" I asked.

"We're going to start moving the detachment tomorrow."

"That soon?" I said. "Does the hospital know?"

"Yes, and so does the marine commander. I told him he could have you for three or four more days, but after that, we would need you at Bien Hoa."

"The marines really do need a doctor in their helicopter ambulances," I said.

"I know. They've already put in an urgent request for their own flight surgeon."

While I was on Guam, the fighting near Da Nang had escalated, and casualties were rolling in. I assisted in the operating room almost constantly. The marines had received orders to "find and destroy" the Vietcong and NVA regulars, so the number of patrols had increased, along with the number of air ambulance flights. We were picking up the wounded at distances farther from Da Nang than in prior weeks, and the dispatcher began calling for a flight surgeon on more flights.

The day before my scheduled departure, the phone rang. It was the air ambulance dispatcher. "Doctor, we need you again. The marines have taken a large number of casualties in a firefight, and some are in bad shape. I've sent a helicopter to the hospital to pick you up."

As soon as we were airborne, I clicked on the intercom to talk to the pilot. "What's up?"

"NVA regulars have surrounded a company of marines at Nam Hoa."

"Where's that?"

"Near Hué."

Hué was an ancient Vietnamese cultural center, about fifty miles north of Da Nang near the border with North Vietnam. Fierce fighting had been going on for days in that area.

"How many wounded are there?" I asked.

"We aren't sure," the pilot answered, "but the dispatcher said there were at least eight."

"We'll need more than one helicopter."

"A second one is right behind us."

That many casualties almost always meant that some would be critical. I had never gotten used to these helicopter ambulance rescues and always suffered anxiety until we had the casualties on board and were airborne again.

"What's the LZ like?" I asked.

"Not good. The marines are defending an open square in front of a temple that they want to use to evacuate the wounded."

I hadn't landed in a hot LZ for a couple of weeks, and the old fear gripped me. The familiar nausea and panic were returning.

The pilot continued, "The marines radioed that the square is too small to land two helicopters at the same time. We'll go in first and pick up the most severely wounded. As soon as we lift off, the other helicopter will drop into the square behind us."

A small landing area meant that the NVA could concentrate their mortar fire. This might be worse than just a hot LZ; it might be a trap. I was frightened and felt that I couldn't get enough air. We turned to approach the town, and I looked down on a scene that resembled newsreel pictures of bombed-out villages in Europe during World War II, with devastation everywhere. None of the buildings still had a roof, and all that remained of many houses was rubble and perhaps one wall. The pilot found the center of the town quickly and immediately plunged into the square.

The beating of the rotor blades, the mortar blasts, and the racket of automatic weapons disoriented me. Our helicopter created a dust storm that obscured the ruined buildings and converted the village into what I imagined a nuclear holocaust would be like. An explosion rocked the helicopter as if we were still airborne in turbulent air. Grime-covered marines appeared, looking like extraterrestrials. Pairs were carrying wounded men toward the helicopter, and sometimes a lone marine was struggling by himself to drag a victim.

Two hospital corpsmen had come on the helicopter this time, and the three of us jumped off to help load the casualties. I saw an explosion across the square obliterate two marines who were carrying a wounded comrade. For a few seconds, the dust from another explosion obscured the helicopter, and I couldn't see it. I was terrified.

I saw one marine fall while trying to carry another. I pulled myself together and ran to help.

I yelled, "I'll grab his legs," and then found that one leg was missing. I froze while the marine looked at me, picked up his comrade again by himself, and staggered on toward the helicopter.

I found another victim writhing on the ground, with blood and dirt coating the front of his shredded uniform. One of the corpsmen noticed and helped me carry the victim to the helicopter deck, which now looked like a medieval engraving of hell. The other corpsman reached to swing us on board, one after the other, and then we shot up into air. The sudden leap tumbled all of us into a twisted scramble, and one of our patients almost rolled out through the hatch.

I struggled to regain my balance as we roared above the town. The square below filled with explosions from a mortar attack, as if we had provoked a nest of hornets—but we were clear. The pilot banked toward Da Nang, and I looked back to see a horrible sight: a North Vietnamese mortar shell had scored a direct hit on the second helicopter, which had just landed. The urge to vomit almost overwhelmed me, but the victims in our helicopter needed my attention.

We leveled off, and I stabilized myself on my knees in order to concentrate on the wounded. All four casualties were caked with a black mixture of blood and dust. One of the corpsmen was already administering morphine to the patient that I had helped carry to the helicopter. Bright red blood oozed through the black, shredded remnants of his shirt. The victim missing a leg had a tourniquet around his thigh, and his skin was pale beneath the dirt. The other two had bullet wounds, one in the neck and the other in the abdomen.

The victim missing a leg had lost a large amount of blood and was barely conscious. He needed a blood transfusion immediately but would have to do with intravenous saline to replace the blood loss until we reached the hospital. I had become faster at inserting internal jugular catheters and hung a bag of saline with the stopcock wide open to try to prevent complete cardiovascular collapse.

I called the pilot on the intercom. "Radio the hospital and put me through."

The connection happened almost instantly. I yelled, "We picked up four patients. All of them need operating rooms right away. One has a traumatic leg amputation and needs blood immediately. I have an internal jugular catheter in place and saline running wide open. His dog tags say O-positive. Two more have gunshot wounds. The fourth victim has a huge anterior chest and abdominal wound from a mortar blast. I'm starting an IV, and we've given him morphine." I looked over at him and then said slowly into the radio, "Oh, no—never mind—he's not going to make it."

David Steiner's voice came on. "We'll be ready for you, Doc."

We continued working frantically, and as we approached Da Nang, the pilot came back on the intercom. "Doctor, after we unload the patients at the hospital, we're going back to Nam Hoa. The *Enterprise* is sending in a flight of A-4 Skyhawks to bomb the perimeter around the marines, and we're going to follow right on their tails. I'd be relieved if you went with us."

The thought of going back into that crucible horrified me. I had known subconsciously that we would have to, but we had been too busy to think about it. We had been lucky to survive, and a second mission would be just as risky.

Reluctantly, I clicked on my mike. "I'll stay right with you. Radio the hospital to be ready to restock our supplies as soon as we land."

"Thanks, Doctor. Wilco."

Chapter 14

NAM HOA REVISITED

As we approached the hospital landing pad, I could see below a gang of doctors and nurses with four gurneys waiting for us. The victim with the huge mortar wound was now quiet; I checked his carotid pulse and felt nothing.

As soon as we touched down, a nurse passed me a unit of universal-donor blood that I hung immediately for the amputation casualty, and the patients—three living and one deceased—disappeared into the hospital. I helped the two hospital corpsmen grab our supplies, and we lifted off for the return to Nam Hoa, not taking the time to wash the blood from the deck.

I looked at the two hospital corpsmen sitting opposite me. I guessed that neither was yet twenty years old. They had done their jobs expertly and bravely. I was glad to have them with me.

Twenty minutes later, we could see the A-4s in the distance beginning their low-level attack, saturating the perimeter of the already-ruined town with their bombs. When the last pair of A-4s began their run, the helicopter lurched forward and almost immediately plunged into the square. The roller-coaster dive and the fear disoriented me again, but this time no mortar blasts filled the square. The stillness was eerie. The three of us dismounted and began helping to carry wounded marines to the helicopter in an orderly fashion, assisting the ones who could walk.

I noticed a marine sergeant signaling to wait for one more wounded marine entering the square and hurried over to help him. That was when it happened.

Explosions erupted all around, and both the sergeant and I dropped to the ground. The noise was deafening, and the ground shook like an earthquake. Rubble flew through the air, and dust obscured everything.

A pause in the barrage allowed me to hear a helicopter high overhead, and the dust in the square cleared just enough so that I could see that mine was gone. I lay there in despair without moving. In time, the barrage stopped, and the marine sergeant lifted himself up on an elbow. He looked at my medical corps oak leaf.

"Welcome to the United States Marine Corps, Doctor. Let's get the hell out of here."

I was too stunned to think of anything clever. "Let me take a look at your wounded man."

The casualty was a marine corporal with a bullet wound in his left shoulder. The sergeant had rigged him with a sling.

"I've got some morphine in my flight suit," I said.

"I already gave him some," the sergeant said. "I always carry it—a marine's best friend."

I was devastated at being abandoned, but the sergeant had a survivor's air about him. Given the circumstances, I had no option but to follow him, anyway.

"Now, if you don't mind, Doctor," he said, "I recommend that we move our asses over into that temple."

I didn't see any temple, but I took the sergeant's word for it that the rubble he was pointing to had been one once. The two marines made a dash, crouching low, and I followed. We stopped behind a ruined wall and waited. I heard gunfire near the area we had just left.

"We're pulling back out of the village," the sergeant said. "There's a whole regiment of NVA moving in on the other side."

We made another dash—waited again behind cover—and ran again. Eventually, we reached the edge of the village and entered into some brush. I hadn't noticed before, but more marines were around us now. They used sign language only; no one spoke. Every time they stopped, they sighted their weapons behind us. Darkness was coming on. After we had distanced ourselves more from the village, the marines stood up and started to walk, spread out, with their weapons ready. We continued for two or three hours the same pattern of walking, stopping, stooping, and listening.

Finally, we reached a small knoll and stopped. I noticed for the first time a second sergeant, who came over to the one I was following. The two began to talk in a whisper. They went around giving orders.

"All right, set up a perimeter. Watch your field of fire."

The marines went about digging in and dragging brush, while I sat useless. They were talking now, but only in whispers. I couldn't hear any of them more than a few feet away.

After a while, my sergeant came over to me and started to whisper. "Doc, we're going to spend the night here. I don't expect we'll have any visitors."

"What's up for tomorrow?" I asked.

"We're going to try for a pickup. Our platoon has been shot up pretty bad. And we lost our lieutenant—killed back in that village."

"I'm sorry."

"Yeah," he said. "We were relieved that you medics could pick up our wounded. We had to get out of that village."

"Glad we could help."

He looked me in the eye for a minute. "I've never seen a doctor in a combat area before."

"We're trying something new," I said. "Maybe we can improve your chances a little."

He nodded and continued to stare at me. Then he held out his hand. "My name's Schiller, Doc."

I took his hand. "Luke Lucas, Sergeant. I'm glad you were around. It was pretty frightening during that bombardment."

"Yeah, we took a pounding."

"I'd like to take a look at your corporal again, if that's okay," I said. "Ideally, we ought to remove that bullet in an operating room before the wound gets infected."

"The helicopters will pick us up at daylight. We're close to a clearing that will work as an LZ."

"Still, it won't hurt to take a look," I said.

The bullet was deep in the corporal's shoulder, and the morphine had worn off. I had no instruments, except maybe a borrowed combat knife, and I knew that trying to retrieve a bullet that way would be brutal and imprecise. I had more morphine, so I decided to treat the pain and wait for the pick up, which might be in less than eight hours. One of the marines offered some soap, so at least I was able to clean the area, but I had no dressings. My years of medical education had no value in the bush without equipment. I hoped those helicopters would arrive on time.

The marines had very little food, but they shared what they had. They offered me some, but I wasn't hungry after all of the stress of the past few hours. I was tired, but in spite of my training in quick naps as an intern, I found sleeping impossible on a marine patrol with NVA soldiers in the area. I just sat up all night with my thoughts. If I got out of this mess, I probably wouldn't tell Lynn about it, at least not until I left Vietnam behind.

There hadn't been any rain for a while, but it came down hard during the night. No one carried rain gear, but the temperature was in the high seventies or low eighties, so it wasn't uncomfortable being rained on. Just before dawn, the rain stopped, and the two sergeants moved everybody out. The clearing was less than a mile away.

We found it but didn't enter right away. Instead, we hid in some high growth. Soon I could hear helicopters in the distance and saw Sergeant Schiller talking in a low voice on a radio. In minutes, the helicopters appeared over the trees. We were about to begin our dash into the clearing when the shooting started.

Machine-gun fire was coming from the other side of the clearing. The NVA gunners hit one of the helicopters as it was attempting to land, and it dropped in a fiery crash. The rest of the helicopters aborted, turning back the way they had come.

I gaped at the wreckage burning out in the middle of the clearing. If the NVA gunners had held their fire until all of the helicopters had landed, most of us might now be dead. There was no hope for the crew in the downed helicopter. They were probably killed on impact. The marines near me were just staring, not moving. Then the two sergeants passed the word to pull back. I turned around to look at the sky several times to see the smoke rising from the clearing as we retreated in the same direction from which we had come. I had seen plenty of men who were wounded in combat, but in the past two days, I had twice seen men die as their helicopters exploded. I wouldn't forget that.

We walked all day in the same pattern of stopping, listening, and moving. It rained several times, and I was now covered with mud and indistinguishable from the marines. Sergeant Schiller walked alongside me for a while.

"We're heading for another LZ," he said. "They're going to try another pickup the day after tomorrow."

I thought of the corporal. "That bullet wound will become infected by then," I said. "Maybe I should try to dig it out with a knife. It will be very uncomfortable for him."

"Whatever you say, Doc."

I moved over to the corporal. "How are you feeling?"

"Not very good," he responded. In marine talk, that meant he felt dreadful.

"The sergeant says we may not be picked up for a couple of days. That's a long time to wait to dig out that bullet."

"What do you mean, Doc?"

"I can try to dig it out after we stop."

He didn't answer right away. We just kept walking. Then he asked, "Will it hurt?"

"Yes," I said. "I still have a couple of morphine ampoules, but even with that, it will hurt like hell."

He was silent for a while before speaking. "What would happen if you didn't dig it out?"

"The wound would become infected. Bacteria would enter your bloodstream. You would develop a fever, and you might die."

He continued walking, now with his head down. "After we stop, Doc, I want you to take it out."

"All right," I said. "I'll talk to the sergeant."

I found Sergeant Schiller. "Can you round up penknives and any other tools that might function as surgical instruments? I wouldn't mind a little more soap and something that might serve as a bandage. Also, see if anyone has any more morphine."

"I'll take care of it," he said. "We'll stop in about an hour."

We still had some daylight when we stopped this time. The sergeant presented me with an astonishing collection of wicked-looking, non-regulation sharp tools. One of the marines used a helmet to scoop some water from a fast-running stream, and I washed the tools I wanted in soapy water. A fire was out of the question. I injected the corporal with two ampoules of morphine and sat him up against a log. After the morphine had time to take effect, I scrubbed the area well with soapy water.

"Are you ready, Corporal?"

He had his eyes closed tightly and was grimacing. "Yes, sir," he said in a voice a little too loud.

Two sharp penknives and a couple of mess forks to substitute for tongs made up my main instruments. I widened the wound with a penknife, using one fork as a retractor, and increased the exposure to try to grab the bullet. The corporal's whole body tensed as he reacted to the pain, but he didn't scream. I pressed ahead and tried to work the bullet out with another fork. Finally, it moved, and I could grab it between the two forks. The marines watching let out low whistles as I dropped the bullet into the helmet.

Sergeant Schiller addressed the patient. "Corporal, you're going to have a souvenir to show your grandchildren."

One of the marines presented me with a pair of clean boxer underpants, the only available dressing not permeated with mud. I cut some strips and tied it on the best I could, and then had the corporal put his arm back in the sling. He stayed propped against the log most of the night.

I found a spot to lie down and slept for a few hours. We began moving again early in the morning, heading for the new LZ with a plan to stop again for the night about a mile short again. The corporal was uncomfortable from the surgery, but the wound didn't look infected, at least not yet. We moved slowly. Sergeant Schiller had one last ampoule of morphine to help the corporal on the trek.

Late in the afternoon, we arrived near the LZ, and the marines set up a perimeter again. The other sergeant picked two men to hide near the clearing to watch for any evidence of the NVA. Before dawn, the two sergeants moved us closer to the clearing and organized scouts to probe the far side. Just after dawn, I heard the helicopters and saw

Sergeant Schiller on his radio again. The lead helicopters dropped smoke bombs, and we all charged to the center of the LZ to jump on as they landed. This time, there was no machine-gun fire and no mortars. We were out. I asked the pilot to telephone for an ambulance to carry the corporal over to the hospital.

In twenty minutes, we were landing at Da Nang. Colt Benson was waiting as the marine helicopters came in, but with my filthy flight suit and stubble, he didn't recognize me at first. I shook hands with Sergeant Schiller and thanked him for leading us out of the wilderness.

"We ought to call you Sergeant Moses," I said.

He smiled, but I don't think he understood.

Colt drove the ambulance, taking the corporal and me over to the hospital. One of the orthopedic surgeons was going to look at the corporal's bullet wound, and I was heading for a shower.

Two days later, I obtained a space on an air force transport plane leaving for Bien Hoa so that I could rejoin VAP 61. Two hours before my departure, another flight surgeon, Henry Lawrence, arrived at Da Nang to begin what the navy called TAD, temporary additional duty. His permanent post was at the dispensary at Cubi Point. He was to remain at Da Nang until the navy could find a permanent replacement for the marines.

We had a chance to talk while walking over to the marine commander's tent. He said that he had been living in officers' family housing with his wife and two-year-old son. His tour of duty overseas would end in six months, and he was already accepted to begin his residency in internal medicine at the naval hospital in Oakland, California.

We met with the marine commander, who explained the fighting in which the marines at Da Nang were engaged. Dr. Lawrence blanched when the commander broached the subject of riding air ambulances into combat areas. I felt a great deal of sympathy, remembering how inadequate I had felt the first time I had to provide care for a major trauma victim in a helicopter. No training was adequate to prepare anyone for the carnage of Vietnam.

After our meeting, Dr. Lawrence and I walked over to the hospital, and I offered him a few tips.

"Your best friend, and that of your patients, is the staff of doctors and nurses at the hospital. In just a few months, they have taught me enough to get by. I recommend that you spend as much time there as possible and learn as much as you can."

"I have no experience in taking care of major battlefield wounds," he said. "I'm not trained for this."

"Neither was I," I said. "None of us were. I've thought about it a lot, though. Most flight surgeons have had only a year of rotating internship and six months of aviation medicine. But at least most of us have spent a little time managing patients in ICUs and emergency departments."

"Only a few weeks."

"Few doctors who are senior to us have even that little experience with critically ill patients. We've had to learn on the fly, and none of us has ever been comfortable. A specialty in battlefield medicine doesn't exist—we have to invent it."

"How do I do that?" he asked.

"Stay close to David Steiner; he's probably seen more battlefield trauma than any other doctor in the world."

I introduced Dr. Lawrence around at the hospital. The doctors and nurses had prepared a little going-away party for me and had painted a big sign in the mess tent—it read "Luke's Far Eastern Creamery." The nurses awarded me a handmade diploma certifying me as an "airborne chest and vascular surgeon."

One of the nurses laughed. "We wanted to change 'airborne' to 'airhead,' to designate someone who would fly in helicopters that land in the middle of mortar attacks."

David Steiner announced that he was nominating me for "Grunt of the Year."

The orthopedic surgeon who had debrided and revised the marine corporal's bullet wound added that he would nominate me to become the first president of the American College of Knife and Fork Surgery.

"I'll be spending some time on the *Enterprise*," I said. "I'll see what I can do to fish another downed airman out of the water to bring to you."

David Steiner said, "If it's all the same to you, we'd prefer the fresh milk instead of the wet airman."

Henry Lawrence was watching our morbid joking with a worried look.

I boarded the flight to Bien Hoa with mixed emotions. I hated to leave the hospital at Da Nang and felt guilty about handing over the responsibility for the marine air ambulances to someone who had to learn from scratch. I wrote up a special flight surgeon's report to send to BuMed and to Pensacola to explain what I thought was the minimum supplementary training necessary for flight surgeons who were going to be involved in rescue operations of combat casualties.

Six weeks after I left, I got word that Dr. Henry Lawrence had been killed on a rescue mission when his helicopter was shot down. On January 1, 1966, President Johnson issued an order grounding all flight surgeons from flying in combat areas in Vietnam.

IV

BIEN HOA

Chapter 15

DOCTOR TRAN'S CLINIC

The air force base at Bien Hoa resembled the one at Da Nang, only larger, but with the same suffocating heat and dust permeating everything. The monsoons of September and October had ended, and we had entered the dry season that began toward the end of each year, a period when temperatures often exceeded 100° F. Constant noise from dozens of taxiing jet engines quickly fatigued anyone not wearing sound suppressors. VAP 61 had five aircraft using the air base, supported by a large number of maintenance personnel.

Instead of just a community of tents, many permanent structures surrounded the runways at Bien Hoa. The nascent South Vietnamese Air Force, equipped and trained by American advisors, had occupied the air base for several years. Since the escalation of American involvement in the war, the U.S. Air Force had almost entirely displaced the South Vietnamese, who had used antiquated, propeller-driven A-1 Skyraiders.

The rapid buildup at the air base had meant shortages of everything, including sleeping quarters. Since we were navy squatters and newcomers, we had to make do with tents again. I would miss having immediate access to a hospital. The nearest major medical facility was an army hospital several miles away.

The air force dispensary had air conditioning. It was the first time that I had experienced it since Guam, and I was uncomfortable walking into the wintry air. The sergeant at the front desk told me that the air force had installed it after taking over the air base from the South Vietnamese. I marveled at the contrast between the tent-and-Quonset-hut navy hospital at Da Nang, where operations on major trauma were taking place around the clock, and this spotless, beautifully equipped dispensary with very few patients.

The desk sergeant introduced me to an air force warrant officer, the dispensary administrator, who showed me around and assured me that I could see patients there any time I wanted. Two air force flight surgeons were permanently stationed at Bien Hoa, but they had a light patient load, just as at the naval air station on Guam. There was plenty of space for me.

After we finished the tour of the dispensary, the warrant officer set me up with a phone connection to the naval hospital on Guam, so I was able to talk to Lynn. I didn't mention anything about helicopter ambulances or my expedition with the marines at Nam Hoa.

"Are you all right?" she asked. "Is there less fighting around Bien Hoa than at Da Nang?"

"It's much safer," I said. "Almost all of the fighting is up near the North Vietnamese border."

"Will you be flying much?"

"No. I'll be spending most of my time in a nice, safe dispensary."

"Be careful about the malaria."

As Stan had warned, the VC were sending a random mortar shell every day or two into the air base, usually without serious damage, but once in a while, someone was killed.

I set up regular hours for sick call and let the VAP 61 personnel know where to find me at specific times, although I assured them that I would be glad to see them any time. I also told the warrant officer at the dispensary that I wouldn't mind seeing air force personnel if it would help.

The morning after my arrival, I learned that a bomb had exploded during the night at the BOQ in Saigon, demolishing the façade of the building. A number of people were killed, and a report published later in the armed forces newspaper *Stars and Stripes* asserted that Vietcong insurgents had somehow gained entry into the lobby. Construction would begin immediately to repair the damage, but meanwhile the BOQ would remain open with heightened security.

Stars and Stripes was also distributed on Guam, and in the afternoon, the phone rang in the dispensary. Lynn had induced the telephone operator at the hospital on Guam to put a call through.

"I was frantic that you might have been staying at that BOQ in Saigon," she said.

"No, I haven't been off the air base."

"Didn't you say it was safe around Saigon?"

"It had been until last night," I said.

"Be careful."

I started to feel uneasy about not telling Lynn the real situation in Vietnam. I was just trying to protect her, and also I wasn't sure anyone would believe what the war was really like. I don't think any of the squadron members who returned to Guam for a few days ever said much. We weren't keeping secrets. In my case, I just didn't think I could find the words to explain it, or that anyone not in the war could understand.

Late in the afternoon, I found Stan White, who had even deeper shadows under his eyes than before. He had just been talking on the phone and was blankly staring at a stack of messages. When he saw me, he stood up and rose to shake my hand.

"Doc, I'm glad to see you. We heard what happened."

"I have the greatest of respect for the marines after that," I said.

"We were pretty worried."

"Is the squadron settling in okay?" I asked.

He sat down again and leaned back in his chair. "Everyone is flying a lot of hours—probably too many."

"Worse than before?"

"Yes," he said. "The attack squadrons can't get enough of the real-time intelligence we produce, now that we have the infrared gear."

I sat down. "I'm sure the extra distance to the targets hasn't helped morale very much."

"The crews are professionals, and they are doing their jobs."

"At least they don't have to use the flash bombs," I said.

"Sure," he paused. "That does help."

I didn't understand the long pause. After the tragedy with John Grayson and his crew, were VAP 61's planes still going to fly such high-risk missions?

"You won't be using flash bombs again, will you?" I asked.

"Not often," he said. "But the high-resolution cameras using flash bombs give us detailed images that can sometimes be important in spite of the delay in developing the film."

I was aghast. "So you'll still use flash bombs once in a while?"

"Well, yes, but not often. Most missions call for real-time images. That's what the attack squadrons want."

We were both quiet for a minute. Stan looked down at his desk. There wasn't much to say about the flash bombs. Stan knew better than anybody about the extreme risk.

"I've set up shop at the air force dispensary," I said.

"We're all glad to see you back, Doc."

At the dispensary, I noticed that all of the cleaning and delivery personnel were Vietnamese civilians. Almost no contact took place between Americans and Vietnamese, who were separated by the language barrier. A few Vietnamese spoke a kind of noisy Pidgin English, and they acted as foremen and interpreters. To me, the rapport between Americans and Vietnamese workers resembled too much the French colonial culture of the old rubber plantations, where the French were masters and the Vietnamese almost slaves.

I wanted to learn more about the Vietnamese people and their views about us. Since many of the citizens in the town were Catholics, I guessed that French nuns and teachers might have played a role in their education. I had studied French in college, but more than six years had passed since then, and my French was rusty. I approached a small, wiry civilian worker who was cleaning the exam rooms that I was using.

"Bonjour, Monsieur, comment allez-vous?"

He looked up suddenly and turned toward me.

"Bonjour, Docteur. Vous parlez français? Je ne savais pas qu'il y avait des Américains qui pouvaient parler français."

(Good day, Doctor. You speak French? I didn't know there were Americans who were able to speak French.)

He spoke French beautifully, much better than I could, but we understood each other very well. He said that he was a Buddhist, but even so, he had attended a Catholic school that the French had established for Vietnamese in the late forties. His parents had attended French schools during the colonial days before World War II, and they sent him to the Catholic school because of the superior education offered.

"Was it unusual for a Buddhist to attend a Catholic school?" I asked.

"Yes, very unusual. I had to pretend that I was a Catholic."

"They wouldn't let a Buddhist attend?"

"No," he said. "Catholics and Buddhists don't get along, and sometimes there is violence."

"Why do they hate each other?"

"The Catholics have more education and more money. They look down on us and think we are ignorant peasants. They own all the looms and clothing workshops, but they won't hire us."

I was embarrassed to remember that I had used the term "peasants" in referring to Vietnamese people, thinking that few of them had any education.

"I'm glad that we could hire you," I said.

"Yes, my job is very important to me."

"What do you think about Americans coming to fight against the Vietcong?"

He looked away from me, evidently weighing the risks of being open.

"When the Americans first arrived," he said in a low voice, "we had hoped that they would make the government in Saigon stop the corruption and the discrimination against Buddhists, but nothing has changed."

"Wasn't there a change in your government just two years ago?"

"Yes. We were glad, because we hated the Diem government, but Premier Ky discriminates against Buddhists, too. And we know he is just a puppet of the Americans."

"Do you think that Americans control your government?" I asked.

He raised his eyebrows. "Of course. You have all of the power. The Vietcong would take over quickly if you left."

I was becoming worried. We viewed ourselves as making a great sacrifice for the Vietnamese people. They saw us as colonialists.

"Do most Vietnamese prefer the Vietcong?"

He shook his head and almost shouted. "No, no! We don't like the Vietcong, but we aren't willing to fight for Americans, who are just like the French. We don't like foreigners to occupy our country."

I felt sick inside. My whole life had been turned upside down by this war. Now I found that the people we were trying to protect didn't want us here. At that moment, the war seemed obscene to me.

My Vietnamese acquaintance said that he lived in Bien Hoa and took the local bus that carried civilian employees onto the air base. French nuns had trained him to be a sort of lay medical practitioner, and he had been running a small children's clinic for several years in Bien Hoa. He worked at the air base to earn money to buy medical supplies on the black market. I imagined how the spotless air force dispensary must have contrasted with this poor man's clinic.

He said his patients called him "Doctor," even though he had told them that he wasn't a real doctor. Real doctors were trained at the University of Saigon, but their numbers were few, and poor people had no access to them.

His name was Tran, so I began calling him "Dr. Tran." He seemed to think my calling him "Doctor" was quite natural. He asked me an unending series of medical questions, paying close attention to my answers, and then followed up with more questions. The dispensary administrator marveled that I could converse with a Vietnamese employee, not recognizing that we were speaking French—or at least Tran was.

I asked about the kind of problems he was seeing in his clinic.

"We see many children with malaria and dengue during the monsoons when the mosquitoes are worse, but during the dry seasons, more come in with diarrhea and hepatitis."

"Don't the people have access to safe drinking water?"

"No. Water from wells is contaminated, especially during the dry season, and some people drink water from the river."

"Do you see cholera sometimes in the patients with diarrhea?" I asked.

"Yes, many cases every year."

I had never seen even one case of cholera, a disease that had been common in the United States and Europe during the nineteenth century, but it was now absent as a result of safe public drinking water and sewage treatment. Patients with cholera often died from dehydration, but even in the absence of any effective antibiotic treatment, victims usually survived if they were given adequate IV fluid support. I asked him how he hydrated his patients.

"The nuns showed me how to measure salt and put it into boiling water to make saline for intravenous use. We boil everything: bottles, tubing, and needles, but the tubing deteriorates after so many uses, and our needles are old."

"Can't you buy tubing and needles?" I asked.

"Supplies for IV fluids are difficult to buy, even on the black market."

I felt angry about the irony of the air force dispensary storerooms being filled with supplies in the face of desperate need just outside the gate.

"Do you have enough to treat all of your patients that need IVs?"

"No, never," he said. "Right now, we have only two sets of IV tubing, so we have to make a decision about which patients we will treat."

"Do you mean that some children die because you don't have enough IV tubing?"

"Yes, that happens every day."

"How terrible!"

I couldn't ignore the misery of people that I might be able to help. I began to think of how to get supplies to Tran. He invited me to see his clinic and suggested that we take the civilian bus that ran very close to it. I worried about the safety of a tall blond American naval officer alone in Bien Hoa. But my indignation about our ignorance of the severe poverty right next to the air base was great, so I accepted.

The ancient, dust-covered Japanese bus had no glass in the windows and spewed smoke like an old locomotive. Passengers crammed into the sweltering oven, and most stood. The small number of wooden benches were jammed full. As in Japan, I towered over the other passengers, who stared at the floor of the bus and avoided any eye contact with me.

We bumped into Bien Hoa through a crowded street, barely wide enough for the bus, where there were rows of tiny stalls selling food, fabrics, simple clothing, and wicker baskets. Roasting poultry and fish generated an oppressive atmosphere of smoke blended with incense that failed to cover the pungent smell of human waste. Naked small children played in the dust, while old people with an air of despair lounged about, staring absently into space.

The dilapidated clinic consisted of four rooms, huge by the standards of the neighborhood, but tiny compared to the air force dispensary. One room contained a small operating table, some cabinets for medical instruments and supplies, and an ancient microscope in the corner. A nurse worked in another room, cleaning and dressing wounds and distributing herbal medicines. The two largest rooms were crowded with cots, all of which were filled with children who appeared to be quite sick. Large windows without glass attempted in vain to capture a breeze. An odor of disease, poverty, and death, stronger than I had ever experienced, permeated the entire interior. A ladder led to the roof, where bandages on clotheslines were drying in the hot sun.

"Bandages are precious," Dr. Tran said. "We reuse them after washing them with soap and drying them in the sun."

I noticed a young girl with extensive third-degree burns and asked what had happened to her.

"We think her older brother was making homemade bombs that accidentally exploded."

"Do you think he is a Vietcong?" I asked.

He paused, not looking at me, apparently deciding how to answer. "It's possible, but he could also be part of the Buddhist Struggle Movement that attacks Catholics. Many young people have nothing to do and are filled with hate."

"Struggle Movement?"

He lowered his voice. "They have weapons, and they are very dangerous."

Dr. Tran clearly didn't want to talk about the war or violent religious and political factions. He quickly changed the subject.

"We have many patients, as you can see."

I noticed an emaciated young girl who was struggling to breathe. She seemed mentally retarded. I asked about her.

"She has been having convulsions," he said, "and she has severe anemia and congestive heart failure. I think malaria is the cause."

"Do you have any drugs to treat malaria?"

"We use quinine, chloroquine, and tetracycline, when we can get them on the black market. But we never have enough."

"It doesn't seem to be helping her," I said.

"We can't spare using any on her, because I don't think she will survive. Most often, the drugs we can get don't have any effect, anyway, especially on patients with severe complications like she has."

I thought of the unlimited resources I had used as an intern to treat patients with end-stage heart disease in order to buy them another few months of life. This young girl looked about five years old and should have lived many years.

"Isn't there something you can do for her?" asked.

"No," he said. "Even if she did survive, she would be mentally retarded from the cerebral malaria. Mentally retarded children don't survive in Vietnam."

I was appalled. I had never faced indifference like that. I was seeing brutal practicality.

"I've heard that orphanages exist throughout Vietnam," I said. "Can't they take care of handicapped children?"

"The orphanages are filled and have no money for food. Young children roam the countryside, and more than half of the babies in the orphanages die before they are one year old."

I felt very uncomfortable and didn't speak for a while. The Vietnamese people were suffering far more than I had imagined, and we Americans had not reached out to them. Dr. Tran and I watched silently while a nurse talked with several young women, each holding an infant. He said that she was trying to explain to the young mothers how to prevent malaria.

"We try to educate them to use netting at night when the mosquitoes are biting, but most of them don't, or say they are too poor to buy the netting."

"Isn't netting cheap?" I asked.

"Yes, but these mothers don't have enough food, either."

I was going to give Dr. Tran as much money as I could, and I wanted to find out more about his needs.

"Who pays your nurses?" I asked.

He looked at me, surprised once again. "I do. I don't make very much money at the air base, but the nurses still work even when I don't have any more money."

I knew the air force paid civilian workers very little, and I had seen at least four nurses that he must have been supporting.

"Don't you have any other source of funding?"

"The Buddhist temple used to give us some money, but since the fighting increased last year, we have received nothing."

I knew the Saigon government wouldn't help a small clinic serving impoverished Buddhists. When I asked about the Vietcong again, he answered in a loud voice, "No! They are worse. They threaten us and steal what little we have."

"Can't you complain about them?"

"If we complain, they will kill us," he said.

I had to do something. "Dr. Tran, like to help," I said.

"What can you do?" he said.

"Let's make up a list of supplies that you need. I can telephone a friend who is a doctor on Guam and ask him to buy your supplies. My squadron will fly them in. We have planes going back and forth between Guam and Bien Hoa all the time."

"I don't have any money to pay you."

"I'll pay for the first shipment and see what I can do to get you a sponsor," I said.

"Why do you want to help me?" he asked. "What do you want from me?"

He didn't understand that I felt ashamed to be watching sick Vietnamese children die when I had the means to try to prevent it. He hadn't imagined that an American might express goodwill toward Vietnamese people with no expectation of compensation. Except for the nuns, foreigners had always exploited him. Nevertheless, he agreed to work with me to compile a list of high-priority equipment, supplies, and drugs. Then he showed me how to catch the bus back to the air base.

The next morning, I was able to patch through a telephone call to Roger Casey at the hospital on Guam. I explained what I had found in the tiny clinic in Bien Hoa and asked if he would buy the supplies for me and take them to the VAP 61 duty officer at the naval air station. He agreed to help.

He also forwarded the call to Lynn so that we could talk for a just a minute. She said that she loved me and wanted reassurance that I wasn't flying or going off-base. I wasn't completely truthful. I said I wasn't doing anything dangerous. I said that I loved her and missed her.

After we hung up, I went to find Stan White to explain about Dr. Tran's clinic and his need for supplies. "The patients there are desperately ill," I said. "And most of them are infants and young children."

I explained that they had almost no supplies and no drugs, and I told him of my arrangement with Roger. "Would you would authorize flying them to Bien Hoa?"

"Why don't you use supplies from the dispensary?" Stan asked.

"I can't just take government property. I'm going to help him with my own money. I'd be happy if anyone else wanted to help, but it's evident that the Vietnamese government isn't interested."

"I'll send a message back to Guam to ensure that you get your supplies," he said.

"Thanks, Stan. We can only make a small gesture, but it will mean a lot to the children. Many would not survive otherwise."

Stan thought for a minute. "Be careful, Doc. You can't carry the whole war on your shoulders. You're a darn good flight surgeon. That's more than enough job for anybody."

Chapter 16

TRAUMATIC STRESS

When I returned to the dispensary for sick call, Jason Lockhart was waiting for me. I had anticipated seeing him sometime and was relieved that he had made the first step. He didn't look at me when I came in, instead staring blankly at the floor in front of him, his elbows on his knees. He seemed almost as withdrawn as during the flight from Guam back to Da Nang.

I tried to sound cheerful. "Good morning, Jason. How have you been?"

He was slow to answer and stuttered, struggling to find words. "Doc, I had a mission scheduled last night, and I had to cancel it."

I wasn't going to hurry him. I wanted him to tell his own story, so I remained silent.

He said, "I told my navigator and photo technician that I was sick, but I think it was all nerves."

Maybe we were getting somewhere. "What makes you think so?" I asked.

"The night before last, we flew a mission up north, and I couldn't make the run over the target."

He still hadn't yet looked at me, and the pauses between his phrases were long.

"Why was that?" I said finally.

"I made an excuse about one of the engines and aborted."

"There was nothing wrong with the engine?" I asked.

He shuffled in his chair, still looking at the floor. "That's right, nothing was wrong."

"How long has this problem with your nerves been going on?" I asked, trying to use his own terms.

"A long time, but it's much worse lately," he said.

"Do you have an idea why?"

He bit his lip while trying to find the words. "Flying stopped being fun for me a couple of years ago. That's when I started worrying more."

"Was there something specific that happened?"

He nodded slowly. "Before I came to VAP 61, one of my friends was killed."

I hadn't been aware of this. "What happened?"

"His plane broke apart when he came in short on a carrier landing."

I thought about my own worries and Dave Andrews's fear of carrier landings. "How terrible! Did you see the accident?"

He closed his eyes and grimaced. "Yes. Ever since then, I've been terrified about landing aboard ship."

"When did the accident happen?"

Jason looked up for just an instant and then lowered his head again. "Almost two years ago," he uttered almost in a whisper.

"And you have been thinking more about it lately?"

"Yes, all the time," he said.

I tried to encourage him to go on. "But it's worse now?"

Jason glanced at me and spoke at a more normal pace. "Yes. When John Grayson was killed, I began having worse nightmares."

"Your nightmares started before John Grayson was killed?"

"Yes. For the past two years."

"What are they like?" I asked.

He closed his eyes tightly and wrinkled his brow. "I'm always trying to catch a carrier deck, but it keeps moving away. Then I wake up screaming."

I paused for several seconds. "Jason, how many missions have you logged in Vietnam since this war began?"

"About 120."

I suppressed my gasp. I knew that the flight crews were flying nearly every day, but I hadn't before guessed at the total number of missions.

"How many have been over the North?" I asked.

"About half—mostly during the past three months."

I wanted to know what he was doing before coming to VAP 61. "You've been flying carrier planes for a while, haven't you?"

"Yes, about eight years. Half of that in A-3s," he said.

I thought for a few minutes, trying to decide on my next step. Jason shifted uncomfortably.

"Do you think you could ground me for a few days?" he asked.

"I could give you a temporary grounding chit, but I don't think it would solve your problem. I might even be able to talk Stan White into giving you a week's leave, but I think you would only become more worried."

"I can't face flying a mission tonight."

I blurted out my own inner thoughts. "Jason, I can't offer you a medical solution to overcome the stress you feel. The stress arises from the reality of the situation."

It was a mistake. He looked up with a panicked expression. "Do you think I'm a coward?"

"No. Of course not. A coward could never have completed 120 missions as you have. What you've done is extraordinary. I don't think I could have done it. You're like a professional athlete who is no longer physically or psychologically capable of competing at the highest level. Sometimes it happens at age twenty, and sometimes at age forty, but it always happens."

Jason was sitting upright now. "I know pilots who are still flying in their old age."

"As a civilian pilot, you might have been able to make some adjustment to avoid stressful flying situations, but in the navy, we don't have that luxury. It's all or nothing. The danger of carrier landings and combat missions raises the stress to an extreme level."

He was more alert now. "What are you suggesting?"

"Jason, you're at a crossroads. Other naval aviators who experience as much traumatic stress as you fail to improve over time. If they continued to fly, their symptoms worsen."

"It sounds like you're telling me to stop flying altogether."

"No, but if you can't fly in combat or land on a carrier, then you can't fly in the navy."

"What do you mean?"

"Giving up your wings."

He paused and looked away from me. "Won't that effectively end my naval career? The navy usually doesn't have jobs for ex-naval aviators with the rank of lieutenant commander."

"Sure, but plenty of civilian jobs exist. It doesn't have to involve flying."

After another pause, his eyes met mine. "Would I get a discharge as a sort of psychological basket case?"

"In my mind, you're no different than the naval aviator that I had to ground because of diabetes. Diabetes and severe traumatic stress are equally disqualifying medical problems to me. I'd say it's time for you to end your career as a naval aviator. You've made your contribution, and you've reached the limit of your capability."

"Are you going to ground me?"

"I think we should make that decision together. I can ground you temporarily, but Stan White will want to know why. I can't conceal anything from him; the stakes are too high. I suggest that we go over to see him right now."

"Can you give me a little time?"

"Sure, but if you have a mission scheduled for tonight, Stan has a right to know what's going on as soon as possible. Take a few hours to think about it and come back to see me early this afternoon."

Jason left. As I thought more about it, I decided I wouldn't let him fly under any circumstance. Too many other people were relying on his competency, especially his two crewmen, and perhaps a number of marines on the ground. If he didn't return by the end of the afternoon, I was going to find him and insist on our talking with Stan White.

Two air crewmen, both photo technicians, came in that morning with vague gastrointestinal symptoms. Neither had eaten off the air base. They had assumed that it was something in the food in the air force mess hall. We weren't seeing other patients with similar complaints at the dispensary. I gave them some Kaopectate and recommended a mostly liquid diet for a few days, but I couldn't give them anything stronger that might interfere with alertness during flights. I suspected that the symptoms of combat stress were spreading.

I went looking for Dr. Tran to tell him that I had made arrangements for his supplies and that they would probably arrive in a couple of days. He became emotional and almost collapsed to the ground.

"It's a miracle! It's a miracle! We have so many sick children and can do so little. You are doing so much."

I felt uneasy that the small amount of money that I was spending on a few medical supplies would mean so much to him and his patients. I didn't want Dr. Tran to feel indebted to me. He had dedicated his whole life to that clinic, trying to make something out of nothing. I was just a foreigner passing through with resources at my disposal.

"The work you are doing is very important," I said. "I am glad to be a small part of it."

He wasn't listening. His mind was on his clinic. My exam rooms received a special scrubbing that day.

Jason returned early in the afternoon and said that he was ready to talk to Commander White. He wanted me to go with him.

He spoke with more assurance. "After talking with you this morning, I felt relieved just getting it off my chest."

"I'm glad," I said.

"I can't do it anymore. I'd be putting others at risk. You're right. I have to resign."

I called Stan and told him that Jason and I had something important that we needed to discuss with him. Stan said to come over.

When we arrived, Stan leaned back in his chair. "What's up?"

"I've not been able to carry out my missions adequately the past few weeks," Jason said, "and I went to see the doc this morning,"

Stan leaned forward and placed his elbows on his desk. "I've known something was wrong. You haven't identified a target once in the past two weeks. You cancelled at the last minute last night and aborted the night before. What's the problem?"

"Doc called it psychological trauma, or something like that," Jason said.

Stan looked at me. "What's that?"

"The army used the term 'shell shock' in World War I and 'combat fatigue' in World War II. Whatever term we use, it means an overexposure to combat stress. Mostly we call it post-traumatic stress disorder. Anyone exposed to repeated, severe psychological trauma over extended periods of time will crack eventually, some a little sooner, others a little later. Everyone has a limit."

"So what do we do about it?" Stan said.

"If we force soldiers or airmen with severe anxiety back into the same stressful environment, they very often become a danger to themselves and to others. They also have a high suicide rate; their anxiety is not solely a fear of dying."

Stan looked directly at me. "That sounds bad. Are you going to ground Jason?"

"That's what I propose to do," I said.

"Isn't there any treatment?"

"So far, the only effective solution to severe traumatic stress has been to remove the patient from the source of the stress. Psychotherapy alone won't fix the problem, nor is there any effective medication."

"You're saying that it's an untreatable disease?" Stan asked.

"No," I said. "But it does require radical treatment. He needs a career change. VAP 61 flies high-stress missions, and Jason won't be the last member of the squadron to suffer from severe traumatic stress."

"I'll want to talk with you about the others afterward," Stan said. "But specifically, what do you recommend concerning Lieutenant Commander Lockhart?"

"I'd like to ground him and send him home with a recommendation for a medical discharge. He has already shown you his deteriorating capability to carry out a mission. I don't think it's going to improve. In fact, I can practically promise you he will get worse if he stays. He's a dedicated officer and has had a distinguished career, but it's over."

"You seem pretty certain," Stan said.

"You talked about Jason's performance yourself when we first walked in. He knows, and he doesn't want his medical problem harming someone else. He doesn't want to end his naval career, but permanent grounding is better for him, and hard as it may seem right now, better for VAP 61. This isn't any different than if he had failed his eye exam. He isn't fit for combat, period."

"You see this as a purely medical problem?"

"That's exactly how I see it," I said. "I'll write it all up."

Stan sighed and looked at Jason, who was sitting with his head bowed again. "You've been a friend and a darned good naval aviator. I don't like this, but Doc says we don't have any choice. We'll get you on a flight back to Guam and then to the States."

Jason looked up. "Thanks, Stan."

Stan turned back to me. "What will we tell the rest of the squadron?"

"You should say that I found a medical problem and grounded Jason and that we're sending him back to Guam and probably to the States."

Stan looked at Jason again. "Are you all right with this?"

"Stan, I can't force myself back into a cockpit again. I love the navy. It has been my career and my life. I don't know what I'll do now, but I know that I can't do my job here."

"I'm sorry, Jason," Stan said. "I wish there were another way. Cancel your mission. We'll book you on a flight back to Guam. Doc, may I speak with you for a few minutes?"

Lieutenant Commander Jason Lockhart gave Stan a professional salute, turned, and left. I felt drained by the conversation.

"Doc, you don't know how that hurt me," Stan said. "Jason is a career officer, a good man, and at one time, a fine naval aviator."

"That wasn't a whole lot of fun for me, either," I said. "Jason is *still* a fine man. He just can't be a naval aviator."

Stan looked down. "I know. You handled it in the best possible way. To tell you the truth, I've known this for a long time. What did you mean when you said that Jason wouldn't be the last case?"

"VAP 61 combat missions are like Russian roulette," I said. "There are only three possible outcomes: crack and quit, die, or keep playing the game. Jason told me that he had logged 120 combat missions, including half over the North. I'll bet that's only about average for your crews."

"Are you seeing more of this combat stress?" Stan asked.

"Just today I had a couple of air crewmen come in to sick call with some minor GI complaints that I thought were stress-related. I know that every man in this squadron has a breaking point, and each is moving closer to it every day."

"What would you have us do?"

I suspected that Stan was considering his own vulnerability to the stress that we were all facing. I know I thought about my own susceptibility more often.

I answered, "What we all do, I guess. Perform the best we can as professionals and try to help each other in a war over which we have no control. That's what you are doing. We're all just living day-to-day."

"But you think this psychological trauma will spread?"

"Sure, if this war goes on and we continue losing flight crews."

Stan thought for a minute. "That seems likely."

"It doesn't help that some Americans at home can't even locate Vietnam on a map and have no idea why we're here. Even worse, we see that the Vietnamese people don't support our efforts."

"Is that why you want to help the Vietnamese doctor and his clinic?"

Stan was playing the part of flight surgeon now. He was right.

"I suppose that's part of it, but mostly it gives me a sense of purpose. He and the sick children in his clinic are tangible to me. With just a little effort, I can improve their lives in a real way."

Two days later, a flight crew arrived from Guam carrying the supplies for the clinic. Stan had talked about it during one of his briefing sessions, and everyone wanted to chip in to help pay for them. I told them I would use the money to arrange regular shipments from Guam. Stan wanted me to use the squadron's loaner jeep to carry Dr. Tran and the supplies to his clinic to let the people in Bien Hoa know that we all wanted to help. It was a big day for Dr. Tran, his clinic, and his neighborhood in Bien Hoa.

Chapter 17

BONSOIR, DOCTEUR

Over the next few days, I made several more trips to Dr. Tran's clinic to help him with some minor surgery, but also to learn more about tropical diseases in their more virulent form, such as cerebral malaria. Children and malnourished adults suffered more from those maladies than healthy marines, and the complications were more devastating. I wanted to see if the supplies were improving treatment outcomes.

"More of our patients are surviving now," Dr. Tran said. "Even the cholera victims get better now that we have adequate quantities of needles and IV tubing. The people in the neighborhood can see the results, and more of them are coming in."

A line of people stood in the street, waiting to be seen. Each nurse was with a patient.

"The nurses look busy," I said.

"They are tired because of the increased work, but they are happy for our patients."

"May I talk to them?"

"They like it when you answer their questions," Dr. Tran said. "They work hard, but they need help."

I asked one of the French-speaking nurses about her work.

She stood up and bowed deeply to me. "Thank you a thousand times, Doctor, for giving us the supplies. We can do so much more now. It's a miracle."

"Dr. Tran says you are tired from too much work," I said.

"We don't care about the extra work. Before, the people expected that their children would die. Now they see that most recover."

Another nurse was watching and broke in. "We used the soap and disinfectants you gave us to scrub the whole clinic. I think that's the reason why our patients are getting better. It used to smell very bad—worse than a sewer. That bad smell made our patients sick."

"I think you are right," I said. "Patients do improve faster in a clean clinic."

I noticed the small, undernourished child that she was examining. He was cranky with a pathetic cry. The whites of his eyes were yellow, and he appeared dehydrated.

"Tell me about the child you are examining," I said.

"He is three years old and has been vomiting for several days. His mother says his urine is dark, almost brown. His sister has the same symptoms."

"What is your diagnosis?" I said.

"I think he has hepatitis. I am going to give him IV fluids until he stops vomiting and can drink normally."

"Have you talked to the family about hygiene?" I asked.

"Yes, and I gave them some soap and told them about washing their hands. They were drinking water from the river. We have had many cases of hepatitis from people who drink water from that river."

I turned to Dr. Tran. "I can see that the nurses are spending more time teaching the patients about prevention."

"It's easier now to convince the people about hygiene," he said, "because they have more confidence in us. See how much difference your supplies made?"

"The supplies would do no good without you and your nurses. You give the people hope."

He put his hands together and bowed.

This humble Vietnamese doctor was saving the lives of many children using my modest contribution of a few basic medical supplies that had cost a small fraction of my salary. I was glad to be a part of it, yet I knew that millions more Vietnamese were suffering.

I wanted to spend more time at the clinic, but I could not abrogate my responsibilities to the squadron. Nevertheless, I stayed until after dark one Sunday evening because of the huge number of patients. Since I didn't want to impose on anyone at the air base for a ride to support my hobby, I rode the local bus, which ran late into the night. I badly underestimated the risk of being out in Bien Hoa at night.

As I was waiting at the bus stop, several men grabbed me from behind and dragged me into a dark building nearby. I yelled and struggled, but there were too many of them. They pushed me down on the floor and held me while one of them poked a gun barrel in my face and screamed at me in Vietnamese. I stopped resisting and froze, terrified that I would soon be dead.

The tiny room, the darkness, the men punching me and shouting, the suffocating heat, and the bad odors all closed in on me. They stripped off my clothes, bound my hands and feet, blindfolded me, and placed a gag in my mouth. They yelled threats that needed no translation. I was certain they were going to kill me, and I feared they would torture me first. I heard Lynn's voice again. "You won't do anything dangerous, will you?"

They stopped shouting at me and began yelling excitedly at each other. A voice from outside the back door seemed to be giving orders. Three or four of them carried me to a rickety cart, covered me with a filthy blanket that had the smell of rat urine, and pulled me along a road for what seemed to be an hour or two. I imagined myself covered with fleas or lice from the blanket. I couldn't move, and the jolting from the rough road felt like punches to the ribs and kidneys. When we hit a pothole, the cart struck me in the temple and caused my scalp and ear to bleed.

Soon the men stopped talking, but I could tell they were still there by the footsteps alongside the cart. There were many of them, and their steps blended into a kind of shuffling and swishing sound. My wrists and ankles ached awfully from the tight ropes. I thought of a horrible engraving I saw as a teenager, depicting prisoners being carted to the guillotine during the French Revolution. Would they start shouting and poking me again soon?

After an interminable time, the men began speaking again. Soon the cart stopped. A group of them carried me into a building, sat me in a chair, and removed my blindfold, gag, and bindings. They turned on some bright lights that blinded me for a few seconds. About a dozen young men dressed in black crowded around me, speaking excitedly in Vietnamese. One of them handed me a black shirt and pants, along with some straw slippers, and waved for me to get dressed.

I rubbed my wrists and ankles as the circulation began to improve in my hands and feet, but my whole body ached from the jolting ride in the bottom of the cart, and my mouth was dry from fear and thirst. The room was revolving, and I almost fell down, but with some effort, I managed to put on the clothes as the men watched. Then I sat down again.

This room was much larger than any I had seen in the village of Bien Hoa. I seemed to be in a large house built of concrete, more like a mansion. The windows were large but had no glass or screens. I could see no furniture, only my chair. None of the bad smell of Bien Hoa was evident; the air was fresh, as in the brush during my three days with the marines.

A wiry man who seemed to be in charge stood in front of me looking down.

"Bonsoir, Docteur. Ne vous inquiétez pas. On ne vous fera pas mal, mais on a besoin de vous comme chirurgien."

(Good evening, Doctor. Don't worry. We're not going to hurt you, but we have need of you as a surgeon.)

At least they weren't going to kill me right away, because they wanted me to perform surgery. I had misgivings about their expectations of my skill level and about the appalling sanitary conditions.

"May I have some water?" I asked in French.

"Of course, Doctor."

Someone went into the next room and came back with a cup of relatively clean-looking water. I was too thirsty to care where it came from.

"Surgery requires equipment, supplies, and a clean operating room," I said.

"We have taken care of all that. Please follow me, Doctor. I want to show you our clinic."

I stumbled behind him into an adjacent room where two wounded men dressed in black were lying on cots. One had a bullet wound to the abdomen, and the other had two bullet wounds, one to the right thigh and the other to the left shoulder. Both men must have been suffering considerable pain, but they were stoic and silent. At least the wounds looked recent, so the risk of infection was not as high as it might have been.

"These men have serious wounds and need an operating room in a hospital," I said. "I have no way to operate on them here. I would need surgical instruments, antiseptics, anesthetics, antibiotics, and an anesthesiologist."

"We have everything," he said. "You will do the surgery here. I will show you."

I followed him into another room that was fairly clean with a long wooden bench that could serve as an operating table in a pinch and several lamps that together might provide enough light. Then he showed me an adjacent room, more like a large closet, with stacks of corrugated boxes stamped "U.S. Army" containing medical supplies.

I knew that Vietnamese civilians delivered supplies to the dispensary at the air base, so I assumed they did the same for army hospitals. The Vietcong probably had little difficultly bribing or coercing civilian workers to cooperate with a clandestine diversion of supplies.

"We have everything you need. You will operate. If you refuse, we will have no further use for you."

My captor was clear about my options. I had no doubt that the Vietcong would kill me immediately if I refused to cooperate. I had survived so far, but they wanted me as a slave, a disposable surgeon. I was to receive a stay of execution for only as long as they needed me.

I began to examine the supplies. One of the boxes was packed with scalpels, clamps, retractors, suture material, and even surgical drains. Other boxes contained bags of IV fluids with needles and tubing, antiseptics, and large quantities of dressings. Much to my surprise, I also discovered a large assortment of drugs and several cans of ethyl ether. I had never seen anyone using open-drop ether as a general anesthetic, but the concept was simple enough. Nurses assisting surgeons had used it successfully for almost a hundred years until very recently. The problem would be administering it: I couldn't give the ether and do the surgery at the same time.

I looked at my captor. "I'll need someone to assist me and to give the anesthesia, preferably a nurse."

He pointed to one of the young figures in black. To my surprise, a woman was among my kidnappers.

"Je suis infirmière."

She was a nurse, and she spoke French.

"Have you ever administered anesthesia with ether?" I asked.

"No."

"I'll explain it. When we have the patient prepped, hold a wad of gauze pads like this over the patient's nose and mouth and begin slowly dripping ether onto the gauze so that he breathes it. But don't breathe it yourself. Do you understand?"

"Yes, I can do that."

I wasn't so sure that she understood. Given the circumstances, she probably wasn't in any position to decline to help me.

"You'll need to keep an eye on his respirations to be sure that you're not giving too much. If he seems well anesthetized, stop the drip and check his blood pressure and pulse. If he starts to become agitated, begin the drip again. Do you understand?"

"Yes."

"We'll boil the surgical instruments and wash the patients with soap and water. We'll operate on the one with the abdominal wound first. I'll start an IV and pass a nasogastric tube; then I'll prep the abdomen with an antiseptic while you start the ether drip."

I had assisted in the operating room at Da Nang on patients with abdominal gunshot wounds, and I knew that the damage could be extensive and unpredictable. The fact that this patient had survived so far told me that the bullet had not hit a major artery, but plenty of other organs could have received considerable trauma. I had never operated alone on a patient with an abdominal bullet wound, and my lack of experience might cause this patient his life—mine too, probably. Of course, if I refused to operate, we were both dead, anyway.

My abductors didn't have sterile operating room gowns. I had to make do with mask, cap, and latex gloves. At least I was wearing what might pass for a clean scrub suit. I needed more light. I turned to the leader. "Could you hold this lamp closer to the operating field so that we get better illumination?"

He took the lamp.

The nurse started the ether drip while I arranged the surgical instruments. When the patient was asleep, I made a large midline incision just as the surgeons at Da Nang had shown me. Next, I did a careful examination to assess the damage. The bullet had nicked the right side of the colon and had smashed the right kidney. I had learned to repair the bowel at Da Nang, but I had never removed a kidney.

The nurse had stopped the ether drip to watch the operation, and the patient was beginning to rouse.

"Please administer a little more ether, mademoiselle."

I repaired the colon and then began freeing the fractured kidney. The first step was tying off the ureter and renal artery and vein. The kidney was not difficult to remove, although I'm sure that my technique did not follow any textbook guidelines. I made another check around the abdominal cavity and rinsed with saline.

In my most confident voice, I said, "Everything looks stable. I think he will do very well."

I began repairing the peritoneum and closing in layers while explaining the post-operative care to the nurse.

"We'll need to apply suction to the nasogastric tube for several days, but since we don't have a machine to do it, you'll have to use a large syringe every hour or so."

"How long should we continue the IV fluids?" she asked.

"Until we can hear bowel sounds, which will be in approximately five days, maybe more."

I helped her set up the IV fluids and explained the rate of infusion and the quantities to give for each twenty-four-hour period. We started IV antibiotics, because his bowel was perforated and the wound was contaminated. Then I explained how to give morphine for pain every three or four hours, something that she apparently already knew.

"For how long should we keep him in bed?"

"We'll try to get him to stand tomorrow," I said, "but he will be very weak. He should begin walking with help the day after."

The second surgery, on the man with gunshot wounds in the leg and shoulder, went easier, although I was certain that the patient would lose some mobility in his shoulder. Shoulder reconstruction was well beyond my capabilities.

One thing missing in the supply boxes was antitoxin for prevention of tetanus. All of my efforts would go for naught if the patients developed tetanus post-operatively, as I knew that very few Vietnamese had received routine childhood vaccinations. At Da Nang, the hospital usually had several Vietnamese patients with tetanus on a ventilator for weeks at a time. Since we had no ventilator, the disease would result in a horrible death. I prayed that the patients wouldn't develop tetanus, because my captors might not understand the cause and blame me.

Daylight was appearing as I checked the vital signs and IVs on the patients. The windows had no coverings, so I could see outside that we were in a hamlet, probably not far from Bien Hoa. They could not have taken me far in the cart. In every room, one or two expressionless young men in black sat in chairs, holding automatic weapons. My chief captor was still there watching everything.

"That was very good, Doctor. You must be tired and hungry. We have some rice and tea for you."

My adrenaline level was still high, and my fear had abated only slightly. Even if the patients recovered uneventfully, my captors had no reason to release me. My situation had not improved much since my capture.

Chapter 18

ANOTHER KIND
OF MASH HOSPITAL

Something hard was poking me in the ribs. I couldn't tell what it was, but the annoying painful jabs caused me to wake. My body still ached, and now I had a headache.

"*Venez.*"

The voice was speaking to me in French and wanted me to follow it somewhere. I opened my eyes and saw a guard standing over me holding an automatic weapon, and then I remembered. After I had finished operating on the two Vietcong soldiers, a guard had led me to a cot on the upper floor where I was allowed to rest. Guards with automatic weapons watched me constantly, even when I was asleep.

I followed the guard down the stairs into the room where the patients were recovering and saw four more cots, each occupied by a patient wearing the same kind of black clothing. At the very least, caring for these four would buy me one more day.

The patients exhibited wounds similar to those that I had seen in the marines at Da Nang: mostly bullet wounds and injuries from mortar fragments. One of the patients was missing his right foot and would soon need an amputation revision. I cringed thinking about the future of a war amputee in an impoverished country like Vietnam. The patients made me imagine how wounded soldiers must have felt during the American Civil War, when long lines of casualties awaited their turns on the operating table. At least I had anesthesia, but these Vietnamese casualties would be terrified just the same. In my case, the surgeon would be terrified, too.

My Vietcong nurse was already there washing the new patients. She had checked the vital signs on the two post-operative patients, administered more morphine, and hung the next set of IV bottles. She said the patient who had undergone abdominal surgery during the night had developed a slight temperature elevation, but I knew that a low-grade fever wasn't unusual after extensive abdominal surgery. I sat him up and encouraged him to cough to try to prevent post-operative pneumonia, and to dangle his legs to avoid clot formation.

I no longer had my watch, but from the unbearable heat, it must have been afternoon already. Operating under these conditions would cause discomfort all around, but we had to get started. The nurse performed her job a little more efficiently this time, and maybe I did, too, but we didn't finish the four cases until well after dark. We now had six post-operative patients with IV fluids running. They were my insurance.

I asked the nurse if we should train someone to be her assistant.

"Non! C'est mon travail; c'est à moi."

(No! It's my job; mine.)

She was fiercely opposed to anyone else helping, and I was learning that the Vietnamese were proud, especially of learning any skill that would elevate them in the eyes of others. Apparently, she had gained prestige by participating in the care of the wounded insurgents. I would have to try to guide her as gently and tactfully as I could.

The guards gave me more tea and rice, my compensation for operating. As I was eating, they brought in another black-clad patient. This one was sick, not wounded. I insisted that they move him immediately out of the room with the post-operative patients. The nurse saw what was happening and became animated, shouting, scolding, and pushing guards and sick patient back into the front room by the entrance. She had them set up a cot there and started speaking in Vietnamese to the new patient, checking his temperature, pulse, and blood pressure.

She translated into French for me. "He has a terrible headache, muscle aches, cough, and high fever. He has a rash, too."

165

"Ask him if anyone else around him has been sick with the same symptoms."

"His wife and baby are sick," she said, "and they have the same symptoms, but only soldiers are allowed to come here."

I had seen similar cases at Dr. Tran's clinic. They usually had typhus. Three different types of typhus were on the rise in Vietnam, because fleas, lice, and mites flourished wherever people could not maintain good hygiene. It was called "trench fever" during World War I, and the mortality rate among soldiers was high.

"Have the guards shave off all of his hair and wash him and all of his clothes thoroughly to be sure he doesn't carry any vermin. I'll start an IV, and we'll give him some tetracycline."

She began scolding the guards, who were resisting. The conflict escalated into shouting, and the man who had been my chief captor reappeared. The nurse continued to aim her finger at one of the guards, reprimanding him in rapid Vietnamese.

"Is this disease contagious?" my chief captor asked me in French.

"Yes," I said. "It usually doesn't spread directly from human to human; but rather, the vermin in hair, clothing, or the fur of rats and other animals can disseminate the disease rapidly in circumstances of poor hygiene."

"Is it serious?" he asked.

"Typhus has caused an epidemic in almost every war in history," I said. "It's not a disease to take lightly."

The nurse resumed her tirade.

He looked at me. "What do you suggest?"

"Everyone must bathe every day and shave all hair, even you and me, and that includes washing all clothing and sheets every day, too. We must separate the sick patients from the post-operative patients to prevent any transfer of vermin, and we must clean the building thoroughly."

My captor didn't flinch when I used the word "must," and he tolerated the nurse's continuing harangue. He snapped some words to the guards and left, while the nurse began to issue orders directing clean-up tasks. Somehow, I found it funny that my captor's fear of a contagious disease had reversed our roles briefly. I was telling him what he must do for a change. It was the only time during my captivity that I was even tempted to smile.

My amusement didn't last long. Early the next morning, more patients dressed in black arrived. Some of them had wounds from firefights, while others were sick, mostly with typhus. The nurse and I operated for hours at a time on the trauma victims and started treatment on the influx of typhus patients. Both floors of the building were now overflowing, and I was hardly ever allowed to sleep. The nurse must have been exhausted, too, although she never seemed to stop. I had lost my appetite, but then they weren't offering me much food, either: only rice and tea twice a day.

Our first surgical patient, the one with the abdominal bullet wound, continued to run a low-grade fever into the third day, and I began to worry. He was up walking with assistance, and his surgical drains and dressings showed no sign of infection. I would just have to be patient and hope that he recovered. If he developed peritonitis, I would have no effective treatment to offer, and he would die. Death from peritonitis would be ugly and disturbing to my captors—to me, too.

By the fourth day of my captivity, so many patients with typhus had arrived that we had to move them to an adjacent house and barn where the nurse took care of them by herself. The guards would not let me leave, even to go next door, but the nurse had watched me start IVs and was learning to do it herself.

I worried about the patient with the lower leg amputation, but he showed no sign of infection. Some of the guards tried to fashion a pair of crude crutches, but rehabilitation of an amputee in the middle of a guerrilla war was too much. The patient said very little to the guards and other patients and spent all day lying on his cot. The nurse urged the guards to help him walk, but he vigorously resisted their efforts to get him standing or even to sit in a chair.

By the fifth post-operative day, the low-grade fever in the patient with the abdominal bullet wound had disappeared. His chances for recovery had improved considerably, and he would probably soon begin taking fluids by mouth, and later, eating some rice.

I recommended to the nurse that we keep all of our surgical patients as long as possible, or at least until I could remove their sutures. In this extremely hot and dusty environment, the risk of infection was high without proper cleaning of incisions and replacement of the dressings. The patients had developed some relatively minor wound infections, but surprisingly, no serious ones yet, in part due to the compulsive wound care by the nurse.

At the same time, I knew that we would soon run through our medical supplies. I assumed that the nurse would keep my chief captor informed about our needs, but I wasn't sure what would happen when critically important supplies were gone. Perhaps the Vietcong had access to stolen supplies, but I had no way of knowing. I had learned from Dr. Tran how to stretch the use of bandages, disposable IV tubing, and needles by washing them with soap and then boiling them, so I broached the subject with the nurse.

"I have been saving and washing everything and have already begun to reuse them," she said.

"Do you boil everything, including the dressings?"

"No, the dressings, the tubing, and the needles won't last long if we boil everything. We will have to make do with just washing."

She didn't ask for my opinion but instead rendered her decision. I was just a slave. From then on, she would make the decisions. Washing alone would probably reduce, but not eliminate, transmission of infection. To her, that was good enough. We had limited resources, so her goal was to treat as many patients as possible, even if the lack of sterility harmed a few. She added that it was she who would decide when the patients could be discharged.

I could tolerate the long hours of work; in fact, the work helped me maintain my sanity. Over time, a crushing fatigue consumed me. I was suffering from chronic sleep deprivation, heat intolerance, and depression. I had been working at least twenty hours a day, operating, examining new patients, and starting most of the IVs. When I could grab a few hours of sleep, a guard would always climb the stairs behind me, and then sit in a chair with his automatic weapon and watch while I slept. I could escape into my own mind by thinking about Lynn. That helped me to keep going. Every hour and every minute had become a burden, but I would not give up. I was determined to stay alive.

In spite of the repressive circumstances, my efficiency in performing surgery was improving just because of the experience gained from such a large number of cases. The distraction of the exhausting work prevented my crumbling from despair. I remained alert during the operative procedures themselves but would suffer melancholia following each day's surgery and enter into a dreamlike, confused state. In my haze, I would see Lynn's face and try to reach out.

A few more wound infections developed, possibly from fatigue-induced negligence, but I also knew that we should expect them. Combat injuries were dirty, the bandages were recycled, and the heat interfered with healing. Nevertheless, I hated to have any surgical complication. I still had pride in my work. It was one thing my captors couldn't take away.

Many of our typhus patients were recovering, as well, although the nurse said that three of them suffered a progressive worsening of their cough and intensification of their headache. She was worried enough that she convinced my chief captor that I should examine the more severely ill patients. Three guards accompanied me during my short walk to the adjacent buildings.

From listening to the patients' chests, I found that all three had pneumonia. The sickest patient also appeared to have encephalitis and had become nearly comatose, a known complication of scrub typhus. All of the patients had received tetracycline, so the appearance of a more virulent form of the disease signaled the development of antibiotic resistance. I tried to explain all of this to the nurse.

"This is no good. No good!" she said.

"Typhus is a bad disease," I said. "Treatment doesn't always work, and sometimes patients die."

"You must do more."

I was surprised at the nurse's reaction to the inevitable deaths resulting from a terrible disease like typhus. Perhaps she felt responsible, because she alone had managed the typhus patients in the other buildings. Maybe she had expected that Western doctors and medicine could cure anything and didn't realize that our antibiotics for treating infectious diseases often didn't work.

She demanded that we do something, so I said, "Double the dose of tetracycline for all three patients."

The increased dose would probably do nothing, and at least one of the patients was likely to die very soon. I feared that she and my chief captor would turn their wrath on me when their unreasonable expectations were not met.

I had been a prisoner for ten days, and I was losing all hope of being rescued. The idea of attempting to escape had always been present, but I hadn't been able to formulate a plan. Even if I managed to slip away from the guards, the Vietcong would quickly spot a tall American with shaved head and eyebrows in black pajamas.

That night, as I was lying sleepless on my cot on the upper floor, automatic weapons fire startled me. Shouting and running outside of the building followed, and I rolled off my cot onto the floor next to the wall. My guard ran down the stairs, and after a brief silence, more firing erupted from different directions, continuing for several long minutes.

Then everything fell silent. I could hear my heartbeat pounding in my ears but no other sound. Nothing seemed to move. I had an urge to scream, but no sound came out. I couldn't breathe. Many minutes passed.

The firing began again—loudly—inside the building this time, right below me. Then silence. I froze and tried to hold my breath.

Are they coming to kill me?

The silence continued.

They must still be there. Could they have left?

No. They're climbing the stairs, slowly.

A light began dancing around as if someone were searching with a flashlight. Footsteps came into the room. The beam caught me squarely in the face, and a man spoke to me.

"*Ça va, Docteur? Nous sommes du gouvernement.*"

They were soldiers from the South Vietnamese Army who had come to rescue me. They quickly led me down the stairs, and we left into the cooler night air. I was so relieved that I broke down and bawled. I stumbled several times, and they grabbed me, helping me up. We walked past what seemed in the dark to be fields or rice paddies to a truck parked a half mile away. As I was climbing in, I heard more shooting again in the direction of the building and looked back. A South Vietnamese officer noticed.

"Don't worry. They probably found some more Vietcong hiding."

I feared they were shooting the nurse and my patients.

While the truck moved off, I tried to regain my composure. I looked at the South Vietnamese officer sitting next to me. I had heard him speak French, and I tried to thank him, but he just smiled, apparently embarrassed at my emotional outburst walking to the truck. We drove for about twenty or thirty minutes, and then I saw the gate of the base. I started to cry again.

The truck drove directly to the VAP 61 area at the Bien Hoa air base. Stan White and Dave Andrews had just returned from a mission and were waiting for me. I tried to control my tears, but they kept coming. Stan and Dave didn't smile, and at first they didn't speak; they just stared at me. Stan shook himself.

"Doc, what have they done to you?"

Then I remembered that my head and eyebrows were shaved to prevent infestation with fleas and lice, and that I was wearing the black pajamas of the Vietcong.

"You've lost a little weight," Stan said.

I needed to regain control of myself. "I'm all right, I was just scared. I thought the Vietcong were going to kill me. They would never have released me."

"Where did they keep you?" Stan asked.

I described the building, the guards, the primitive operating conditions, the constant flood of patients, and the meager rations.

"How did the South Vietnamese soldiers find me?" I asked.

Stan said, "One of your young patients in Bien Hoa saw you being kidnapped and told Dr. Tran. He came to the base that same night and found me, and I contacted the U.S. Army command center. The big break happened when some friends of Dr. Tran heard about wounded Vietcong insurgents being carried to the house where they were keeping you. It was pretty obvious what was happening. He came and told me."

"How did the South Vietnamese Army become involved?" I asked.

"The army gave the responsibility for the raid to the South Vietnamese, because they could blend in more easily than we could. We were worried the Vietcong might kill you if we attempted the raid ourselves. The South Vietnamese planned the whole thing."

"Maybe I could thank them properly sometime," I said.

"Your Dr. Tran saved your life," Stan said.

"I'll wait to thank him when he comes in. I don't want to go anywhere near the town."

"Wise decision. You stay right here."

I managed a small smile. "Aye aye, sir."

I didn't mention anything about the firing that I heard after the rescue when we had reached the truck. I wouldn't be able to prove an atrocity had occurred even if I insisted on an investigation. I knew that this was a vicious war all around.

Stan said, "I'm sure that someone on Guam would like to talk with you. I didn't realize that you had a special friend at the hospital. It's nearly 6:00 AM Guam time, so why don't we see if we can get her on the phone?"

Stan put the call through from his office and handed me the phone a few minutes later. Lynn was already sobbing when I got on the line.

I was determined not to cry again, but to no avail. "I'm all right," I sobbed.

Lynn cried some more. "Roger found out what happened and told me."

"Everything is okay."

"It sounded horrible," she said.

"It's all over now."

"Don't do those dangerous things!"

She resumed crying.

"Just so long as you're safe," she said.

I told Stan that I wanted to go back to work immediately. I wanted my life back as quickly as possible. He didn't think it was a good idea, but he allowed me to have my way. I took a quick shower, went to bed, and got up in the early afternoon. I put on a clean uniform, had lunch, and went off to see patients at the dispensary. I was in a defiant mood. The Vietcong controlled me no more.

I saw Dr. Tran and thanked him for saving my life. He was embarrassed and tried to downplay his role.

"I am very glad that you are safe," he said.

I told him that I would continue to send him supplies, but that I couldn't leave the base from then on.

Three days later, I learned that a bomb exploded in Dr. Tran's clinic, killing him, his nurses, and many of their patients.

V

THE SOUTH CHINA SEA
AND BEYOND

Chapter 19

TWENTY SECONDS
OVER HANOI

I didn't cry when I found out about the bombing. First I was angry, then I was sad, then I became morose, and then I was angry again. Everyone could see that my mind was somewhere else. Dave Andrews came to see me at the dispensary. He found me just staring out of a window.

"Doc, we're worried about you," he said.

"I'm all right."

"No, you're not," he said. "You've changed a lot since the kidnapping and bombing."

"The kidnapping isn't what's bothering me. It was a rough ten days, but it's over. Bombing a children's clinic, that's something I can't understand."

I hadn't slept much since the bombing and imagined that I was responsible. I thought if I had never been rescued, the Vietcong wouldn't have cared about the clinic. They probably found out that Dr. Tran had told American authorities where they had taken me. I was sure the bombing was revenge. I had been naïve in thinking I could reach out to the Vietnamese people, and a lot of them had paid with their lives.

"You didn't bomb that clinic," Dave said.

I stood up and started to pace. "I as good as did it."

"No, you didn't."

I said, "I can't understand hatred so profound that could bring the Vietcong to commit a mass murder of sick children. The children didn't do anything."

"It was a terrible thing."

"How could they do that?" I yelled.

"Everyone in the squadron admires what you tried to do with that clinic," Dave said. "We're all sick about the bombing."

I stopped and looked at Dave. "Our airplanes can fly two hundred miles away and take pictures at night that identify the name written on the stern of a ship, but we can't do anything about children dying from starvation and disease right outside our gate."

"I get the point."

I paused and lowered my voice. "I'm sorry. I didn't mean to flare up. I'm still exhausted. I have difficulty sleeping and terrible nightmares about children hemorrhaging, and I can't stop the bleeding. It just flows and flows. I could shake off the kidnapping, but the bombing just kills me. It might take me a while to calm down."

"That's okay."

"And it's not just the children. I still see the faces of that photo technician with his leg torn open, and a sweating marine struggling to breathe."

Dave just stared at me. I said, "Did you ever see a direct mortar hit on a helicopter ambulance?"

"You saw that?"

I stopped pacing and sat down again.

Dave said, "Doc, I didn't know all that you'd been through."

"I haven't cried since I was eight years old, but now I cry for no reason."

Dave didn't say anything. He just looked at me.

"I tried to read an article in *Stars and Stripes*," I said. "I read the same sentence over and over, but still I didn't understand it. Sometimes the words just blur."

"Give it time. It will come."

"Food tastes awful."

Dave told me a terrible joke about food. "The trouble with eating in the air force mess hall is that four or five days later, you're hungry again."

I didn't understand the joke. "Yesterday, I couldn't find my socks, and I just sat alone for half an hour trying to think of what to do. I looked everywhere. It turns out, they were on my feet."

We were silent for a few minutes, and then I said, "Maybe I should start attending the skipper's meetings again and try to put all this behind me."

"Can you do that?"

"I can attend the meetings."

"No, I mean can you put all those terrible things behind you?"

"I don't know. Probably not." I hesitated. "I can try."

"What are you going to do?"

I realized that building a shell around myself wasn't fair to other members of the squadron. It wasn't helping me, either. I had to stop thinking about myself.

"I'll try listening to other people's problems. Maybe it will distract me."

After Dave left, one of the crew chiefs, Barney Daniels, came into to see me about a boil. Many of the maintenance personnel got them working in the intense tropical heat. I had to lance this one, so I tried to engage Barney in a conversation while I was setting up.

"What's the biggest maintenance problem you face?" I asked.

He didn't think long for an answer. "Spare parts."

"What's the hang-up?"

"We keep all the replacement parts on Guam and all the planes here," he said.

That sounded to me like the punch line of a Dave Andrews joke.

"Just a little Novocain," I said. "What happens if you can't get the part in time?"

"We scavenge," he said.

"How does that work?"

"We cannibalize one aircraft to keep the others flying."

I incised the boil, packed it, and started applying a dressing.

"That feels much better already, Doc."

"Cannibalizing means you have to do double the work, doesn't it?" I asked.

"Yes, it's a lot of work."

"And the squadron is now flying longer missions, and more of them."

"I never get more than four hours sleep at a time."

Now, the joke wasn't at all funny. The ground crews took great pride in having an aircraft ready when the flight crew called for it, and doing so under such adverse conditions amplified that pride. Yet I worried that fatigue could lead to maintenance errors. Although aircraft mechanics were not flying in combat, they were under plenty of stress all the same. I had something new to think about now.

Before he left, CPO Daniels stopped for a minute. "Doc, we know what you tried to do at that clinic, and we felt terrible about the kidnapping. We're awful glad to see you back."

I had a lump in my throat. The squadron was a close-knit family all right.

I saw Stan at the air force officers' club in the evening, and he asked me to make the rounds of the other detachments to mix with the flight crews and look for any unmet health needs. I think he meant that I should observe the men to see whether any more were close to cracking. I think he also wanted to improve my psyche by getting me out of Bien Hoa for a while. He was right about that. When I was around the exam rooms in the air force dispensary, I thought too much about Dr. Tran.

Stan was due to take his turn on the *Enterprise* in the Gulf of Tonkin and was replacing his photo technician, which meant an empty seat. He proposed that I fly to the ship with Dave and him. The replacement photo technician would fly to the ship on the COD from Cubi Point.

Each flight crew rotated for about a week aboard the *Enterprise,* where we usually parked two or three aircraft. They hunted only targets in North Vietnam, mostly in mountainous areas, so the navigators were constantly challenged. The limited carrier space for the RA-3Bs meant that the aircraft were sometimes flying more than one mission each night.

As we approached the ship, I was disappointed that it appeared tiny from the air, just like the *Coral Sea*. Yet I knew that the *Enterprise* displaced twice as much tonnage and was the longest ship in the world. After we trapped aboard, I could better appreciate the immensity of the deck. The tall, square island in the center looked more like the control tower at a major airport. There was no vent for diesel engines; a nuclear core powered the *Enterprise*, the world's first nuclear aircraft carrier. The ship still needed refueling at sea, but only for aviation fuel for the air wing, which contained many more aircraft than the air wing on the smaller *Coral Sea*. Consequently, crowding still existed as a result of more aircrews, more aircraft mechanics, more deck crews, more cooks, more everything.

On board, Stan and Dave went immediately to the CIC, Combat Intelligence Center, for an update, while I looked for other members of the squadron. I knew that any navigator on board would be either poring over maps or sleeping. I found Stuart Blake, Jason Lockhart's old navigator, who was now flying with a pilot named Jim Newland. They had been on the *Enterprise* for nearly a week and had flown eight missions.

"Hi, Stuart! How are the missions going?" I asked.

"You can't believe how bad it is, Doc," he replied. "It's like the Fourth of July when we're crossing the beach."

"How's flying with Jim Newland?"

"He's a good naval aviator with lots of experience, but I worry about our photo technician."

"How come?"

"He's been flying with us for only a short time, but he's very nervous before each mission."

"You're flying dangerous missions."

"Yeah, that's for sure." He turned to face away from me. "To tell you the truth, I'm feeling the stress a little myself."

I noticed that Stuart had lost weight and had bags under his eyes, just like Stan. "Are you able to catch some sleep once in a while?"

"Not much. I spend most of my time on the charts. But then, I've never been able to sleep on board the ship during the day."

I had not seen Stuart that dejected before. We didn't say anything for a minute, and then I said, "I'll be on the ship for a while if you want to talk to me some more."

He stopped me. "Doc, thanks for taking care of Jason. You did the right thing. I couldn't say anything, you know."

I tried to reassure him. "It wasn't your job. That's why we have flight surgeons."

I headed toward the ready room to see if Stan and Dave had any news from the CIC. From the beginning, the Vietcong had been pulling off deadly ambushes against marine and army patrols at night and then disappearing during the day. But now, organized NVA units were showing up in large numbers, completely replacing the VC and mounting large scale attacks against marine outposts. They also intensified the shelling of the air base at Da Nang. One of the operating tents at First Med was hit, but miraculously, it wasn't in use at the time. No one was killed.

Stan had on his serious face.

"What's on for tonight?" I asked.

"We're going to Hanoi."

I gasped. "Hanoi!" They were going directly into the jaws of the tiger. "How can you tell what you're seeing on infrared in all that population congestion?"

"We're not going to use infrared," Stan said. "This will be a photographic mission."

"You're going to use flash bombs near Hanoi?"

Dave had been listening and looking down at the deck. He turned toward me. "I'm afraid so."

I remembered the terror I felt on the mission that we flew over Haiphong Harbor, but that was easy compared to flying over the most heavily-defended target in North Vietnam, fifty or sixty miles inland with no quick escape over water. I wanted to ask why the target was so important, but they weren't in a position to question their orders, and my nagging them wouldn't improve anything.

"When do you launch?" I asked.

"At midnight," Dave answered. "That seems to be our special time."

He headed for a quiet nook with his maps, while I began looking up other squadron members and talking with the crew on the hangar deck. I planned to stay close to the ready room after they launched to wait up for them and to listen to any radio traffic that was broadcast there. The flight from launch to recovery probably would consume only a little over an hour. They would return to the ready room at 2300 hours for a last-minute weather report and discussion of the route to the target, and then they would leave for the plane.

After midnight, I was agitated and pacing like an expectant father. This mission seemed crazy to me. For awhile, no radio traffic from them came in over the loudspeaker hooked up in the ready room. I hadn't expected to hear right away, because they would have remained radio-silent for the dash from the gulf into the target. Just before 0100, I heard Stan's voice.

"Yankee Station, Quiz Show Niner Zero One."

"Roger Nine Zero One."

"Possible airframe damage. Request priority recovery. Niner Zero One."

"Nine Zero One. Affirmative priority recovery."

Something had happened to cause structural damage to the aircraft that caused Stan to request permission to land on a priority basis, and to warn the ship of the weakened state of his A-3 that could cause the plane to come apart on trapping aboard. I ran to the sick bay to pick up a couple of hospital corpsmen, stretchers, and some emergency equipment; then we rushed to the flight deck. I speculated about the "possible airframe damage" and wondered if they had taken a hit from triple-A during their run over the target. At least they were able to return to the ship rather than bailing out—or worse. Stan had made no mention of anyone being wounded.

We stood inside a hatch in the island just off the flight deck to avoid any lethal flying parts that might careen around the deck during a crash. Only the deck crew essential to the landing remained, and they were moving aircraft around the flight deck and down to the hangar below on the two elevators. Then everyone stopped, signaling that Stan's plane was on final.

Stan's voice came on a loudspeaker next to the hatch broadcasting to the flight deck. "I've got a problem. The flap warning light came on. Niner Zero One."

I could now hear the sound of the plane.

"I'm going around, Niner Zero One."

The big A-3 waved off and roared over the deck at low altitude with engines at full power, climbing out.

Huge flaps on the wings created the lift necessary to fly the airplane slowly enough to land on a carrier deck. If those flaps weren't fully down and locked, the plane could either stall on final, which would be fatal, or collide with the deck at too great of speed, snapping the arresting wire, or worse. On a long runway, the big plane could use a drag chute released from the back of the fuselage in order to stop, but the nearest air base was Da Nang, forty minutes flying time away.

"Nine Zero One, please advise. Yankee Station." The ship wanted to know what Stan planned to do.

"I'm low on fuel," Stan said. "I'm going to have to come in."

Deck crewmen began scrambling to move more airplanes.

We searched the blackness beyond the aft end of the ship, trying to will the plane down safely. I stopped breathing. A hushed stillness enveloped the ship. For the first time, I could actually hear the sound of the ship's hull plowing through the waves.

The aircraft suddenly appeared out of the black and immediately slammed down on the deck. The engines roared, and the tail hook caught—the arresting wire held—the plane was in one piece. Stan pulled back on the throttles, folded the wings, and followed the commands of the deck crew. At first, nothing seemed amiss.

I ran to the aircraft as the bottom hatch opened and saw Dave handing the big film cassettes to photo lab technicians, who ran off with their trophies. Two deck crewmen were pointing to the flap on the port wing on the other side of the aircraft. I stood behind the CAG, Captain Leigh again, who was waiting by the aircraft for Stan to climb down. Dave appeared first and stumbled when he hit the deck.

"What happened?" Captain Leigh asked.

"The shaking was horrible." Dave said. "I've never been so scared in my life."

"Did the controls work normally?"

Dave was too distressed to notice the question. "I can't believe we made it down."

Then Stan emerged, and for the first time ever, he appeared hesitant, dazed, and bent over.

Captain Leigh asked again if the controls were working.

"No," Stan replied. "The port flap wasn't all the way down. We were coming in fast, but the stall warning alarm was on, and the plane was shaking hard just before we hit the deck. It was a wrestling match."

The photo technician had climbed down and was on his hands and knees on the deck crying.

"What happened to the airframe?" Captain Leigh asked.

"A SAM almost got us," Stan said. "We passed through the red line into the mach buffet; it was loud and scary."

"Why were you up at high altitude?"

"A thick curtain of triple-A—halfway through our run—don't know how they missed us." Stan wasn't looking at Captain Leigh but just staring absently. "We had no chance. We had to climb to get above it. I knew we might be in trouble with the SAMs, but we were dead down low."

"Did you actually see the SAM coming up?"

Stan began to focus on Captain Leigh. "Dave saw the whole thing on his radar. My only option was to dive."

"Did the yoke work all right?"

"I wasn't sure it would respond, but it did—and then I didn't know if the wings would hold as I pulled out."

"Jesus!" Captain Leigh said.

"I don't think this plane is safe to fly again," Stan said. "I don't know how we survived."

"Where were you when the SAM locked on?"

"Almost to the coast."

I followed as they started walking toward the war room for the debriefing.

"Did you consider diverting to Da Nang instead of attempting to trap aboard?" Captain Leigh asked.

"Yeah," Stan said. "I had to make a decision. It was a close call. The aircraft was handling all right, and I didn't know about the damage to the flaps until I lowered them. I decided to return to the ship, because I knew the pictures were important, and we don't have our photo lab people at Da Nang anymore."

I decided not to follow them into the meeting, since I had no active role in the mission. I would wait until the debriefing was finished and then see if there were anything I could do for Stan or Dave. Meanwhile, I went looking for the photo technician.

I found Petty Officer Williams shivering violently, still on the flight deck, sitting with his head in his hands. "It was horrible, horrible."

"Tell me what happened," I said.

He looked up at me. "The shaking—and the noise. The cameras were jumping off their mounts."

I sat down next to him. "What happened with the SAM?" I asked.

"We were still climbing. Then Commander White flipped over the airplane and put it into a dive."

"Did you see the SAM?"

"I saw the quick flash of the exhaust pass us right outside the canopy," he said.

"That close."

He looked directly at me and frowned. "I'd rather be court-martialed than fly another mission."

There was nothing I could do except to tell him that I admired his bravery. I suspected that Commander White would not be flying more missions around Hanoi, but I couldn't tell that to a photo technician. There was no point in giving him sedatives. His adrenaline level was so high that nothing would faze him. He would have to come to grips in his own way with the danger he had just faced; his lifetime supply of risk tolerance was just about exhausted.

I went to the war room to wait outside until Stan and Dave came out. They appeared less agitated now, just stooped over and tired.

"You two look like you need more time to unwind," I said.

"Doc, I've been flying for a long time and have logged a lot of combat missions," Stan said, "but that was the worst scare of my life."

"I just saw your photo technician, and he is still shaking. He said he actually saw the exhaust of the SAM pass by the canopy on your way down."

"I know," Stan said. "He told me."

"I'm placing him on my list of airmen who may not tolerate any more combat missions. He's cracking."

"So was our aircraft."

"I heard you notify the ship of airframe damage and your request for priority landing," I said.

Dave spoke. "We learned the hard way about the limitations of the RA-3B over North Vietnam. We don't have the speed to avoid the SAMs at high altitude. Captain Leigh is going to restrict the targets that he assigns us to."

"We won't be going back over Hanoi with flash bombs," Stan said. "Luck got us through this time, but the odds were against us. I'll remember forever that curtain of triple-A. We had almost made it when that SAM locked on during our run to the coast."

They were reliving those awful minutes. From the time they turned away from the triple-A, their dash to the coast probably lasted only about ten minutes, but that was too much time in the crosshairs of a SAM radar system. Then they experienced the terror of trapping aboard with the damage to the flaps. The ship's maintenance crews would probably replace the stressed arresting wire.

For the rest of the night, they continued to recount every detail, interspersed with long minutes of reflection. Dawn was not likely to bring them any relief. Remaining up with them and absorbing myself in their frightful experience masked my own nightmares, giving me a temporary reprieve from my nightly specters of children bleeding and dismembered marines.

Stan and Dave had survived their mission over Hanoi somehow, and I had survived ten days in captivity with the Vietcong. I could no longer weigh the benefits and risks of our actions, because I was having difficulty identifying any benefit at all. I found that I could continue to provide medical care aboard ship, participate in rescue operations, and play the role of the good listener, but I could not imagine how Stan and Dave would ever be able to climb into a cockpit again to fly a combat mission. I knew that I wouldn't have been able to. I was certain that Petty Officer Williams would carry the psychological scars of that night's mission for the rest of his life.

Chapter 20

THE SUMMIT

The next afternoon, I went looking for Jim Newland and Stuart Blake, who had flown at the same time as Stan's close call with the SAM. They were sitting in the ready room.

Stuart looked up at me. "Have you heard? They intend to push the skipper's aircraft over the side. The photo technicians have pulled all of the cameras out of the plane, and now the electronics technicians are cannibalizing other equipment. Have you seen Stan?"

"No," I said. "I know that he and Dave didn't get to bed until after dawn, but I expect they'll be around soon. We might check the bowling alley."

They were there, sitting alone in the near-empty compartment. Flight operations didn't start for another eight hours, so most aircrews would not arrive until later. Stan signaled us to come over and sit down.

"Your aircraft is in bad shape?" Jim asked.

"I can't be sure about the integrity of the airframe. Luckily, the plane didn't come apart when we trapped aboard, but I wouldn't trust it again, especially not for a catapult shot. The air boss needs the deck space, so there's no choice but to dump it."

Jim looked straight at Stan for several seconds. "Will we be doing more missions like yours last night?"

"No," Stan said. "I've talked with Captain Leigh about it. That's the end of using flash bombs over the North."

"What are you planning to do now?"

"Dave and I are taking the COD back to Cubi Point. We'll hitch a ride to Guam to pick up another aircraft. Doc, could you come with us, too?"

My spirits soared. I was giddy. It was Christmas, a birthday, and Fourth of July all in one. When I first arrived on the island the year before, I remembered thinking how dull a place it was. Now, with Lynn there, a nice boring tropical island with beaches and palm trees sounded perfect.

"I'd love to go to Guam," I said.

He smiled. "I'm sure you would, but I'm going to need you there for another reason." Stan leaned forward toward me and lowered his voice. "Captain Leigh took me aside and told me about something big happening on Guam, and I'll need you to be there. I'll tell you about it later."

I couldn't imagine anything that qualified as big ever happening on Guam, except for Lynn, and maybe World War II.

Stan said, "The COD will arrive in about an hour and then launch for the return to Cubi Point twenty minutes later, so we only have a little time."

The COD was a propeller-driven, twin-engine airplane that looked like something out of the 1930s. It contained four seats for passengers and exhibited a characteristic found exclusively on naval aircraft: it had a tail hook. Stan said the landing speed was only seventy knots, so with the ship's speed of close to thirty knots and a headwind of twenty, the COD appeared to make its approach in slow motion, almost as though it were struggling to catch the ship. When it touched down, it didn't even bend the arresting wire that a heavy jet would have pulled out for half the length of the deck.

A few passengers got out, and the deck crew quickly unloaded the plane and towed it over to one of the catapults. I wasn't certain if a catapult was even needed for launching, but Stan said the extra margin of speed made the launch safer. The catapult crew reduced the amount of force for the cat shot, which felt relatively mild after experiencing the violence of a launch in an RA-3B.

The noise level inside the cabin during flight precluded conversation, and we all sat back and enjoyed the leisurely eight-hundred-mile flight to Cubi Point. Normally an A-3 could fly that distance in an hour and a half, but the COD with its propeller engines took nearly four hours. I didn't mind at all.

Subic Bay looked like a pristine tropical harbor from the air, except for the presence of several naval warships, including one carrier. I could see the parking areas filled with gray naval aircraft at the Cubi Point naval air station, enough for two or three carriers. I could even pick out several A-3s, mostly the tanker version.

After we landed, the three of us checked into the BOQ with plans to meet for dinner at the officers' club. I asked Stan about his important news.

"Let's get changed first. We can sit down and talk about it over dinner."

Stan was being mysterious, and I suspected he had more bad news.

The officers' club was crammed with naval aviators and navigators from the air wing attached to the USS *Oriskany*, which was returning to Vietnam after a brief refitting in San Diego. Most of the aviators present in the club had not participated in the previous tour and were in high spirits as they headed to their first combat experience. Alcohol flowed freely, and the noise made conversation difficult.

The three of us had recently experienced life-threatening situations and were in no mood to participate in a wild bacchanal, so Stan collared the head steward and obtained for us a small, private dining room out of the din. The menu offered choices we hadn't seen in months, including fresh fish, fruit, and vegetables.

I prodded Stan. "Okay, what's the big secret?"

He looked at each of us. "President Johnson is flying to Guam for a mid-Pacific summit meeting with Premier Ky."

"Wow! That is big news. I assume that President Johnson is going to declare victory and bring us all home," I said.

Stan laughed for the first time since the SAM incident. He was the great stabilizing strength in the squadron, but even he had a breaking point. I had come face-to-face with my own, and I had been looking carefully at Stan. That laugh reassured me—temporarily.

"If you were the president," Stan said, "that's probably what would happen. No one knows what the subject will be, or whether this is just for show."

"When are they arriving?" I asked.

"In three days. The meeting will include Ambassador Ellsworth Bunker and General Creighton Abrams, deputy to General Westmoreland. McNamara is staying home."

"This is a very big deal," I said. "Maybe something good will come of it."

Stan explained further. "President Johnson will deliver a short speech from a small platform to be erected next to Air Force One, and then he'll be driven to the Top O' the Mar. The place is undergoing emergency renovations, and workmen and secret service agents are swarming over the whole area. They are installing miles of temporary telephone cables, along with a large electricity generator."

I was now completely relaxed, until I noticed Stan looking intently at me. "The White House has requested that an emergency medical station be set up inside the civilian air terminal and manned by a navy physician," he said. "The presidential party will be traveling without a physician this time."

Stan had my full attention. "Why are you looking at me? There are lots of doctors at the naval hospital. That's right next to the Top O' the Mar."

Stan said, "One of the heart doctors from the hospital will be available during the meetings, but they want another doctor to handle any emergency that might arise at the airport."

Stan paused. "Doc, you are going to be the doctor on duty at that emergency medical station. You can pick out a hospital corpsman from the naval air station dispensary to assist you, but I don't want anyone but you to be in charge."

Stan didn't realize that he was asking a lot of a physician with limited post-graduate medical education. Two and a half years before, I had been a lowly medical student at the bottom of the hospital pecking order, holding retractors in the operating room. During the last year, I had been responsible for the emergency care of victims of major trauma in a combat zone and had participated in the treatment of a variety of tropical diseases that few American physicians had ever seen. Stan was now placing me in the position of being responsible for providing emergency care for the president of the United States. Even though it would be for just a few minutes, I thought it was completely beyond my competence level.

"Three days isn't much time to prepare," I said. "I'll call Bethesda to see if I can get some medical records, or at least a list of his significant medical problems and medications."

"Somebody in the White House already thought of that," he said. "A coded message with the information is waiting for you at the VAP 61 area on Guam. You can get it as soon as we arrive."

"If the president is going to give a speech, what are the security arrangements?" I asked.

"The whole naval air station will be locked down, and every person entering the gate will be searched by the marines. No one without an invitation will be admitted anywhere near the president."

"All the same, I'm going to put together a surgical kit like the ones we use on rescue helicopters in combat zones. How about the civilian terminal? It's very small. I'd need some space."

"No one will be allowed in the terminal except for you, your hospital corpsman, Ambassador Bunker, and General Abrams. Premier Ky will already be up at the Top O' the Mar."

It occurred to me that I might also have to treat Ambassador Bunker or General Abrams. Somehow that didn't cause me the same trepidation as being responsible for the president of the United States.

We were all dead tired and returned to the BOQ immediately after dinner. I knew that sleep would not come and that I would think about everything that could go wrong once Air Force One arrived on Guam. We were scheduled to fly there early the next morning on an R-5, an ancient, propeller-driven transport plane that would require eight hours for the trip. The navy wasted no money on airplanes that didn't have a tail hook. This noisy, old relic had an unpressurized cabin and so would fly low, dodging the storms. I was impatient to get to Guam to see Lynn and miserable with worry about the president's visit at the same time.

She was at the naval air station to meet me. The minute I descended, she ran to the plane and hugged me as if I might escape. We stayed that way for a long time. The relief of being with her on that peaceful island, protected from the violence of the war, swept over me.

She started pulling me toward Roger, who was waiting in his rusty old car. Roger's wife Jill and several of their friends had invited us to the hospital for a little reception.

When we had a minute together, she said, "You're a scarecrow. I'm going to fix that."

I ignored her comment. "I think I'm in paradise," I said.

"I feel that way, too. Do you have a few days' leave?"

"I have to attend a small ceremony for the president's arrival at the naval air station, but I won't let a little thing like that bother us too much."

"You don't have to go back for a while, do you?" she asked.

I didn't know. The thought of reentry into that firestorm caused me to shudder. She noticed.

"What was that?" she said.

"I'm just happy to be here with you," I replied.

"A little malaria, too?"

"No. I think what I have is curable."

We couldn't have dinner at the Top O' the Mar because of the renovations for the summit, so we went to the beach with Roger and Jill and had a barbeque. Their daughter was now a toddler, playing in the sand and wading in the water. Roger had learned how to climb trees to cut down coconuts. We amused ourselves opening them with a machete, drinking the milk, and eating the meat. We all sat on the beach, leaning against a log, watching the clouds turn pink. Slowly the whole sky became bloodred.

Jill exclaimed, "Have you ever seen anything so beautiful—so romantic—as that sunset?"

To me, the redness was horrible. I saw gauze pads soaked in the blood of an airman and the abdominal wound of a marine blown open by a mortar blast. I knew what lay waiting for me over the horizon behind that sunset.

When it was dark, we lit a fire and told stories. I had many to tell, but not that night, and maybe not ever. I had my arm around Lynn and listened as she recounted the story of Lenny and George from *Of Mice and Men*, how big-hearted, clumsy Lenny with his great strength would unintentionally kill the people and animals he tried to protect. I thought of the Vietnamese people dying in the war and about Dr. Tran's clinic. Lynn felt my shudder once more and looked at me as if to ask why. I gave her a weak smile.

The next morning, the day before the arrival of the president, an entourage of White House staff arrived, including his personal cook, who came directly to the dispensary and presented himself with a sore throat. Luckily for me, he was a man who loved to talk about his job, so I peppered him with questions about the president's diet, a backdoor way into obtaining a medical history.

"I catch hell from Lady Bird if I don't watch the calories and reduce the cholesterol."

"Can you give me an example?" I asked.

"The president loves popcorn, but I can't put any salt on it, and he gets only one cup. She says I have to make it with olive oil. Can you imagine that? He's the president of the United States, and he can't have popcorn with butter and salt."

Based on these few phrases from the cook, I knew that the president had cardiovascular disease. The coded message from Bethesda Naval Hospital confirmed the diagnosis of heart disease with angina pectoris and a prior history of a myocardial infarction. My first aid station was going to be stocked with everything that the best hospital coronary care unit would normally contain, and the hospital corpsman who was my assistant was going to be drilled extensively in cardiopulmonary resuscitation in order to help me in the event of a cardiac arrest.

I worried about sniper bullets, too, and planned for managing wounds like the ones I had seen during my weeks at Da Nang. What I dreaded most was the ten-minute drive on winding roads from the air terminal to the Top O' the Mar, but Stan had assured me that security would be tight all the way. I also worried about administering care in a careening ambulance, so I requested a nice, level-flying helicopter to stand by, just like at Da Nang. Stan didn't think it was necessary.

"No!" he said. "This isn't a battlefield, and the president will be at the air terminal for about ten minutes."

"Would you deny the president the same care that we give to the marines?"

"Doc, there are times when you can be a real pain in the ass. I'll get you your damn helicopter."

The big day arrived. We were in the middle of what was called "the dry season" on Guam, which meant that we had a cloudburst only about two or three times a day. Towering clouds rolled across the island and dumped deluges, limited sometimes to an area of less than one square mile. One end of the runway might be in bright sunlight, while rain flooded the other end. We all hoped for clear weather for the president's speech.

The hospital corpsman and I, both dressed in service dress whites, found ourselves alone inside the small terminal when General Abrams and Ambassador Bunker arrived. The general looked like a kindly father and had an easy smile. The ambassador looked like a British diplomat, tall, slender, serious, and gray-haired, dressed in a Bond Street blue suit. They came over to us, politely introduced themselves, and shook hands. General Abrams asked me if I was the flight surgeon who had been kidnapped by the Vietcong.

"Yes. I'm surprised that you know about that."

"I had to approve your rescue attempt," General Abrams said.

"I didn't know," I stammered. "You saved my life."

"How did the kidnapping happen?"

I told him the story.

General Abrams raised his eyebrows. "Do you think that the Vietnamese doctor in Bien Hoa was a Vietcong?"

"No," I said. "He was the one who found out where the Vietcong had taken me and alerted my squadron CO. The Vietcong bombed his clinic in retribution, killing him and many of the children he was treating."

"I'm sorry. Do you think many of the people in Bien Hoa are Vietcong?"

"I doubt it. The ones with whom I talked complained bitterly about the South Vietnamese government's persecution of them, but they said the Vietcong were thugs."

"What did they think about Americans?"

"They saw that we were protecting the government in Saigon that they hated. They viewed us as just another foreign invader like the French."

I was a little surprised about the questions, because I thought the Pentagon and State Department would have had excellent sources of information about the Vietnamese people and intelligence concerning the Vietcong.

General Abrams hesitated. "Do you know if the Vietcong are the ones shelling the air base at Bien Hoa?"

"Probably," I said, "but the Buddhist militant group called the Struggle Movement might possibly be behind it. They fiercely oppose the Ky government and Catholics in general."

"How did you find out all of this?"

"The Vietnamese doctor knew both sides, because he was a Buddhist but educated by French Catholic nuns."

Ambassador Bunker asked, "What did you think of the Vietcong?"

"The ones who kidnapped me were fanatical and well armed. Bombing the children's clinic was a ruthless act of terrorism."

"Did they harm you?" General Abrams asked.

"They were a little rough at first, but they didn't really hurt me. The depersonalization and isolation as a slave were worse."

General Abrams kept up his questioning. "Did they have medical supplies?"

"Plenty," I said. "All stamped 'U.S. Army.'"

The ambassador and the general looked at each other for several seconds.

General Abrams said, "Thank you for telling us about your experience. I'm glad you got back safely."

Air Force One was approaching the runway. Tall cumulus clouds swept in from the other end, and the downpour began just as the president was descending the portable stairway. He stepped to the podium and cracked a joke while two aides held umbrellas.

"I'm going to tell everyone in Washington that the heaviest rain I've ever seen was during the dry season on Guam."

The president did not mention the summit he had traveled so far to attend, and in about one minute, he was gone. My preparations had gone for naught—so much the better. President Johnson and Premier Ky then engaged in closed sessions, excluding the press, and issued a joint statement affirming strong American support of the Saigon government against the Communist aggressors. After the statement was read, I walked to a lonely spot where I could see the Philippine Sea and stared numbly for a long time. Vietnam was still out there—waiting.

Chapter 21

DOWN IN THE SOUTH CHINA SEA

After a few short days in paradise, I had to fly back to Vietnam. Lynn was very quiet, and I caught her crying as I packed. I reminded her that my tour of duty with VAP 61 would be coming to a close in a few months and that we might think about our future. She gave me a brief smile.

The replacement RA-3B that had arrived for Stan and Dave at the naval air station caused a stir—it was all black. All of the identification marks, including the word NAVY on the wings and fuselage, were painted in small letters and numbers, so that the aircraft appeared solid black, even from a short distance away. The tough-looking paint job produced smiles all around among the ground crew. Everyone thought the blackout paint would generate envy on the *Enterprise*. It might be an old whale stuffed with cameras, but it would at least look dangerous like a harmless snake with coloring that matched a poisonous one.

Dave was grinning. "It's a beauty, isn't it, Doc?"

"Do you think it will hide you from the North Vietnamese radar?"

"It couldn't hurt."

I had never before appreciated that black paint could serve as an effective remedy for a stressful combat experience, but Dave seemed almost cured of his brush with the SAM. He wasn't always open with his feelings, though. I knew his tour of duty with VAP 61 would end soon, and probably he was just enjoying this little misdemeanor—like painting a mustache on the face of a politician on a poster or a senior prank in high school. In the navy, we called this "short-timer syndrome."

The three of us were flying back to Cubi Point, where Stan and Dave would pick up a photo technician. They would fly their mission and land back aboard the *Enterprise* soon after midnight. I would catch the COD the next day from Cubi Point to the *Enterprise.*

We climbed up into the cockpit, familiar to me by now, with the same infrared gear and electronic countermeasures devices that were found on all of the other aircraft in the squadron. Under its dark skin, this was the same as any other RA-3B. We flew to Cubi Point, where I made the rounds and ran into Jim Newland and Stuart Blake, who had finished their rotation aboard the *Enterprise* and were now flying a reduced number of missions from Cubi Point.

Stuart Blake looked better than when I had last seen him on the *Enterprise* at the end of their week-long turn flying over the North. I was sure that he was much more comfortable flying with Jim Newland, his pilot after Jason Lockhart's grounding. Jim was calm, steady, and unflappable, exactly what a more spirited navigator like Stuart needed. Although Jim had only recently become a lieutenant commander, he obviously was destined for his own command someday, and the way this war was going, it might be sooner rather than later.

Jim had some interesting news.

"We might open a detachment at Bangkok."

I looked for any hint of a joke. "That sounds like a whale's tale."

"No, not at all. The air force wants us to reduce the number of aircraft in the detachment at Bien Hoa."

"Is Bangkok any closer to the targets?" I asked.

"It's closer than Bien Hoa to many targets in North Vietnam and much closer than flying from Cubi Point," Jim said.

"And you think the Thai government would allow it?"

"The air force already has a number of squadrons there."

The ground crews would love to swap our tent city at Bien Hoa for Bangkok. There was no war in Bangkok, and the occasional mortar shell lobbed into the air base at Bien Hoa caused tension twenty-four hours a day. Just the name "Bangkok" sounded exotic. It was probably too good to be true.

"If you're not leaving until tomorrow, why don't you join Stuart and me for dinner at the officers' club tonight?" Jim asked.

"Love to," I responded.

Usually, squadron members were less tense at Cubi Point than aboard ship or at Bien Hoa, because the Philippines was not a combat zone. Although it wasn't Bangkok, there were certain comforts like air conditioning and a swimming pool at the officers' club. The *Oriskany* was no longer in port, so the officers' club was quiet, and I enjoyed a rare, relaxing time with Jim and Stuart. We were joined by the pilot and navigator of an A-3 tanker, Ed Bailey and Don Miller. Ed looked nearly forty, old for a carrier pilot. He had an engaging, fluid way of speaking and moving that had earned him the nickname "Liquid Ed." He told jokes with exaggerated movements of his arms that made everyone laugh, and he had a certain reassuring self-confidence. Don Miller was senior among navigators, too. He was quiet and obviously enjoyed being the partner of a colorful character like Ed.

Tankers were A-3s that the navy had adapted to perform in-flight refueling to allow combat aircraft to stay aloft longer, reducing the need for repetitive launching and recovery from the carriers and increasing the number of aircraft airborne. Tanker crews were more relaxed than VAP 61 air crewmen, because they never had to fly over North Vietnam. They could just patrol off the coast over the gulf. I was scheduled to catch the COD to the *Enterprise* the next morning, but Ed and Don were flying there, too, and offered me the third seat on their tanker.

Meteorologists had forecast some stormy weather over the South China Sea for our flight to the Gulf of Tonkin, and I was glad to avoid four hours of turbulence at lower altitude on the COD. The bad weather would have no effect on an A-3, which could easily fly above storms. Since we would be leaving late in the afternoon, the weather would already be clearing in the Gulf of Tonkin by the time of our arrival at the ship.

The flight began without incident, but less than an hour out of Cubi Point, Ed began making anxious comments about the airplane. Tankers had a huge fuel capacity, and the pilot could normally transfer fuel between tanks, to the engines, or to the in-flight refueling hose, but now a light was flashing on the instrument panel. He clicked on the intercom.

"We have a problem. The low-fuel warning light just came on."

We were out in the middle of the South China Sea, a long way from land and in the middle of a storm, a bad place to run out of fuel. I had been relaxed, and now the familiar fear of a combat flight gripped me again, beginning with the awful nausea and anxiety. I tried to deny what was happening, because this was so improbable.

"We had plenty of fuel when we ran through the preflight check," Don Miller said.

Ed's face was buried in the instrument panel. "I know. Something isn't working with the fuel transfer system. We're carrying plenty of fuel, but I can't feed it to the engines."

"What'll we do?" Don asked.

"I'll keep trying to get it working. You contact the ship and see if we can talk to an aircraft maintenance officer."

Ed continued troubleshooting in the cockpit, and in less than a minute, the voice of a maintenance officer from the *Enterprise* crackled in our earphones.

"What's the problem?"

Ed clicked on and explained, describing his attempts to transfer the fuel.

"You must have a failure of the main transfer valve."

Ah, there we may have a solution, I thought.

"Okay, how can I transfer fuel around it?" Ed asked.

"You can't. We could easily replace it on the ship, but I don't know any alternative way to transfer fuel in-flight except through that valve."

I was crushed. The maintenance officer sounded matter-of-fact, but there was a possibility we were going to die. I wanted to scream at him.

"We have only about ten minutes of fuel left if I can't make the transfer."

"I wish I could tell you another way, but there isn't any."

Ed swore. "Connect me to the CAG."

In less than thirty seconds, Captain Leigh came on. "What's the trouble?"

Ed quickly described the situation and gave our coordinates. "We don't have much fuel left, so I've started a slow descent to stay airborne as long as possible in order to close with the *Enterprise*. We'll jump when we flame out."

That was it. We were going down. It wasn't fair. This wasn't even a combat flight.

"A rescue helicopter will launch right away," Captain Leigh said, "but it will take more than an hour to reach you."

"We'll try to hang on," Ed said. "Do you have an update on the weather?"

"You have a bad storm below you with gusts to seventy knots and fifteen-foot waves. It should clear in a couple of hours, but you'll be jumping into near-gale conditions."

"Damn!" I had survived antiaircraft fire over Haiphong Harbor and mortar attacks while picking up wounded marines in a helicopter, but now I was going down over the ocean in the middle of a storm during what was supposed to have been a shuttle flight. And all because a mechanical problem was starving the engines on the airplane with the biggest fuel capacity in the fleet. I longed to be on that noisy, bouncing COD about twenty thousand feet below.

Having participated in air-sea rescues, I knew the drill, and I also knew the odds. We were almost five hundred miles from Cubi Point, and about three hundred from the *Enterprise* and the *Oriskany*. I had never seen fifteen-foot waves and doubted that anyone could survive in such heavy seas. At best, we would have a long wait for the helicopter to arrive, and even then, I wasn't sure they could find us. We might have to survive the best we could in the water for a long while, possibly all night. Ed came on the intercom again.

"We're almost out of fuel. Get ready to bail out."

I was carrying two flares in my vest and a strobe light, and we each had a one-man life raft in our seat pans. None of us spoke while Ed frantically repeated his attempts to transfer fuel. Then we all felt the sudden loss of power.

"That was a flameout of the port engine," he said. "I've notified the *Enterprise* of our position. We're on autopilot. I'll follow you. You two go now."

My flight instructor in Pensacola had warned that orders to bail out would not be repeated, so I got up, opened the bottom hatch, and jumped. There hadn't been enough time to feel terror. It was like diving into a cold swimming pool to avoid the torture of a slow entry. The blast of air whacked me, and I lost all sense of direction. I felt chilled through and through, and a kind of paralysis set in. After what seemed to be more than a minute of falling, I began to regain my senses.

An altimeter was supposed to automatically open the parachute at a lower altitude, but I didn't have much confidence in mechanical devices at that moment. I could open the chute manually if the altimeter failed to work, and that gave me some comfort, but visibility was almost zero in the clouds and rain. I could not see the water to judge my height. I decided to pull the D-ring, but before I could locate it, the chute popped opened spontaneously and jerked me to what felt like a halt. It seemed as if I were no longer descending, just hanging from a giant hook while the wind and rain battered me like a rag doll.

Suddenly huge waves came into view, and I plunged into the water. Immediately the wind in the chute began to drag me, but my survival instincts recovered. *Bottom clips first—top clips last.* I was free.

The high waves disoriented me, moving me up and down as if I were on a roller coaster, and the rain lashed my face. I could see no farther than the top of the next wave and had no hope of locating Ed or Don. The tropical sea felt almost warm after my freezing descent, but I knew from my experience as a swimmer that I would eventually begin to feel chilled, even though the water temperature was probably nearly eighty degrees.

I inflated my life vest using the two compressed-air cartridges and rode the giant waves up and down. Then I pulled the one-man raft from the seat pack attached to my parachute harness, making sure that its lanyard was firmly attached to me. I didn't want to lose that raft in the high winds. I inflated the raft easily—the hard part would be mounting it. Pulling myself up in a placid swimming pool during drills had required a certain amount of strength and dexterity, but doing the same in the ocean in the middle of a storm would take all of my might and willpower. The wind and the waves would soon tire me if I failed, so my best chance of success would be my first attempts.

When I was in a trough between giant waves, I grabbed the raft with both hands and heaved myself up with a mighty lunge. My balance was off, and the raft immediately flipped over, punishing me with a nose full of salt water. I grabbed for the raft in a panic as I bobbed up to the crest of the wave, but the lanyard had held. The raft was still attached to my harness.

I rested a few minutes riding up and down, trying to regain my strength. This time, I was going to lunge just after a crest had passed.

I guessed wrong, and ended upside down again. I began to despair, thinking that I'd never make it, and waited to catch my breath for another try.

With a mighty effort, I made it into a precarious seated position, one foot dangling over the side of the raft and the other over the end.

I was in! Now, I just had to straighten myself a little.

My elation lasted only seconds. Just as the raft reached the crest, the full force of the wind flipped and hurtled me down the other side into the trough. I tumbled helplessly, submerged and disoriented, but something was tugging me up: the raft, still attached to my harness by the lanyard. I burst to the surface and gulped a big breath of air. I rested a long time, just clutching the raft in the powerful up-and-down motion.

I wouldn't last long unless I mounted that raft. The last attempt had almost succeeded, so I doggedly tried again. This time my timing was perfect. I wasn't sure how I did it, or if I could ever do it again, but I centered myself in the raft with both feet over the end. At least I wouldn't become exhausted from struggling in the water.

Still, I couldn't rest, because the whitecaps at each crest demanded my full attention. Each time I rose to the top of a wave, a blast of wind and spray would try to flip me over and plunge me down. Even in the raft, my strength wouldn't last long battling this storm.

I checked my watch. Only twenty-four minutes had elapsed since we had bailed out. Maybe my watch had stopped. I would check it again in a few minutes.

Gradually, I developed my own subconscious timing, leaning to counter the tendency of the raft to capsize, but I still had to concentrate to avoid capsizing. It was becoming more automatic. Just as I was gaining confidence, a sudden strong gust at a crest almost flipped me again.

I checked my watch one more time: twenty-seven minutes since we had bailed out. My watch was working. I had been in the water less than half an hour, yet I was already tired and beginning to feel cold.

I thought about yelling.

Then I realized how silly it was to think that anyone could possibly have heard me over the howling of the wind. Even if Ed and Don had heard, they would have been just as helpless. I tried to think of something positive and thought about Lynn. I had a big reason to keep up the fight.

The weather forecast for our expected time of arrival at the *Enterprise* predicted clearing. Maybe the storm would blow over soon. Then I realized that the *Enterprise* was three hundred miles away. It might take hours for the storm to clear where I was. By then it would be night. How was I going to survive overnight?

Maybe I could see Ed and Don. I might catch a glimpse of them when the raft reached the crest of a wave. As I strained to search for my comrades, a gust of wind punished me with yet another dunking. I tumbled down into the whirlpool once more.

Several minutes passed before my energy returned enough to try pulling myself up into the raft again. I could feel my strength fading, but my technique had improved. I succeeded in landing squarely once more.

After several cycles of waves, I tried a quick peek straight ahead when I reached the crest. Success—I didn't capsize—but then I didn't see anyone, either. It became a game: watch the wave, carefully, carefully—peek—and zoom down into the trough. I counted twenty cycles looking in all directions with nothing in sight except for rain and the next crest. I glanced at my watch again: less than one hour in the water.

My mind was becoming blank with the rolling motion of the waves and the stinging of the rain. Gradually, I noticed that the wind and rain were beginning to diminish. I could see better. I started my lookout again at the wave crests: still nothing in sight.

The sky began to darken further—dusk was turning to night, and I began to shiver. I checked my watch again: an hour and a half since bailing out. The wetness, the wind, and the fatigue had chilled me to the point of losing my concentration. I thought I saw Lynn's face in a wall of water and tried to reach out before I realized that it was just in my mind.

I didn't see it coming. Another gust caught me at the top of a crest and flipped me over, tumbling down the other side yet again. I felt too weak to climb back into the raft this time, but I had to try.

No luck.

Several attempts failed, and I just clung to the raft, not knowing what I was going to do. The sky was growing ever darker, and Lynn's face appeared again. She was telling me to hold on. My grip on the raft tightened.

I began to hear a faint noise. It sounded familiar, but my mind couldn't register what it was. It grew louder.

A helicopter!

I grabbed for one of my flares, but my fingers weren't working very well. It seemed to be stuck in the pocket of my vest, and in my haste and clumsiness, I lost it into the sea before I could fire it off.

Don't panic! Take your time.

One flare left. I was very careful and grasped it firmly. I fired it, and the flash arced up into the low clouds and floated for several seconds, drawing the beating of the helicopter blades closer. Then I saw the spotlight.

They were over me.

The hoist was coming down, but I decided that I would not grab it until it reached the full depth of a trough. If I grabbed it at a crest, I might be left hanging without securing the sling under my arms, and then I might lack the strength to hold on during the lift up to the helicopter.

Several minutes passed as the helicopter pilot attempted to drag the harness to me. Finally, enough line had played out for me to safely loop it over my head and under my arms. The rescue crewman saw that I was ready and immediately started the winch. In seconds, I was inside the helicopter with someone handing me a cup of coffee. It was Stan.

"I wasn't sure we would find you, Doc—and we wouldn't have without your flare."

I was shivering, holding the warm cup in both hands, overjoyed to be alive. I wanted to shout.

"I didn't think there was any chance you'd find us in this storm," I said.

"You knew we'd come to get you, didn't you?"

"I was sure, but it's a big ocean, and I lost one of my flares."

"Good thing you had another. We've been circling for twenty minutes."

A realization hit me. "And you haven't seen Ed Bailey or Don Miller?"

"No. Have you?"

"No." I had assumed they were maneuvering to fish the other two out of the water. My elation turned to dismay, and I sprung close to the hatch to see below. We were hovering just above the heavy sea, but nothing was visible beyond the circle of the spotlight.

"I bailed out first," I said, "and they were going to follow. I never saw them, but they can't be far away."

"Did you see them at all after you bailed out?" Stan asked.

"I couldn't see anything coming down, and then after I landed, the high waves and driving rain blinded me."

"Had the aircraft lost all power when you bailed out?"

"No. Ed said we had a flameout of the port engine and then ordered Don and me to bail out. Don was supposed to be right behind me."

A helicopter crewman handed me a blanket, a dry flight suit, and some sneakers. We all continued staring at the light dancing on the sea below. We wanted to see a flare, but there was nothing but empty waves.

Without looking at me, Stan asked, "Was it pretty bad down there?"

"I don't think that I would have made it through the night."

After a few minutes, Stan said, "Those look like fifteen-foot waves."

We both continued to stare below. A coldness invaded me. If they were still alive down there, we should already have found them.

Stan said, "I don't have a good feeling about this. We'll continue to search for awhile until our fuel runs low."

"Is another helicopter coming?" I asked with alarm.

"The *Oriskany* has agreed to relieve us with one of their helicopters so that we can return to the *Enterprise* and refuel. We'll continue our relay through the night."

"What if we don't find them tonight?"

"At daylight, Cubi Point can send a fixed-wing airplane that can stay airborne all day if need be," Stan said. "The weather is supposed to clear by then."

Just as our fuel level was becoming critically low, the helicopter from the *Oriskany* appeared, and we left the area. No one said much on the way back. Near the *Enterprise*, the helicopter pilot came on the intercom.

"Captain Leigh wants to see you both in the war room as soon as we land."

A crowd of naval aviators and navigators, clamoring for news, surrounded the helicopter as soon as we settled onto the deck.

Stan yelled, "We haven't found the other two yet, but a helicopter from the *Oriskany* is still searching the area."

We went directly from the helicopter to the war room.

Captain Leigh met us. "What can you tell us?"

I told him my story.

He looked at Stan. "How about the search for the others?"

"Visibility was poor because of the low ceiling, the rain, and the oncoming night. By the time we picked up the doc, it was completely dark."

"Doctor, you've been on a number of search-and-rescue missions. Do you think there is any hope of finding them?"

I chose my words carefully. "That storm would have tested anybody's endurance, but they may still be alive. Maybe their flares didn't work, or maybe they lost them. I'd like to go back when we're due to relieve the *Oriskany's* helicopter."

"All right, Doctor, but you look worn out. Someone else will make the next trip."

I blurted out, "Please let me go, Captain. There's nothing wrong with me. I have to go; it's my job."

Captain Leigh snapped his head toward me and frowned, glaring for several seconds.

"All right, Doc," he said finally. "For anyone else, I would have denied that request." He closed his eyes and turned away. "Go get your tail end onto that helicopter."

"Aye aye, sir," I said and dashed to the flight deck.

Chapter 22

THE BLACKBIRD

We reached the *Oriskany's* helicopter in a little over an hour and joined the slow, methodical search. The limited visibility during nighttime searches had always severely reduced our chances of finding downed airmen, but the turbulence of the water made it even worse. The whitecaps that formed on the tops of the waves could obscure a small raft, even if a survivor had been directly in the beam of the searchlight. The search would be fruitless without Ed or Don sending up a flare. I was despondent, but at least I was doing something.

The other helicopter left to return to the *Oriskany* around midnight, and we continued the search alone. The storm began to abate in the early hours of the morning, and the rain stopped. We were seeing big swells now instead of whitecaps, but the sky remained pitch black, and our visibility was still limited to that tiny circle of light. No one spoke as the sense of futility and finality grew, and my despair deepened.

The sky would begin to lighten soon, but we were low on fuel and had to depart. A fixed-wing antisubmarine plane was to arrive from Cubi Point to take up station over the site for the day, but Captain Leigh had withdrawn the helicopters for good. I rationalized, that with excellent visibility, the search plane could effectively cover a large area. Who was to say the survivors weren't still down there? I spent most of the day in the ready room, waiting to hear any scrap of news about the search and becoming more and more depressed.

Dave Andrews came in and tried to cheer me up by telling about the reaction of the aviators in the air wing when the black RA-3B trapped aboard. The VAP 61 crews thought it was beautiful and called it the Blackbird, but everyone else was envious and labeled it Moby Dark. My mood was dark enough. I didn't want to talk about black paint, or black airplanes, or anything else. I liked Dave a lot, but I just wanted to be alone. I made a feeble attempt at being civil.

"Who authorized the color change?" I asked.

Dave smiled. "Remember that old principle, that it is easier to beg forgiveness than it is to get permission?"

"Do you think Stan put the maintenance crews up to it?" I asked.

Dave just laughed and shrugged his shoulders.

"I'll bet Captain Leigh will hold a little meeting with all of the squadron commanding officers to avert any further art projects," I said.

"He already did. Yesterday, during Captain Leigh's briefing with the flight crews in the ready room, he referred to Stan as 'Count Dracula.'"

"How did Stan react?" I asked.

"He didn't say a word," Dave said, "but I think he rather enjoyed the nickname. Captain Leigh had a smirk on his face when he said it, so he must have thought the black paint was pretty cool, too."

"Are we going to have more black airplanes?"

"No way!" Dave laughed. "Stan is the only squadron commanding officer who could have gotten away with it. No one else would have dared."

I had been wrong about the black paint. Stan knew just how to relieve the stress in the squadron at a time when we needed it most. Captain Leigh's nickname for Stan was perfect. No one could have been more different from Count Dracula than Stan. It was like nicknaming a tall basketball player "Shorty."

I wanted Dave's opinion about the current level of stress.

"I suppose the triple-A and SAM situation is the same?" I asked.

Dave shook his head. "It's worse. We're finding it almost impossible to fly under their radar, except in the mountains."

"Are the attack squadrons still taking losses?"

Dave leaned back in his chair, his smile gone. "Too many. One was shot down over North Vietnam yesterday, and two A-4 pilots had to eject over the gulf a couple of days ago."

I probably didn't know the pilots, but it pained me just to hear about it, especially in my current state of mind.

"Were they rescued?" I asked.

"Yes, the two who made it to the gulf were."

"Anybody wounded?"

"No," Dave said, "and both rescues happened in clear weather, so the helicopter crews spotted flares from the downed pilots quickly and fished them out."

I had to look away from Dave. I nodded my head slowly. "That's good."

Dave was silent for a minute, realizing what I was thinking. "I didn't mean to make you feel worse," he said. "I know you're distressed about the tanker pilot and navigator."

He got up and left to attend to his maps. I continued to fret over the lack of news about Ed and Don coming in from the search plane. Stan came into the ready room looking for me.

"Hi, Doc. You feeling okay?"

I looked up. "No. I still feel rotten."

He sat down where Dave had just been. "Did you know the tanker pilot and navigator very well?"

"No, just from the flight and dinner the night before."

"You've had a bad string," he said.

I turned toward Stan. "You haven't exactly had such good luck yourself."

"I'm fine," he said.

"I hope that the fuel transfer system will be checked out thoroughly on all of the A-3s."

Stan nodded. "Our maintenance crews are looking at it, and we've already contacted Douglas Aircraft about the problem. You mentioned some concern about the survival equipment."

"I have to write a flight surgeon's incident report. I'll recommend that we scrutinize the one-man raft design. Perhaps Ed and Don couldn't inflate their rafts, or maybe their lanyards became detached. Maybe the flares didn't work. Something didn't work for them."

"Do you think equipment failure is why they didn't survive?"

Stan's question stopped me. The airplane went down because of a mechanical failure in the fuel transfer system, and now I was blaming everything else that happened on equipment failure, too. A much more logical explanation is that Ed and Don became exhausted in the water and overwhelmed by the storm. I was certainly near the end of my endurance when the helicopter spotted my flare.

"No, you're right," I said. "It was a bad storm. The wind scattered us, and you found me and not them. Perhaps it was all chance."

"Are you feeling guilty because you were rescued?"

I looked directly at Stan. "Do you think so?" I wasn't so sure. "Maybe you're right, but I know rationally that my rescue had nothing to do with the failure to find them. I don't feel responsible for the inevitability of death of a patient in the face of a fatal disease, but I feel drained in the case of a random accident like this. It seemed so unexpected and preventable. I think that's what is really bothering me."

I thought about my conversation with the maintenance chief Barney Daniels at Bien Hoa, who talked about having to scavenge for parts and not getting enough sleep. Stan wasn't getting enough, either, nor was I. Overwork and fatigue could have caused this accident. In my confused state of mind, I couldn't work it out.

Stan remained silent for several minutes. "Doc, I have to tell you something. The search plane has seen nothing all day and is returning to Cubi Point. We're calling off the search."

I hadn't completely accepted that Ed Bailey and Don Miller were dead, but this made it final. I leaned forward with my elbows on my knees, looking blankly at the floor, and then I nodded my head.

Stan got up to leave. "You're a good man, Doc."

I sat in the ready room for a long time and then went back to my compartment to lie down in the dark. I cried for a while, and then my nightmares of the bleeding bodies returned.

About 0130, I got up and went looking for Stan and Dave, who were returning from their night mission. I was almost surprised when they landed back aboard unharmed. In recent weeks, the series of combat losses, the accidents, the kidnapping, and the clinic bombing had made

211

life seem fragile. One by one, the attack planes returned without any losses. I was surprised.

Two other tanker crews were aboard the *Enterprise*, and I approached them the next day. They were sitting alone together in the bowling alley speaking in low voices.

"May I join you?" I asked.

They moved to make room for me at their table.

"I had known Ed and Don for less than twenty-four hours," I said, "but I liked them a lot."

They all nodded. One said, "They were good men."

"I wish I knew what we could have done differently. It was a terrible storm. Ed put the aircraft on a glide path to conserve fuel to close with the *Enterprise* as much as he could. He probably saved my life. I was completely exhausted when the helicopter arrived, so the shorter distance from the ship made a difference. I can't thank him, but I can at least thank you."

"Thanks for telling us, Doc. We're going to miss them both."

They told stories about the two men, and after a while I got up and left. Stan had entered the bowling alley and was watching. He got up to leave with me.

In the passageway, he stopped me. "Doc, I have a mission for you. Let's go to the ready room."

He said we were going to set up a detachment in Bangkok as rumored. Between the *Enterprise,* the *Oriskany,* and Bien Hoa, we still didn't have space for enough aircraft, and the distance between Cubi Point and our targets made us inefficient. He wasn't sure we could get medical support in Bangkok, so he wanted me to fly there to set up whatever I could. Since the air force had squadrons deployed at several air bases in Thailand, he suggested that I find out if we could get some help from them.

"There had been rumors about a possible detachment in Bangkok," I said. "So it's really going to happen?"

Stan said, "We don't have much choice."

"I'll see what I can arrange."

He told me that a tanker with an empty seat would be flying to Bien Hoa the next day and that I could take the air force ground shuttle between Bien Hoa and Tan Son Nhut International Airport near Saigon to catch the commercial Pan American flight to Bangkok. The trip would also give me a chance to check on VAP 61 personnel at Bien Hoa.

I was happy to see what I could do in Bangkok, but I now had an irrational aversion to A-3s. Worrying about a bizarre mechanical failure happening twice was silly. Still, my old nausea had come back. But I had to make this trip, if for no other reason than to show my confidence in the tanker crews. I told none of this to Stan. If he and Dave could fly over North Vietnam again, I could handle the simple shuttle flight to Bien Hoa.

This time, the flight on the tanker from the *Enterprise* to Bien Hoa went smoothly. Upon arrival, the bottom hatch opened, and the cockpit filled with suffocating heat, bringing back horrible memories of the kidnapping and clinic bombing. I thought of the hatred between the political factions in the small town: Catholics, Buddhists, and Vietcong. To me, Bien Hoa symbolized the impossibility of developing a peaceful democracy in Vietnam. Just the name made me feel remorse and fear.

I managed to get a phone call through to Lynn. I asked if she had received news of my rescue from the VAP 61 administrative offices or the *Enterprise*.

"Yes, but the message was very short. It said that you had to parachute into the sea, but that you were already on the ship after a helicopter picked you up. I was terrified."

"I'm all right. I'm sorry there was no way to call you from the *Enterprise*."

The message she received must not have mentioned that the pilot and navigator were lost. I decided not to tell her.

"The plane had a mechanical malfunction," I said.

Maybe, after my tour in Vietnam had ended, I would reveal more about it to her. I felt like I was living two lives, and I didn't want to tell her about the other one, the dreadful one.

"Where are you now?"

"I'm in Bien Hoa at the moment."

"Oh, no," she said. "Bien Hoa scares me."

"It's just another air base," I lied. I had been nervous ever since the plane landed. "I'm going to Bangkok tomorrow."

"Bangkok? What's there?"

I told her my assignment. "There's no war going on in Thailand. If I have to be on a detachment, Bangkok is the safest place I could be." That was my hope, at least.

"Will you be spending a long time there?"

"I don't think so—possibly only a week or two."

"Please be careful and don't get kidnapped or do any more parachute jumps."

I didn't feel right about telling Lynn half-truths, but I didn't see the point in frightening her more. I would tell her everything later—much later—if she still wanted to know.

I made the rounds at Bien Hoa and confirmed my impression that tension had decreased, in part as a result of lower-risk missions in the North after Stan's encounter with the SAM, but also because more requests were coming in for low-risk daylight photoreconnaissance over the South. The NVA wasn't launching SAMs south of the border, and the photography could be conducted at high altitude using high-resolution telephoto lenses. But the improved mood didn't change the fact that everyone knew, sooner or later, his number might come up for a risky mission over the North.

Jim Newland and Stuart Blake returned from a mission just after my arrival and came over to greet me.

"Hi, Doc. We're glad to see you," Jim said. "You gave us a scare, bailing out in the middle of the South China Sea in a typhoon."

"The storm didn't quite rate typhoon status, but it was bad enough."

"Will you be here long?"

"No," I said. "I'm supposed to fly to Bangkok tomorrow to scout out the medical resources for the new detachment, in case any of you catch some shrapnel in your rear end. We have authorization to use commercial hotels, and I'm going to sample a few restaurants to make sure it's safe for you to eat there."

"Commercial airlines, fancy hotels and restaurants—are you sure you can handle all of that?"

"Come and join me."

In the morning, during my ride from Bien Hoa to the international airport at Tan Son Nhut, I saw some burned-out buildings, evidence of fighting only a few miles from Saigon. The people standing on the side of the road looked ragged and dazed. For many Vietnamese, American intervention in this war had improved nothing.

The Tan Son Nhut airport terminal showed none of the scars of the war. A visitor might not immediately become aware of the carnage going on outside of the gate. Air conditioning cooled the terminal building and the neatly dressed travelers who waited there.

After I had boarded the Pan American DC-8 and had sunk into my seat, the ultimate in spacious luxury after flying in naval aircraft, a smartly dressed flight attendant brought me iced guava juice while the rest of the passengers finished boarding. A cocoon of comfort separated me from the impoverished, discontented Vietnamese people that we were supposedly rescuing.

In less than an hour, the plane was landing in Bangkok at Don Mueang International Airport. The tarmac was filled with commercial airplanes that showed logos from countries scattered around the world. Off at some distance from the terminal, I saw a parking area filled with U.S. Air Force planes, furnishing the only hint that Bangkok was not solely a busy tourist destination.

Taxis competed to transport incoming passengers to fashionable hotels in the center of the city. Within minutes of landing, a driver deposited me safely at an air-conditioned Hilton that was indistinguishable from that chain's hotels in the United States, except for its extraordinarily low prices, made possible by a favorable exchange rate and the appallingly low wages of the hotel's employees. Even the sumptuous Erawan Hotel, the height of extravagance in Bangkok dating from British colonial days, was no more expensive than a navy BOQ in the States. But I was no aristocrat. The Hilton was luxurious enough.

VI

FROM BANGKOK TO GUAM

Chapter 23

BANGKOK

My survey of American medical resources in Bangkok required very little time. An air force flight surgeon who had arrived only a few weeks before held sick call during limited hours in a one-room clinic at Don Mueang Airport, and a doctor at the American embassy provided care for State Department civil service employees. Both handled anything more serious than colds or muscle strains in the same way: air evacuation. The embassy physician was reluctant to see occasional navy patients, but the air force flight surgeon was willing. I planned to help him out as much as I could and hoped that he would reciprocate when I was with the squadron at one of our other locations. The amount of work for both air force and navy patients combined would probably not total more than an hour or two per day. But one big problem we faced was a lack of support services, such as X-ray and lab.

I knew that Bangkok's Chulalongkorn University School of Medicine, located in the center of the city, provided relatively advanced medical care as a result of British influence from many years of colonial occupation. The faculty taught all courses in English; likewise, most of the books in the medical library were in English.

When I made a visit to the hospital, a medical student recognized me as an American and asked if he could speak with me to practice his English language skills. He told me his name was Waen and explained that it was a nickname for someone who wore glasses. Then he boasted that his real name contained twenty-four letters, and that no foreigner could ever pronounce it. He dressed in the usual white shirt and pants of all the medical students, along with the straw sandals common throughout Southeast Asia. Waen spoke perfect English as he showed me the hospital's X-ray department, clinical laboratory, and operating rooms. He also showed me huge wards with patients on IV fluids recovering from infectious diseases, including cholera and typhoid fever.

I learned that the hospital would be glad to provide support services for anything my patients needed, and I went back to the Hilton reassured that I could patch something together, as long as the air force maintained their small dispensary at Don Mueang Airport. Stan, Dave, and their newest photo technician had just arrived.

"Hi, Doc. What's happening in Bangkok?" Stan asked.

"Not a single mortar explosion in the past twenty-four hours."

"Dull place, huh?" he said. "Sounds good."

They were flying a mission that night and had no time to become tourists. Stan would need to work on messages out at the airport before their flight, and Dave was buried in his room with charts of North Vietnam.

"What's the medical situation?" Stan asked.

"American medical facilities are a bit skimpy here," I said. "The air force has just one flight surgeon, and he's got a small examining room at the air terminal and some basic equipment. He's not very busy, and he's willing to help out when I'm not here."

"That's all they have?"

"I found another option; Chulalongkorn University Medical Center has good X-ray and lab facilities, and they are willing to provide us with service anytime. I looked it over. The quality is pretty decent."

"Whatever you say, Doc."

Another flight crew and some maintenance personnel arrived the next day. Because most of the missions took place at night, no one was in the mood to play tourist or to spend an evening in a fancy restaurant. I had very little to do.

The air force flight surgeon wanted to fly to Tokyo for a few days and asked that I cover for him at his one-room dispensary at the airport.

It was an opportunity for me to show some goodwill that might benefit our squadron whenever I was away. I learned from him that the air force detachments had lost some planes to SAMs, and like the aircrews of VAP 61, they were a somber bunch, not much interested in revelry.

From some of my new patients, I learned that the air force had recently equipped some supersonic F-4 Phantoms with the same kind of infrared equipment that VAP 61 was using, and they were trying a new kind of radar-controlled autopilot that followed the terrain for low-level flying in the mountains. It nearly eliminated the risk of crashing into a hillside. I hoped that we would get similar equipment and made a note to ask Stan about it later.

One of the air force F-4 pilots, Major Sean Callahan, came to see me for sick call. He had the look of someone with a chronic illness, something that no one else seemed to have noticed, as in the case of Bill Spencer with his out-of-control diabetes. Almost every American who served in Vietnam lost weight—I certainly did—but to me, there was a different look about someone who was sick. For one thing, Major Callahan was pale, almost ashen.

"Doc, I know that our flight surgeon is away for a few days," he said, "but with all this heat and humidity, I've got no appetite, and I'm tired all the time. Can you give me some medicine to help me out until our doctor returns?"

The major was wearing a uniform much too big for his frame. He had no excessive thirst or frequent urination, so this wasn't diabetes. On physical examination he had a slight fever, some enlarged lymph nodes in his neck, and a big spleen. Had we been on Guam, I would have hospitalized him immediately.

I tried to gather my thoughts. "I think you have a serious illness," I said, "and I would like to order some tests to be more certain of the diagnosis. I'm sending you in a taxi to Chulalongkorn University Hospital in downtown Bangkok for a chest X-ray and a blood count. I'll call and tell them to hand you the X-ray films so you can bring them back for me to read as soon as you finish. They all speak English, by the way, and they're well trained."

Major Callahan glared at me. "I've got a mission in six hours."

I knew that he was severely ill. But he was in denial. Someone who belonged in a hospital had no business flying supersonic jets over North Vietnam. Under no circumstances would I let him near an airplane.

"I'll notify your commanding officer," I said. "I'll have to ground you until we get to the bottom of this."

He started to stand. "I didn't come in to be grounded."

"Not many people ever plan to be sick, but you're sick all the same. You're in no condition to fly. I have no other choice."

"You're a navy doctor. You can't ground an air force pilot, can you?"

As an intern, I had occasionally seen a patient who refused to accept a diagnosis. But there had been time to allow those patients to adjust to the reality of their disease in their own way. Occasionally, patients became angry at first like Major Callahan. A mission scheduled in an F-4 Phantom in six hours eliminated any flexibility. I was going to have to be firm.

"I'd be glad to call your CO for his opinion."

Major Callahan sat down, still angry, and turned his head away from me. "Okay, Doc. Tell me where I have to go," he said.

I arranged everything. After he left, I called the pilot's CO to explain the situation.

"Can't he fly his mission first and then get the tests later?" he asked in a loud voice.

Neither Major Callahan nor his CO wanted to hear about the disruption in their lives that I seemed to be causing. They were both in complete denial of what I thought was obvious. I was frustrated.

"I think Major Callahan has a serious disease that is progressing rapidly," I said. "He's extremely weak and probably anemic. He could easily pass out with the kind of G-force that your pilots experience."

"You think it's that bad?" This time, his voice was not quite as loud.

"I'll have a better idea about the diagnosis when I see the test results in a few hours," I said, "but you've probably lost a pilot."

"Christ, Doctor. I hope you're wrong. Let me know what's happening immediately as soon as you know anything more."

Soon the major came back with his chest X-rays, and I telephoned the hospital for the results of the blood count: marked anemia. The X-rays showed enlarged lymph nodes in his chest like the ones in his neck, consistent with a lymphoma.

I looked at him. "I think you have Hodgkin's disease. Do you know what that is?"

He leaned forward, slightly bent over with his elbows on the arms of his chair. His anger was gone. Finally, in a low voice, he said, "I've heard of it, but I don't know what it is. It sounds bad. Are you telling me that I have cancer?"

I felt awful for him, but I had to tell him the truth.

"Yes, I think you have cancer. Hodgkin's disease is a type of lymphoma, and lymphomas are a kind of cancer."

He looked down at the floor, trying to find some words. "Is that why the glands in my neck are swollen?"

"Yes, that's what I suspect."

"Are you sure it's cancer?"

"Not without a biopsy," I said, "but I can't do one here. And even if it turned out to be something else, you have a fever, anemia, and a lot of weight loss. You would get the best care at a medical center in the States where diagnosis and treatment are more advanced."

"Is it fatal?"

"A few years ago, Hodgkin's disease was universally fatal, but researchers have recently developed extraordinarily effective new treatments. You might live a long and healthy life."

"What do I have to do?"

"The best course of action is air evacuation directly to one of the major air force hospitals. I recommend David Grant Hospital at Travis Air Force Base near San Francisco, because the most advanced research on Hodgkin's disease is going on at Stanford University only about an hour away. Your doctors are going to want to confirm the diagnosis with a biopsy and more specific testing that we don't have in any military hospitals in the Far East. Then they will probably want to start treatment that you can get in only a few places in the world ..."

My patient had stopped listening. He stared into space, lost in his own thoughts, devastated. I had confronted him directly, because the advanced state of his illness required urgent treatment, and Southeast

Asia was no place for him. Major Callahan was struggling with a new reality that had suddenly threatened his identity and his life.

"I hate to let down the other pilots in the squadron," he said.

"This disease isn't your fault."

"My squadron has already lost some pilots over North Vietnam, and the stress level is high. It will be tough for everybody to lose another one. Have you told my CO?"

"Yes, but that was before your chest X-ray and blood test. We should go see him now. I'm going to recommend your evacuation as soon as possible."

Upon hearing the diagnosis, the air force colonel furrowed his brow and glared. "Are you certain about this?"

"Of course not," I said. "I can't tell for sure if this is Hodgkin's disease without a biopsy, and the kind of pathology lab needed doesn't exist here. But Hodgkin's disease is certainly the most likely diagnosis. Major Callahan is anemic, he has lost a lot of weight, he's running a fever, he has big lymph nodes in his chest, and he has an enlarged spleen. Among the other possible diagnoses, the rest are just as serious as Hodgkin's disease, and all require specialized treatment. He could become a lot sicker quickly. Time is critical here."

The colonel twisted uncomfortably. He was in no position to argue with me. "Okay, Doctor. You've tied my hands. I'll take it from here. We'll set up his transportation."

That night, I ran into Stan, who had a big smile.

"I got a call from a certain air force colonel. He wanted me to thank you for taking care of a Major Callahan. The colonel said he was so upset about losing another pilot that he forgot to express his appreciation."

"He seemed very skeptical when I talked with him."

"He probably was at first. But he knew that something was seriously wrong and was relieved to get it resolved, even if it meant losing his Major Callahan. I told him that he had received the most expert medical advice west of San Francisco."

"That's a gross exaggeration. Any doctor could have figured that one out. I felt badly for the air force pilot, because he has a wretched disease."

"Is it fatal, Doc?" Stan asked.

"Major Callahan asked me the same question. It was until recently, but researchers have developed a radical new method of radiation therapy that shows good results so far. Not long ago, patients like him had only a few months to live, but patients with advanced Hodgkin's disease are surviving many years now with no evidence of recurrence. I hope that he will be one of them."

"He was lucky that you were around."

"That diagnosis wasn't difficult. Thank you all the same."

I wanted to tell Stan what I had learned from my air force patients. "Major Callahan and some of the other F-4 pilots have started flying reconnaissance missions using infrared gear like ours. They also have some special autopilot system that uses contour-conforming radar to make low-level flights at night less dangerous in the mountains. Will we get the same equipment?"

"Doc, you must have your own radar system. You find out about top-secret information as soon as I do. I don't know the answer. For the present, we still have to rely on the skill of our navigators on our low-level flights."

The air force flight surgeon returned from Tokyo not long after. He thanked me for helping the squadron during his absence. He wondered how I had arranged for the X-rays and blood count, and I gave him some names and telephone numbers and suggested that he take a tour of the medical school and hospital. I also recommended that his squadron find a way to channel a modest sum of money to the hospital, explaining that a small donation might establish invaluable goodwill and save some lives.

With the air force flight surgeon back, I had very little to do. My tour of duty overseas would be coming to an end soon, and I began to think about what might be next. I knew that I would make every effort to avoid returning to Vietnam. I had stopped losing weight, and my nightmares and early-morning crying had greatly diminished, but some exhaustion still remained. The navy gave priority for specialty training to physicians returning from Vietnam, and I had originally planned to apply for a residency to become a surgeon, but now I was feeling less certain about that. My concentration and reading comprehension were still not back to normal, and I had little interest in planning my future professional life.

Late in the afternoon the day after the air force flight surgeon returned, Stan knocked on the door of my room at the hotel.

"I wanted to talk with you alone for a few minutes," he said. "Your tour of duty with the squadron is about finished, isn't it?"

"Yes, in about eight weeks, I think."

"I haven't received any orders for you," Stan said. "Have you heard anything?"

"No, I don't know what I'll be doing."

I sat on the bed, and he took the chair.

"I thought you had plans to complete your specialty training in surgery," he said.

"I missed the application deadline."

"You've been busy. I'm sure we could induce BuMed to make an exception about the application and send you wherever you chose. I know plenty of people in Washington."

I didn't say anything right away. "Stan, I didn't apply for a reason. I'm not sure that I want to spend the rest of my life as a surgeon operating on people with diseases of old age. Dr. Tran added more years to his patients' lives in a week than a Philadelphia surgeon could in a year."

"I thought you admired that surgeon at Da Nang, the one who you said saved quite a few lives."

"That's true. David Steiner is the best surgeon I've ever met. But no one wants to make a career out of battlefield surgery. He wanted to go home as much as any of us. Just as with naval aviators, there's a limit to how much stress a surgeon can take. Operating on hemorrhaging marines every day and night takes its toll, psychologically and physically. Nobody has to face the carnage of this war quite like a surgeon."

"I hadn't thought of that. What do you think Dr. Steiner will be doing now that his service obligation has ended?"

"Near term," I said, "he's probably just looking forward to a full night's sleep once in a while. Long term, he'll probably operate on older people with blocked arteries and lung cancer. I want to do more than that."

"Dr. Tran still haunts you?"

"I wouldn't say 'haunt.' He showed me the desperate needs of people, especially children, in impoverished countries like Vietnam."

"If I were going to twist some arms at BuMed," Stan said, "what kind of duty would you choose?"

I leaned back on the bed and thought about it for a minute. "I'd like to get away from the war zone and from having to face young marines and sailors who've been blown apart." I could have added that, occasionally, I was still suffering gruesome nightmares, bleeding war victims spinning around in a kind of scarlet vortex. It was another reason that I didn't want to do a surgical residency, at least not right now.

"The navy usually grants stateside duty for anyone who has spent time in a combat area."

I thought some more. "My classmate Roger Casey from Philadelphia has a position at the hospital on Guam taking care of marines with a variety of infectious diseases that they acquired in Vietnam. He and Colt Benson at Da Nang have organized radio conferences with a group of doctors in Vietnam to try to develop better treatment methods. He enlisted the participation of the Naval Medical Research Unit at Taipei and the Communicable Disease Center in Atlanta. I know Roger will be going home soon. I wouldn't mind picking up where he left off."

Stan thought for a moment. "I'll look into it."

There was no reason for me to stay in Bangkok, and the squadron was flying its most stressful missions from carriers in the Gulf of Tonkin. The *Enterprise* had been relieved, and we were now using the *Oriskany*. Stan was going to take another rotation there and wanted me to join him. I flew by Pan Am back to Tan Son Nhut, and from there to the *Oriskany* by A-3 tanker.

On board the *Oriskany*, VAP 61 had been flying only at night and only over the North. An uneasy aura pervaded the group, as flight crews were risking their lives, but not for a common goal of which we could be proud. We were not defending our country, nor was there any real chance that we could help create a brighter future for the people of

South Vietnam. The world did not look upon our efforts favorably, nor would our friends and neighbors at home regard us as having sacrificed for a great cause.

I could count on joining Stan, Dave, and the other aircrew members in the bowling alley each evening before their missions, and I would wait up until they returned in the early hours of the morning. The number of missions over the North had not declined, and those flights were still perilous, so conversation in the bowling alley was subdued.

One night, I sat next to Stan to ask him about the continuous combat exposure. "Isn't there a limit to the total number of combat missions for a naval aviator or navigator?" I asked.

"No, that happened in World War II, but we don't have that policy now. We're short of replacements, and the RA-3B requires a lot of training and experience."

"The navy must place some limit on a tour in VAP 61."

"Yes," he said, playing with his empty coffee cup, "but the navy can also extend those limits on a temporary basis."

I couldn't imagine how the flight crews mustered the courage to climb into their airplanes night after night. Stan received more requests for targets than he could serve, and I suspected that he was discouraging higher-risk ones. But anything over the North was high risk. The A-3s had little defense, except for flying under the radar and the element of surprise.

"What does 'temporary' mean? For how long?" I asked.

"I can't tell you, Doc." He looked at me. "We've never faced a situation like this. It will depend on how long this war lasts."

I couldn't see an end to the war anytime soon. The only hope for the squadron was replacement with a supersonic F-4 squadron for the infrared reconnaissance missions over the North.

"The demands on you are extreme," I said. "I couldn't do what you do."

"I think you could," Stan said, "but I agree that the demands are high."

"How about the photo technicians? I've noticed the turnover."

"Yes, and that's a problem. Your prediction about combat stress was on target. Some of them request reassignment after only a few months. It doesn't take as long to train enlisted replacements as it does to train naval aviators and navigators, so the navy tries to accommodate enlisted men as much as possible."

"I remember your photo technician after that close call with the SAM," I said.

"I didn't hesitate to grant him a change of duty, because he wouldn't have been any use flying more combat missions. They're always enthusiastic at first—and then they see the reality of the job. I've had three different photo technicians in just the past four months."

I remembered with a chill my one experience as a substitute photo technician in the mission over the harbor at Haiphong. I couldn't imagine the courage that it took for an air crewman to climb into that cockpit every night.

I told Stan that I was seeing a greater number of patients coming in to sick bay, and that each of the flight surgeons had seen a marked increase in symptoms related to fatigue and anxiety. Even the maintenance crews were stressed, just like Barney Daniels at Bien Hoa. I wondered if the long hours of work and the high level of stress were going to lead to mistakes.

Then it happened.

Chapter 24

CONFLAGRATION

As I was talking with a patient in the sick bay, a deafening series of explosions reverberated through the ship with a trembling that felt like an earthquake.

"Jesus! What was that?"

I didn't register whether it was one voice speaking or several. Perhaps we had hit a mine, or a Soviet submarine might have slipped in undetected and fired a torpedo.

"Do you think we're going to sink?"

I still didn't recognize the voice. Was it *possible* that we could sink? I didn't know. But I was sure that we would have many victims from whatever had happened.

The voice said, "The ship is going to blow up!"

It startled me to discover that the voice was my own. My subconscious had taken over, and I was frozen with fear and not in control of myself. Terror had caused me to panic again. I began to notice that hospital corpsmen were pulling stretchers out of a locker and making their way forward. They had regularly conducted drills based on our disaster plan, and each one knew his role without waiting for instruction. A few of them started setting up cots, anticipating mass casualties.

A sickening smoke began penetrating the ship, accompanied by the sound of scurrying feet. Soon, stretcher-bearing corpsmen were returning with victims blackened by burns, two of them still wearing flight gear.

I stopped one of the corpsmen. "How many victims?"

"I don't know, probably hundreds. We need more stretchers."

Our emergency plan called for certain sailors in the ship's company to report to sick bay in case of fire or other emergency. As they came in, a senior corpsman heard the call for more help and sent the sailors off with stretchers. Soon they began returning with more victims.

"What happened?" I asked.

One of the stretcher bearers answered, "Something blew up in Hangar Bay One—maybe a bomb. There's a big fire."

I saw that some of the victims were suffering agonizing pain from extensive burns, and I snapped out of my daze. I grabbed a corpsman to help me administer morphine to the continuing flood of victims.

"Morphine first for the victims in pain," I shouted. "We'll clean them up and dress the burns later."

The panicky voice I had heard earlier was now quiet, and I was back in control. In less than twenty minutes, the sick bay and our supplementary treatment compartments were overflowing, and the corpsmen were hurrying to set up more cots in any space they could find. We couldn't use the hangar deck as a treatment area, because the smoke was too dense. I directed the hospital corpsmen to stay in the sick bay to treat the victims, while sending off the untrained sailors to pick up more casualties.

Two sailors brought in a victim that was obviously dead.

"What should we do with him?"

"How many dead are there?" I asked.

"Lots. We don't know how many."

"Find an area on the hangar deck aft to use as a morgue," I said. "We can't help any more in sick bay. A corpsman will show you a locker where there are flags to cover them."

The ship's loudspeaker blared out orders to firemen, aircraft mechanics, and ordnance handlers to move anything explosive away from Hangar Bay One, indicating that the fire was still out of control. Victims continued to pour in, including some who were ambulatory. It was evident that we couldn't launch aircraft, but we could use our helicopters to evacuate our most seriously burned patients. I began to worry that we would exhaust our supply of dressings, and I thought about requesting helicopters to bring in more supplies from the nearby carriers USS *Constellation* and USS *Franklin D. Roosevelt*.

I called the ship's captain and got through right away. He wanted to know our situation.

"We have more than a hundred burn victims, some very serious."

The captain swore. "How many dead?"

"I don't know," I said, "because the stretcher bearers are taking them aft directly to an area in the hangar bay that we're setting up as a morgue. The corpsmen say there are dozens."

There was a long pause on the line. Then the captain said, "What do you need, Doctor?"

"I'd like to use our helicopters to fly as many victims as we can to Da Nang for immediate air evacuation to the States. We'll pick out ones with the most severe burns. A few patients are too badly burned to survive for long, and we'll keep them on the ship."

"The helicopters will be at your disposal," he said. "What about the rest of the injured?"

"We can take care of the ones with only moderate burns here, at least for a while until the situation stabilizes. But we'll soon run out of supplies. I'd like to ask *Constellation* and *Franklin D. Roosevelt* to send over more supplies by helicopter, and maybe a doctor or two. We could ask to use their helicopters to help with the evacuation of victims, too."

The captain sounded despondent. "I'll call the other two carriers with your request. We'll give you communication priority to talk to the other two ships and Da Nang."

"Thank you, sir. I'd like to talk to the hospital at Da Nang first."

In less than a minute, Colt Benson came on the line.

"Colt, we've had a huge explosion in one of our hangar bays, with a large number of burn victims, possibly several hundred."

"That's terrible! Can we help you?"

"I'd like to air evac a number of victims right away to special burn treatment units in the States. If we send them to you by helicopter, can you arrange for immediate medical evacuation flights?"

"Yes, of course," he said. "I'll handle it on our end. We can give your patients priority by keeping some of our malaria and post-operative patients for an extra day. How are you holding up?"

"The situation here is still unstable. Two other carriers are sending us more supplies and maybe some doctors. Thanks for helping us. Has the hospital been quiet?"

"Not this morning," he said. "Twenty-four marine casualties came in during the early hours, and our operating rooms are going full out."

"Is David Steiner still there?"

"No, he finished his tour. We have some new surgeons, and they've been working all night."

"I hate to add this to your load," I said.

"Don't worry; we can probably transfer them directly from the helicopters to the transport planes for immediate evacuation."

"You're a prince, Colt."

The support and sympathy that had materialized from all quarters was reassuring, beginning with the corpsmen, the volunteer stretcher bearers, the captain, and now Colt Benson in Da Nang. We were not alone. When adversity hit, everything clicked perfectly to respond to the disaster.

Next, I talked to the two other carriers. They were going to use their own helicopters to send four doctors, eight hospital corpsmen, and more of the dressings that we needed. All arrived on the *Oriskany* less than thirty minutes later.

One of the flight surgeons from the *Constellation* approached me. "You still have plenty of smoke pouring out of the hangar deck forward. Is the fire under control?"

"I don't know," I said. "Since the explosion, I've been here taking care of patients and arranging air evacuation for the ones who will need specialized care."

"How can we help?"

"What we need most is to triage the seriously burned patients for medical evacuation, clean up and dress the burns, and start IVs," I said. "I've identified a few patients who are going to need emergency surgery for what look like shrapnel wounds, and one who needs an amputation revision."

"Shouldn't we try to send them all to Da Nang?"

"We might send some, but there are too many for the number of helicopters we have, even using the ones from all three carriers. I've just talked to a doctor at Da Nang. They received a large number of marine casualties early this morning, and their surgeons are still in the operating rooms. I've spent some time at Da Nang, and I know they are constantly stretched to the limit."

"So what do you suggest we do?" he asked.

"We should use the helicopters to fill up the transport planes with burn victims first, so they can leave immediately for the States, and then try to take care of the moderately burned victims and a few of our less complicated surgical cases right here if we can. If we sent low-intensity surgical patients to Da Nang, the patients would have to wait a long time for an open operating room and a tired surgeon."

The newly arrived flight surgeons were uncomfortable about operating on a burning ship, but we had little choice, and as long as we stayed afloat, we had a perfectly good operating room. If the other flight surgeons could help manage the moderately burned victims, I could handle some of the less complicated surgical cases.

I worked with the other doctors to triage and prepare the highest-priority burn patients for evacuation. We sent a hospital corpsman on each helicopter to manage the IVs and administer morphine as needed during the trip. Then I turned my attention to the victims that needed surgery.

Once again, I employed the operating room experience I'd gained at Da Nang. The surgical cases that we retained were not difficult, and I could easily manage them post-operatively. We now had patients spread all over several decks aft, but each compartment had either a doctor or hospital corpsmen checking and treating the patients.

The loudspeaker continued to bark out orders, confirming that the crisis had not yet passed. Finally, about two hours after the explosions, the captain made an announcement.

"We have experienced a series of explosions in Hangar Bay Number One that we think may have been caused by the accidental ignition of a magnesium flare. Unfortunately, the flare ignited other flares nearby.

A number of men on the hangar deck were killed instantly, and the fire raced through five decks in the forward part of the ship, causing significant additional casualties. The fire is still burning, but it is now under control. The blast did not damage our engines, and the ship is seaworthy. We have already received additional medical help from the *Constellation* and the *Franklin D. Roosevelt,* and helicopters from those ships are in the process of transporting some of the victims to Da Nang for medical evacuation to the States. Many of you reacted quickly, rescuing wounded pilots still in their aircraft and moving ordnance away from the flames. The entire crew and I thank you for your bravery and for preventing a bad situation from becoming worse. We are leaving Yankee Station immediately and sailing for Subic Bay, where we will transfer the remaining victims to aircraft for transportation to the States."

In the evening, we counted up the carnage. Forty-four men had died, and 243 had been burned or wounded, many seriously. The help from the other carriers had allowed us to begin treatment on a huge number of victims in a timely fashion. Flight surgeons, hospital corpsmen, and helicopters were able to return to their respective ships. Our own doctors and corpsmen could provide all of the patient care during the two-day sail to Subic Bay, but we would be busy.

A concern gnawed at me: were any of the VAP 61 crews among the dead? For the first twenty-four hours, I was not able to leave the area around the sick bay. I tried calling Stan to find out about the squadron.

"Are you and the other members of the squadron all right?"

Stan took a few seconds to answer. "Doc, Jim Newland, Stuart Blake, and their photo technician had just returned from a mission when it happened. Apparently, they were very close to the explosions. Stuart and the photo technician were killed. The photo tech was new, and I didn't even know his name. Jim is alive, but he was badly burned. He's on his way to Da Nang."

I had been thinking about our casualties in a professional way. This was completely different. These were my friends. They had logged a huge number of combat missions, but wound up killed or badly burned in the safe haven of the carrier, not over North Vietnam. Like Ed Bailey and Don Miller, they were victims of accidents. It was so unfair that men who had survived the greatest of dangers could die when they were home safe. I took a big gulp before responding to Stan.

"I can't believe it," I said. "I was talking to them just a few hours ago. What a senseless thing to happen."

"I've known Jim a long time. His wife and two children are on Guam," Stan said. "I managed to patch through a personal call via radio and telephone to Jim's wife and the parents of Stuart and the photo tech back in the States."

The horror of John Grayson's death and our visit to tell Mary came back to me. I felt another of my shudders and could hardly speak.

Stan continued, "I made sure that someone called Lynn to let her know you're okay. We're notifying the families of everyone on the ship from VAP 61. How are you holding up?"

"We're very busy down here," I said. "There are hundreds of wounded. Do you know any others?"

"No, but one of the attack squadrons lost two naval aviators. They had just returned from a mission, too."

"This on top of all of their other losses," I said.

"I think it may be the worst navy disaster since World War II," Stan said.

The tragedy had affected Stan deeply—I could tell as much from his tone. It had to have been a terrible experience for him. It was for me.

"It's been an awful year." It was the first time I had heard Stan express his feelings so bluntly.

"Does anyone know what ignited the flare?" I asked.

"Nobody who was near the blast survived, so we have no witness to tell us exactly what happened. Something, or someone, may have jarred a bomb or a flare, but we just don't know."

"Have you heard anything about the condition of the ship?"

"The steam catapults and the forward elevator were damaged," he said, "so we can't conduct flight operations. We're just riding the ship back to Subic Bay. How are your patients?"

"A lot of severe burns. We transferred the most serious ones to Da Nang for air evacuation to the States. Most of the patients remaining are going to be all right."

I didn't mention that a few victims had third-degree burns over more than 80 percent of their bodies and thus had no chance for survival. All we could do was make them comfortable.

"Keep up the good work, Doc," Stan said. "I'll see you after we arrive at Subic Bay."

The other two flight surgeons and I planned to take turns catching a little sleep during the remaining twenty-four hours before arrival, but none of us was able to break away for long because of the workload. It was a long trip.

Chapter 25

GOING HOME

We were exhausted when the ship tied up at the pier just after midnight, but we had plenty of help carrying patients to ambulances for transportation to Cubi Point and the waiting medical evacuation airplanes. I needed some sleep, but I wanted to find Stan and Dave Andrews first. Stan found me. "Doc, you look awful. If you're not careful, we'll be evacuating you back to the States, too."

"I'll be fine soon," I said. "I just need a little sleep."

"Dave and I going to spend the day here while the deck crew off-loads our aircraft and tows it to Cubi Point," Stan said. "Why don't you meet us for dinner tonight at the officers' club?"

"I'd like that. I'll probably spend most of the day in bed at the BOQ, but I should be fine by dinner."

In spite of my exhaustion, I couldn't fall asleep right away, ruminating about the past two days. The aircrews had suffered combat losses, but the number of deaths from the fire was far greater. We might never know the cause. I fell into a troubled sleep.

Late in the afternoon, Stan knocked on my door. "May I come in? I have some news for you."

"Of course. What's up?" I asked.

"After our conversation in Bangkok, I called BuMed to see what I could do about orders assigning you to the hospital on Guam. I talked to them again early this morning, and they tell me it's a lock if you want it."

I hadn't been thinking about it since we left Bangkok, but suddenly the idea of spending a year at the naval hospital on Guam had a lot of appeal. Guam was also the home port for VAP 61, so I could stay in contact, especially with Stan and Dave, at least for a while. The biggest question was Lynn.

"If I accepted those orders, is there any chance you could get BuMed to extend Lynn's orders at the same time?"

"Probably," he said, wrinkling his brow and looking up at the ceiling. It didn't sound definite. "Have you asked her about it?"

"No, but I could try to get a call through right now."

"I learned that BuMed tries to make special accommodations for married couples," he said with a little smile.

That inspired another idea. "Maybe I can fix that," I said.

"You can call her right here from your phone if you like. And you might consider taking the R-5 back to Guam tomorrow in case you need to discuss this a little."

I grinned. "Aye aye, sir."

The call to Lynn went through easily for a change. "I'm coming to Guam tomorrow."

"Oh, I'm so glad! How long can you stay?"

"I'm not sure, but more than last time. My tour of duty with VAP 61 ends in about six weeks."

There was a pause. "What will you do next?"

"Stan has been talking to me. He said that he has arranged orders for me to take Roger's place on Guam. He said that he might be able to induce BuMed to extend your orders, too."

"Can he really do that?"

"He said that it would be a sure thing if we were married." I took a deep breath. "So—will you marry me?"

"Oh, yes! Of course I will."

I was on a roller coaster, from the depths of depression to the heights of euphoria. At that moment, all of the disasters and tragedies of the past year seemed far away. I knew my specters would be back, especially at night, but this was the greatest joy I had ever experienced.

"I'll be there tomorrow," I said. "I'm coming in on the R-5."

"I wish you had a rocket ship so you could be here right now."

After I hung up, I gave a little whoop and did a little dance.

Stan had heard everything and wore a broad smile. "Congratulations, Doc. We'll have a special celebration at the officers' club tonight. We've had nothing but bad news for months. We need something positive for a change. I'll get a private dining room so everyone won't think we're nuts."

Suddenly, I thought about the squadron and frowned. "I don't have to spend all of the next six weeks on Guam. I can still support the squadron wherever you need me."

"Don't worry," Stan said. "If we need you, you'll hear from me quickly enough. We can always send an airplane to pick you up. Right now, you might be better off spending a little time with Lynn. I think you'd be pretty useless to the squadron right now."

I worried about Stan. "How about you? Can't you ever take some time off?"

"Not now. We're a bit shorthanded again as you know." A dark cloud seemed to pass over him. Jim Newland was at the San Diego Naval Hospital, and Stan hadn't been able to make a telephone connection yet.

Our dinner at the officers' club at Cubi Point turned out to be the last time together for the three of us. Stan and Dave were flying a mission and landing on the *Constellation* the same night, and I was going back to Guam in the morning. I had bonded closely with my navy friends and was haunted thinking about the ones who had died. Stan and Dave tried to make it a celebration, but the *Oriskany* fire dominated our thoughts and conversation.

Many other members of the air wing of the *Oriskany* were at the officers' club. The mood in the main dining room was funereal. Workmen were making repairs on the ship for the long trip back to California, where a major overhaul would take place. Everyone in the air wing was to receive new orders, because the work on the *Oriskany* would likely take at least six months. The navy couldn't afford to pull veteran combat aviators out of the line for that long. A replacement carrier was probably already en route.

The next day, Lynn was waiting at the naval air station with Roger's rusty old car. She ran to me when the hatch on the R-5 opened. I held her for a full minute before we started walking toward the car.

"Tell your Commander White that, after you, I love him second-best for sending you home," she said.

"I'm sure he knows," I said.

She stopped and looked at me. "Tell me, did he really say that we couldn't be stationed together unless we were married?"

"No, I lied about that. I only said it to make sure you wouldn't say no."

She punched me and giggled. "That's what I had hoped."

Lynn had never looked more beautiful to me. She drove toward the hospital.

"Where are we going?" I asked.

"You're going to get cleaned up, and then Roger and Jill have invited us to have a little celebration together at the Top O' the Mar."

"Giving orders already, huh?"

"Yep."

It was a beautiful evening out on the terrace, but I made sure to have a seat facing away from the sea. I didn't want the sunset to spoil a single moment.

Jill asked, "When's the date?"

Lynn and I looked at each other and laughed. "We have it number one on our 'to do' list," I said.

Lynn wrinkled her brow while looking at me. "I'd like to have the wedding in San Francisco. I know my parents would like that."

"That's a wonderful idea," I said. "I think we could both get leave, and you could show me the city. I've only ever spent a few days there."

Lynn called her parents. Her mother would make all of the arrangements. They lived in a fashionable area called Saint Francis Woods close to the schools Lynn had attended, the beach where she had surfed, and UCSF where she had earned her master's degree. The wedding would take place at the Saint Francis Episcopal Church on Ocean Avenue near to their home. Two weeks later, Lynn and I flew to San Francisco on a Pan American flight.

San Francisco was beautiful in the springtime, with a complete absence of any evidence of the war, as long as we avoided newspapers and television news programs. It was as if Vietnam had just been a bad dream. We encountered a large number of people engaged in an antiwar demonstration and expressing antipathy toward members of the armed forces. We weren't in uniform, and some of them asked us to join them. I felt sad and a little angry. I hadn't volunteered to go to Vietnam. The flight crews in VAP 61 hadn't, either. Nevertheless, they had served with great courage and made unthinkable sacrifices.

My parents flew to the West Coast for the wedding. We were reunited for the first time in more than two years. My mother asked me to tell her all about my navy experiences. She was the only one who asked me anything about the navy. I told her about living aboard an aircraft carrier, my trip to Australia, and the hospital on Guam.

"I'm glad to hear you talk about it," she said. "I'm so thankful that you weren't in any danger."

My father listened silently with a slight frown.

After the wedding, we became tourists. Lynn led me to the opera, the Geary Theater, Golden Gate Park, the de Young Museum, and Muir Woods. We noticed that a three-day conference on scientific advances in treating infectious diseases was going on at UCSF and decided to attend some of the meetings, thinking that it might help us care for our patients on Guam. The agenda was filled with talks on hospital-acquired infections and other diseases of affluence, but there was not a single session on malaria or any of the other diseases that I had seen commonly in Vietnam, or that we had seen in patients evacuated to the hospital on Guam. It was as if half of the world's population didn't exist.

When our leave time expired, we flew back to Guam. As if by fate, our orders were waiting for us, extending our tours of duty for the following year at the U.S. Naval Hospital, Guam. Our friends there were glad to see us, and I immediately felt more comfortable than I had in San Francisco. Roger and Jill were due to return to Philadelphia in a few weeks, so I spent that time helping Roger at the hospital.

"I'm leaving you a huge pile of raw data," he said. "I have the impression that some of the drug combinations for malaria are working, but documenting it with the evidence will take long hours of crunching numbers. I've been busy taking care of patients and spending time with my family, so I've had to put off the research."

"Is Colt Benson still involved?" I asked.

"He finished his tour at Da Nang while you were in San Francisco. We don't have anyone to organize our radio conferences anymore."

"I think I'm your man," I said. "Why don't I try to take it on now? I may get a call from VAP 61, but until then, I might as well get started."

Stan never called me during those entire six weeks. After I left the squadron, the air force took over some of the infrared reconnaissance missions, using supersonic F-4 Phantoms equipped with their special radar. Stan White and Dave Andrews survived the war, and I saw Dave a number of times. He left the navy and went to law school, later entering practice in Los Angeles. I never saw Stan again, but I learned that he remained in the navy and became a vice admiral. That was no surprise.

Lynn stayed busy in the lab, and we worked together on the malaria studies. She began asking more questions about what I had seen in Vietnam and listened in on the radio conferences. The infectious disease specialist at the CDC continued to provide advice, as did the tropical disease researchers at the Naval Medical Research Unit in Taipei.

One evening, after we had been married several months, I was able to tell her part of the story about Dr. Tran, the kidnapping, and the bombing of the clinic. We were relaxing on the veranda at the Top O' the Mar, and she listened very quietly. I told her that thinking about her and seeing her face kept me going and made me determined to survive. I said that I loved her. There was a long pause after I finished. She stood up and began to pace; then she sat down again and started to cry. We never talked about Bien Hoa again. In fact, I avoided talking about Vietnam completely.

We were both due to finish our active-duty obligations at the end of the year and had not decided what we would do next.

"We could go back to San Francisco," I said.

She looked at me with a quizzical expression. "What could be there for us?"

"I could apply for more training or look for a practice. You could work in a hospital lab or get more training, if you like."

"That sounds like settling into a routine middle-class life," she said. "I'm not so sure it would work for us right now."

She was right. I was still troubled from my Vietnam experiences, and she had come to Guam in the first place to find something other than the routine of a hospital lab.

Then someone from BuMed contacted us to see if we might both be interested in extending another year in the navy to work with the Naval Medical Research Unit at Taipei. They were looking for researchers with clinical experience to do fieldwork at a detachment in Thailand. The malaria and other common infectious diseases in Thailand were nearly identical to those in Vietnam. They offered us an opportunity to work as partners. We could continue our project examining treatment combinations for malaria, but this time on a civilian population using laboratory facilities at Chulalongkorn University in Bangkok.

Our year on Guam came to an end eventually. Several of our friends accompanied us to the civilian terminal at the naval air station to catch the Pan American flight. The lone agent in the small terminal examined our tickets and passports.

"Everything is in order: two passengers, economy class, one-way to Bangkok with a change in Manila."

Afterword

VAP 61 no longer exists, and the RA-3B Skywarrior they flew was retired from service in the early 1990s. The navy has decommissioned all of the aircraft carriers involved in the action in the novel, the *Coral Sea, Enterprise,* and *Oriskany.* The U.S. Naval Air Station at Cubi Point on Subic Bay in the Philippines has been closed, and the one at Agaña, Guam, was converted into the Agaña International Airport. The Naval Air Training Command in Pensacola no longer uses Saufley Field.

American involvement in Vietnam ended in April 1975 with the fall of Saigon to Communist forces. Phnom Penh in Cambodia fell to the Khmer Rouge, the Cambodian Communists, in the same month, and the Pathet Lao overthrew the royalist government in Laos in December 1975. Over the next four years, the Khmer Rouge killed about 20 percent of all Cambodians, more than one million persons, and in 1978, the Vietnamese invaded Cambodia.

Americans killed numbered 58,193, plus approximately 150,000 wounded. An estimated 830,000 suffered post-traumatic stress disorder. Approximately three to four million Vietnamese and two million Laotians and Cambodians died as a result of the war. Three million more fled from Southeast Asia, many as "boat people," and approximately 1.4 million have entered the United States as refugees since 1975. More than one hundred thousand young Americans fled to Canada to avoid the draft.

NAMRU-2, Naval Medical Research Unit Number 2, moved its administrative offices from Taipei to Jakarta in 1970 at the invitation of Indonesian Ministry of Health officials. It still exists, and its research on malaria, dengue, infectious diarrhea, and avian influenza continues, contributing greatly to improving the health of the people of Southeast Asia.

Glossary

A-3 Skywarrior. A generic term for the largest operational carrier jet aircraft ever designed and built, in bomber, tanker, electronic surveillance, and photoreconnaissance versions. Sailors on the carriers called it "the whale." The letter "A" signifies that the plane is used for attack, rather than as a fighter for defense. See also **RA-3B**.

A-4 Skyhawk. A small, highly maneuverable carrier jet aircraft used extensively as a bomber in Vietnam. It was one of the last carrier aircraft designed with some mechanical controls, as opposed to the electronic and hydraulic controls used exclusively later. Consequently, naval aviators called the A-4 "the tinker toy." The Blue Angels used A-4s for many years. Senator John McCain was flying an A-4 from the *Oriskany* when he was shot down.

Abrams, Creighton. Deputy to General William Westmoreland, head of the Military Assistance Command in Vietnam until 1968, when Abrams succeeded Westmoreland. Westmoreland had used "search and destroy" tactics that gave way to Abrams's "clear and hold strategies." Abrams placed more emphasis on training the Army of the Republic of Vietnam, abbreviated ARV, and helping civilians to defend their villages against the Communists. He had a low opinion of Robert McNamara and especially disliked defense contractors who he thought were war profiteers.

air boss. The officer responsible for all aspects of operations involving aircraft, including the hangar deck, the flight deck, and airborne aircraft out to five nautical miles from the carrier.

aircraft handling officer, or AHO, or handler. The officer in charge of moving aircraft around the carrier deck. He attempted to avoid the problem of "locked deck," where the carrier lacked the space to either launch or recover aircraft.

arresting wires. Four cables stretched across the aft end of the flight deck of a carrier used to catch the tail hook of landing aircraft. The ends of the cables, attached to heavy weights deep in the hull of the carrier, provided resistance to stop an aircraft. Large aircraft, like an A-3, drew out a cable "to the stops," while lighter and slower aircraft like the COD barely bent a cable.

ARV. Army of the Republic of Vietnam. The South Vietnamese Army.

attack aircraft. Naval aircraft designed as bombers, as opposed to fighters that intercepted enemy airplanes. Attack squadrons were designated by the letters *VA*. The letter *V* stands for fixed-wing, and *A* stands for attack.

BOQ or bachelor officers' quarters. A kind of hotel restricted to officers in the armed forces, where they could rent a modest room with a bath by the night or long term. Unlike enlisted personnel, officers had to pay for their own lodging and meals, even aboard ship.

Bien Hoa. A town of five thousand inhabitants in 1966, located twenty miles northeast of Saigon, where the South Vietnamese Air Force had built an air base that Americans used during the war. Buddhists comprised most of the population until textile and clothing light industries attracted Catholic workers, mostly refugees from the North, resulting in sometimes violent clashes.

BuMed. The Bureau of Medicine, the navy's administrative headquarters for the medical corps located in Washington, DC.

Bunker, Ellsworth. American ambassador to Vietnam from 1967 to 1973. He strongly supported the war efforts of Presidents Johnson and Nixon.

carrier task force. A fleet of one or more aircraft carriers surrounded by a ring of guard destroyers. Oilers carrying diesel fuel for the ships and aviation fuel for the aircraft intermittently join the task force.

CAG or commander, air group. The commanding officer of the air wing aboard a carrier, responsible for coordinating the missions of all of the squadrons on the ship. The term "CAG," for carrier air group, is left over from World War II and persists because it sounds better than "CAW." The commanding officer of each squadron on the ship reported to the CAG, who in turn reported to the commanding officer of the aircraft carrier.

CAP or combat air patrol. Carrier fighter planes that patrolled above a carrier task force to protect against any attempted attack by enemy aircraft or ships.

catapult officer, or shooter. The deck officer in charge of catapult launches. He received the signal from the pilot, who flicked the navigation lights to order the launch.

COD or carrier onboard delivery. A twin-engine, propeller-driven aircraft that ferried personnel and supplies back and forth from a naval air station to a carrier.

CPO or chief petty officer. A senior enlisted sailor.

Da Nang. A major South Vietnamese city of one hundred thousand people during the war, located about eighty miles south of the border with North Vietnam. The South Vietnamese Air Force had built a small air base there that the U.S. Air Force enlarged by adding a second parallel runway. The U.S. Air Force launched "Operation Rolling Thunder" from Da Nang early in the war.

Diem, Ngo Dinh. First premier of South Vietnam following the end of French colonial rule. His administration was noted for corruption and persecution of the Buddhist population. His regime ended in 1963 with a *coup d'état* encouraged by the CIA.

Dien Bien Phu. Fortified French stronghold northwest of Hanoi near the Chinese border where, in 1954, the Viet Minh crushed the French defenders, effectively ending French colonialism in what had been called French Indochina.

dirty shirts. Deck crew in colored shirts (the shirts identified specific responsibilities on the flight deck of a carrier to move, launch, and recover aircraft).

Dixie Station. The navy's name for the area of the South China Sea off the coast of South Vietnam, where units of the U.S. Navy were on station.

Don Mueang International Airport. The major commercial airport for Bangkok, just outside of the city. It was also used by the U.S. Air Force for attacks against North Vietnam, and, on a more limited basis, by navy carrier planes.

F-4 Phantom. A supersonic carrier plane used as a fighter by the navy, later adapted as a fighter-bomber by the air force. The air force used a version of the plane for infrared reconnaissance later in the war.

First Med. The navy's First Medical Battalion was a frontline mobile hospital attached to the Marine Corps at Da Nang and located at the air base. Navy hospital corpsmen were embedded with the marine patrols and were trained as flight crewmen on the marine helicopter rescue ambulances.

Fleet Marine Force. Highly mobile marine infantry that could launch by helicopter or amphibious landing craft from special assault ships that resembled aircraft carriers. The marine infantrymen were lightly armed to facilitate speed. By contrast, the U.S. Army favored artillery and heavy tanks. The marine divisions were elite, all-volunteer units.

flight surgeon. A navy medical doctor with at least one year of internship or residency who then received six months of special training at Pensacola, Florida. Mornings were spent in intensive aviation medicine courses, and afternoons in basic flight training. During the Vietnam War, flight surgeons earned certification to solo in the T-34, the navy's basic trainer aircraft.

Green Berets. Elite U.S. Army rangers who organized the training of South Vietnam Army recruits early in the Vietnam War. The Green Berets later engaged directly in combat.

hangar deck. The deck immediately below the flight deck, used for maintenance and storage of aircraft. Two huge elevators transported aircraft between the decks.

head. Short for headquarters, more commonly known as the toilet.

Ho Chi Minh. Chairman of the Communist Party and head of state of North Vietnam during the war. He was educated in Paris and had been an ally of the United States during the Japanese occupation in World War II. Following the war, the United States helped equip the French to fight against Ho Chi Minh.

Hué. A South Vietnamese city with a population of about 113,000 during the war, located near the North Vietnamese border. Hué was an important cultural center. Much of the action of the violent revolt by Buddhists against the Saigon government, called the "Struggle Movement," happened in and around Hué during the Vietnam War.

ICU or intensive care unit. A specialized area of a hospital used for care of the more critically ill patients. Typically, one nurse is assigned only one or two patients. The units arose during the 1960s in American hospitals as a result of innovations in advanced cardiovascular resuscitation and support, and also because of the development of improved ventilators for treating respiratory failure. Techniques developed in ICUs were widely adopted in American military and naval hospitals in Vietnam.

internal jugular catheter. A venous catheter inserted into a deep vein in the neck through a large-bore introducer needle, with the tip of the catheter advanced into the superior vena cava to allow for rapid transfusion in trauma patients suffering severe hemorrhage. The catheters were originally developed to monitor central venous pressure in ICU patients with severe congestive heart failure or cardiogenic shock. See also **subclavian stick**.

Ky, Nguyen Cao. Premier of South Vietnam during most of the Vietnam War. He was raised a Catholic and was hated by Buddhists. In 1966, he led ARV forces against Buddhist rebels who had defected from the army in a civil war of Catholics against Buddhists. See also **Hué** above.

mach one. The speed of sound, generally about 720 nautical miles per hour at sea level. Mach two would be twice the speed of sound. Supersonic aircraft are structurally designed to fly faster than mach one, but the A-3 was not supersonic.

McNamara, Robert. Secretary of Defense under Presidents Kennedy and Johnson. He supported President Johnson's policy of escalation of the war.

naval air station. An air base dedicated to naval aviation. For example, the U.S. Naval Air Station, Miramar, near San Diego, is the major support air station for carrier fighter planes on the West Coast.

naval aviator. The official title of a pilot in the U.S. Navy. Many are U.S. Naval Academy graduates. On a carrier, the commanding officer, executive officer, CAG, and air boss are all naval aviators.

NVA or North Vietnamese Army. North Vietnamese Army regulars that sometimes fought as guerrillas, and sometimes as organized units in the field.

photo technician. A navy enlisted sailor who had basic skills related to photography, and, in VAP 61, was often trained for the in-flight operation of the large high-definition cameras on RA-3B aircraft.

prop wash. Turbulence behind an airplane caused by a propeller.

R-5. The navy version of a C-54, a four-engine, propeller-driven cargo plane used at the end of World War II and during the Berlin

Airlift. They were reliable but slow, and they flew at lower altitudes where there was greater turbulence.

RA-3B Skywarrior. The photoreconnaissance version of an A-3. In this case, the *R* indicates reconnaissance and the *A* means attack, because it was designed originally as a bomber. The number "3" indicates the basic design, also designated by the name "Skywarrior." The letter *B* refers to a more recent, updated model.

RAAF. Royal Australian Air Force.

SAM or surface-to-air missile. Radar-controlled and heat-seeking missiles launched on the ground against enemy aircraft. They were very effective against aircraft at high altitude, especially the slower RA-3Bs.

Seventh Fleet. All U.S. Navy warships deployed in the Western Pacific. Those same ships were part of the First Fleet when they were in home waters on the West Coast of the United States or in Hawaii. The First and Seventh Fleets had separate command structures.

steam catapult. High-powered catapults on the forward area of a carrier deck for launching heavy, jet carrier planes. These replaced the older, less-powerful hydraulic catapults.

subclavian stick. Insertion of a venous catheter through a large-bore introducer needle into the subclavian vein located just under the collarbone. The subclavian vein is even larger than the internal jugular, and placing a venous catheter in it was an innovation that surgeons in Vietnam used for rapid blood replacement while operating on trauma victims that had suffered near-terminal hemorrhage.

Tan Son Nhut. The international airport for Saigon, now Ho Chi Minh City.

tanker. In naval aviation, the term refers to a large aircraft used for in-flight refueling, typically an A-3.

Blair Beebe

trap aboard. A salty term meaning a carrier landing facilitated by snagging an arresting wire with a tail hook.

Triple-A or AAA, antiaircraft artillery. Long-barreled cannons on the ground for defense against aircraft. In Vietnam, triple-A was effective against American aircraft flying at lower altitude.

VAP 61. A navy photoreconnaissance squadron flying RA-3Bs off carriers in the Western Pacific during the Vietnam War. The letter *V* indicated fixed wing, and *A* stood for attack, because the plane was originally designed as a bomber. The letter *P* indicated photoreconnaissance. Sixty-one was the squadron's number. The letters SS on the tail identified the squadron, and the radio call sign was "Quiz Show."

Vietcong or VC. South Vietnamese Communist insurgents fighting against the South Vietnamese government in Saigon, with escalation beginning about 1960.

Vietminh. North Vietnamese insurgents led by Ho Chi Minh who successfully overthrew the French colonial government in 1954. The Vietminh fought against the Japanese during World War II.

Yankee Station. The area of the Gulf of Tonkin off North Vietnam where U.S. Navy carrier task forces patrolled.

The Author

Blair Beebe, MD, served as a navy flight surgeon in VAP 61 early in the Vietnam War. At that time, the squadron was regularly conducting nighttime photoreconnaissance over North Vietnam, launching from carriers in the Gulf of Tonkin and bases in Vietnam, Bangkok, and Cubi Point in the Philippines. He later became assistant chief of medicine at the Saint Albans Naval Hospital in New York City and left the navy as a lieutenant commander near the end of the war.

Dr. Beebe is certified by the American Board of Internal Medicine and is a fellow in the American College of Physicians. He served ten years as the physician-in-chief of the Kaiser Permanente Medical Center in San Jose, and later as associate executive director of the Permanente Medical Group in northern California. He held a clinical faculty position in the Division of Endocrinology and Metabolism at the Stanford University School of Medicine and has served on the Medical

Advisory Committee of the Technology Evaluation Center, Blue Cross/ Blue Shield Association. He has acted as a senior medical consultant to Computer Sciences Corporation, consulting on new medical technology and electronic medical records.

After retiring from clinical practice, he returned to Stanford University where he earned a Master of Liberal Arts degree. He has published a collection of short stories called *Doctor Tales* and a book on health promotion and disease prevention called *The Hundred-Year Diet.* His short story "The Hero" was published in *Tangents,* a Stanford University journal devoted to the liberal arts.

Doctor Beebe lives with his wife Sue in Portola Valley, California. They have four children and ten grandchildren. Regular interests include several book groups, both in English and in French, participation in Pacific Masters Swimming, and mountain biking in the nearby Santa Cruz Mountains.